KINGSMAN

KINGSMAN

Eric Firth

Matador
5 Weir Road
Kibworth Beauchamp
Leicester LE8 0LQ, UK
Tel: (+44) 116 279 2299
Fax: (+44) 116 279 2277
Email: books@troubador.co.uk
Web: www.troubador.co.uk/matador

ISBN 978 1848766 877

British Library Cataloguing in Publication Data.
A catalogue record for this book is available from the British Library.

Other than actual historical persons, portrayed according to my interpretation and
understanding, all characters appearing in this work are fictitious. Any resemblance to real
persons, living or dead, is purely coincidental.

Typeset in 11pt Aldine401 BT Roman by Troubador Publishing Ltd, Leicester, UK
Printed and bound in the UK by TJ International, Padstow, Cornwall

Matador is an imprint of Troubador Publishing Ltd

This book is dedicated to my parents, Vera and Eric Firth. It is the culmination of ten years of hard work by Eric, accompanied by Vera's on-going critique as the chapters rolled from Eric's pen. I take immense pleasure in putting this book before you and hope you will enjoy the read as much as I did.

Sue Firth

"In accordance with the promises already made to My Indian peoples, My Government will do their utmost to promote in conjunction with the leaders of Indian opinion, the early realization of full self-government in India."

Extract from Address by King George VI on the opening of Parliament August 15th, 1945

Chapter 1

A savage jarring, followed by the crashing of tortured shock absorbers hammered him into wakefulness. The Jeep he was driving had swerved across a broken verge and left the road.

He had been driving, under the burning heat of the Indian sun, without a break for over four hours. His thoughts being variously focussed on cold beer, a shower, freshly laundered kit and a wireless schedule with Calcutta timed for 1900 hours, his concentration had drifted, even to the extent of grabbing catnaps at the wheel. A slackness he would never admit.

Now the steering wheel juddered in his hands, responding to violent track changes as the wheels bounced over the hard-baked earth. A final bump and the engine stalled, the differential housing grounded on the exposed roots of a dead tree and his head smashed into the windscreen frame.

★ ★ ★

When Sergeant Harding of the Royal Signals had been ordered up country by Captain Reeder of the Intelligence Corps, his orders – unwritten and very brief – were to "Base yourself at Headquarters Assam Area where you will be attached for pay, rations, accommodation and discipline. Arrangements have been made for you to be issued with a wireless transmitter, receiver and associated kit. Just pick up what you think is suitable and available. The chaps here will maintain a twenty-four hour listening watch on an agreed frequency, but if you arrange a timed schedule with them, make damned certain you keep it. If you don't, we will immediately assume that you are in trouble; not that we will be able to do much about it, but we do like to know

1

what's happening to our chaps in the field. Don't use codes, no call signs, stick to short, plain language transmissions and try to work your schedules just on the edge of atmospherics when it will be difficult for casual listeners as reception conditions go down just after last light. Now the war is over there is little chance of any organised intercept, but you never can tell who might be listening and as you well know, codes and call signs are an absolute giveaway. You will be given a frequency allocation and authentication groups. Stick with them."

"OK sir, got all that. Now, what am I supposed to be doing up there?"

"After the fall of Singapore in '42 a hell of a lot of Indian Army people were conned by one Subhas Chandra Bose to form what he called the Indian National Army and fight with the Japs to liberate India from the Raj. Bose is a renegade politician with Fascist connections. They failed, of course, and when the war ended the rabble disbanded and fled. Many returned to their villages and disappeared into the community, but a hard core, including some named Indian Army officers, are known to be still hanging about in the jungle. Some have since been caught, court-martialled and are now awaiting sentence. The remainder are a danger to internal security and we want to clear 'em out a bit sharp. Your job is to make contact with the headmen of the Naga hill tribes on the Burma side of the border and get all the intelligence you can about these INA wallahs. Pay for their info with gold half-sovereigns; the Paymaster will fix you up with fifty pounds' worth – that should keep you going for a month or two. Finally, if anyone gets a bit curious about what you are up to, your cover story is that you are doing some communications survey work on behalf of Indian Posts and Telegraphs. Roger?"

"Good, sounds interesting. What about personal arms? Could get a bit tricky if the INA people get the wind up and turn nasty."

"Just take the usual, a pistol and twenty-four rounds. That should see you through. If you think you need anything else just have a word with the Camp Commandant at HQ Assam District. I'm sure he'll fix you up."

★ ★ ★

"Oh Sergeant Sahib, we see many INA wallahs coming in from jungle. They come to buy food and try to pay with Indian rupees we do not want.

Sometimes they try to pay with evil smoking thing. Now since ten days ago we see aeroplanes fly to Tamu where British were in war. Headmen from other villages tell me of these things. Very bad things going on. Tell boss we very happy working for King George at England and his gold."

★ ★ ★

Harding tried to focus through a migraine-like geometrically imaged vision to see the time. His watch was missing. As he fought to engage his fragmented memory he picked up the sound of whispering. It sounded to him like Urdu. He quickly pieced together sufficient to tell him that he was being robbed. With controlled chest movements to take in deep breaths without alerting the thieves, he summoned sufficient energy to leap from the Jeep.

"You thieving bastards," he yelled, with all the power his lungs could muster, and lashed out with fists and feet at the two men going through the kit on the rear seats. They fell back in fear, making the sign of supplication with their hands and begging to be forgiven.

"O Sahib, we see accident and sick man, we try to help. We only poor bullock cart drivers and not do bad things." Harding could see the cart and patient bullock standing on the road.

"So that's why you didn't make a run for it? Couldn't get far on that thing, could you? Now, to the count of three, hand over my watch and any other stuff you've pinched or I'll slaughter your bloody shit buffalo." He drew his pistol, cocked it and counted in Urdu, "*Ekh … do,*" Before he could deliver on his ultimatum the hapless pair scrabbled through their dhotis to produce his watch and some packs of 'K' Rations. A quick body search failed to produce any more of Harding's belongings. Satisfied with the result, he waved his pistol in the direction of the cart which they mounted with haste. "Now bugger off," he said, and fired a shot over the animal's head. Startled from a standing sleep it reared up and made off at a heavy gallop with the drivers whipping it into greater effort.

Harding was sweating heavily. Dried blood packed his nostrils, his head ached from the injury suffered in the pile-up, and his face and arms were burned raw from sun exposure after he had collapsed with his body hanging over the side of the Jeep.

The scuffle with the thieves had opened up a head wound which he washed as clean as his stale water supply would allow, then applied a field dressing with its khaki bandage fastened round his head in a bandana fashion. He scraped the dried blood from his nostrils but he had no means of relieving the pain from his sunburned face and arms. With his vision fully restored he checked the time. Two hours to go for his wireless schedule and he estimated about thirty miles yet to cover.

An inspection of the Jeep revealed only some superficial damage to the offside bumper bar. The differential housing where he had impacted on the tree root was intact, and, thankfully, not leaking oil. He rocked the vehicle clear of its landing point, started the engine and re-joined the road.

Chapter 2

As Harding accelerated away from the scene of his mishap he caught sight of some vultures abandoning their vigil over their intended feast as they swayed into a wing-flapping trot to take off. He shivered with disgust at the obscene creatures, relieved that, most likely due to the two thieves, he had been saved from their hooked beaks and razor-sharp talons. Although it was generally believed that the scavengers only went for dead flesh, he had often seen them go for the soft parts of a fallen buffalo calf.

He kept his speed down to about twenty miles an hour, finding it difficult to split his concentration between making the fast approaching wireless schedule, an explosive headache and keeping the Jeep on the road. As he drove, an object appeared in the road ahead of him, the shimmering heat making it impossible to identify.

As he closed up on the object he saw it was a Chrysler station wagon carrying civil number plates and apparently abandoned with its bonnet propped open. He continued past it for about fifteen yards, stopped the Jeep, drew his pistol and, taking advantage of the available cover, moved with great care to a point from where he could take a closer look.

She was sitting on the ground with her back leaning against the shaded side of the vehicle. White, and young. A floppy brimmed hat perched on the back of her head revealed sweat-soaked strands of fair hair. The front of her khaki shirt was stained with engine grime and she looked miserable. Before Harding could say anything she raised her voice and said, "Damn this bloody place. I've been sat here on my arse for absolute ages and no sign of any help. God knows where the nearest telephone might be and I can't start walking in this heat, I have no water. What the hell is one supposed to do in an emergency? And who are you? I saw your Jeep crawl past so I suppose you must be in the British Army."

"Yes, of course I'm in the army. Harding is my name and I'm on my way back to Shillong. I'm already late so if you want any help, say so. If not I'll leave you to it."

She pointed to his pistol and said, "You can stop waving that thing about, it might go off. I'm not about to attack you, and yes I do need help."

He holstered the weapon and realising that, dressed as he was, in jungle green vest and shorts with socks rolled down over his boots and a blood stained bandage on his head, his appearance was rather scruffy. Little wonder she was uncertain about his identity.

She stood up, gave the front tyre a symbolic kick and continued in a more even tone. "If it's not too inconvenient for you I would like a lift. I can get this thing towed in later. We seem to be both pointing in the same direction."

Harding looked at her, trying to work out what this female was doing out here alone in the bush. She sounded and looked to be English. Not many English women around – a few nursing sisters at the military hospitals and some army wives to be found in the garrison towns, but they usually stick together in their tightly organised cantonments.

"Yes Miss, I can give you a lift but I wouldn't leave your wagon out here for long. There's a lot of bandits about and they would have it away in double-quick time. I've just had a run in with a couple but fortunately they didn't get away with any loot. I'll have a quick *dekko* at your wagon and see if I might be able to get it going. If you do need a tow, how far do you have to go?"

"About eight or nine miles, I think. I'm from the Erskine-Jalpai tea estate, just off the Shillong road ... do you know it?"

"Don't think so. Only been up in this area a few weeks and I haven't been around much locally. Spend most of my time cabbying around the *khuds* up on the border. Can't waste too much time;

let's have a quick look and see if it can be made mobile. You've got petrol, I expect?"

She was about to re-ignite at the idea she had run out of petrol, but, remembering he was there to help, didn't wish to ruffle him and nodded her agreement.

He primed the fuel pump until some petrol oozed from the carburettor. Satisfied with the result of that check he raised his head, smiled, touched his forelock in a mock salute and said, "Never take anything for granted, always follow the drill."

She gave a deep sigh and said, "Well … that's satisfied you and what's the next step, pray? Look, I'm getting a bit pissed off with this ritual. I'm dying for a drink, I'm absolutely famished and most importantly I need a bath. Now you can either give me a lift, a tow or hurry and get the thing started if you think you are so clever."

"Don't panic, lady, I think I know the problem. I don't suppose you have a spare stocking by any chance?" She hitched her trousers to knee height to display a pair of slim ankles and well proportioned calves. "Does anyone wear those things out here? The answer is no. Now can you get on with it … please?"

Harding turned abruptly and set off back to his Jeep. He had barely covered ten paces when she ran after him, grabbed his arm and, trying to hold back her tears pleaded with him, "I'm sorry, please forgive me, don't leave me out here…."

He looked down at her and said, "Your fan belt is bust. I'm going to see if I have something I can replace it with. The standard 'get you home' substitute is a silk stocking. It's strong and flexible and it usually works well. I'm trying to do my best for you, so will you stop behaving like a spoiled brat and let me get on with it?"

She let go of his arm and sat down again.

He returned with a length of parachute rigging line which he measured over the engine, generator and fan pulleys, tied the ends together with a bound-in reef knot, dropped the bonnet and said, "Show me a starting handle and we'll give the engine a whirl."

The engine coughed into life after a few turns and settled down to a steady rhythm. He listened until he was satisfied the knot was not fouling the fan-blades then turned to the girl.

"There, that's OK now, so off you go. I'll follow just in case you hit any snags. Keep your revs down and not too fast either."

★ ★ ★

She pulled into the side of the road alongside a track signposted Erskine-Jalpai Estate. Harding drove up alongside and said, "That's me finished, I'll be on my way now."

"Don't go," she said. "Thank you, I can cope now. I'm sorry I was horrible to you back there, it was unforgivable of me." She reached into the Jeep for his map case and wrote 'Shillong Civil 27' on the Perspex cover with her lipstick. "You can reach me at this number. If you are going to be free, please join us for *tiffin*, and perhaps stay for dinner either next Saturday or Sunday or some other time if that's not suitable. You have been really super and I want to thank you. Oh, by the way my name is Laura … Laura Erskine."

★ ★ ★

It had been almost two years since Harding had seen or even spoken with an English girl. A few moments, hurriedly shared at a village near the embarkation port. A tearful 'good-bye and keep safe' and a promise to write if he let her know his address. The only address Harding had was a draft destination code, RMFZL, stencilled on his kit-bag. Could have been any bloody where – North Africa? Italy? Egypt? Palestine?

Laura Erskine was of a different breed – intelligent, spirited, determined, accustomed to having her way and bloody attractive. Early twenties perhaps, terrific shape but … she was wearing a wedding ring. No mention of a husband.

Chapter 3

The Viceroy eased the patch from the empty eye socket and wiped it with a red handkerchief the size of a table napkin. He replaced the patch, carefully folded the square of linen and slipped it into his pocket. He was sitting in the gardens of the Viceregal Lodge, the splendid Lutyens-designed centrepiece of New Delhi.

"Damn this heat, don't know how much longer we'll have to put up with it." He nodded in the direction of the empty chair. "Good of you to come over, Claude. I want to talk to you about the present situation."

The Commander-in-Chief accepted the invitation to sit down and said, "Do you have any information we might share, Your Excellency? I understand that London doesn't seem to be making any progress with the Congress Party or Jinnah's Muslim League about handing over control of the country to them."

"When I took on this job, it was my firm belief that we should go for partition – split the country in two, a Muslim state and a Hindu state leaving them to get on and rule themselves separately. The Cabinet Mission which came out last March has a fixed notion that independence can only be granted to one entity: the All-India Congress which includes Muslims, of course. I had hoped that we could hand over power to an agreed administration within eighteen months of the war ending but that's now a remote possibility. The major players are fighting like cats in a bag whilst the Mahatma is chuntering on about civil disobedience, or passive resistance as it is known in some quarters. Whatever they choose to call it, we are going to be in trouble up to our necks and trying to hold the centre ground as usual. What I want to know is, do we have the military capability to hold the line if we are faced with a rumpus?"

The Field Marshall took a sip of *nimbu-pani* and glanced around the gardens. He and the Viceroy were seated under a canvas parasol in the middle of the well-watered lawn distant from listening ears. Information travelled rapidly and not even the security-vetted domestic staff could be trusted to maintain silence, especially on matters of national sensitivity.

Satisfied it was safe to talk he said, "If there was to be an outbreak of violence we would be compelled to take action in support of the civil power, given that the appropriate authorities made a proper request, even down to the level of a district magistrate. Our task would be limited to the protection of lives and property and to keep essential services running. As you know, contrary to popular belief, India is a very integrated society and we have British nationals living and working alongside Hindus, Muslims and mixed races. To try and protect one group and ignore others would lead to a rapidly deteriorating situation."

"I well understand all that you are saying," the Viceroy responded, "but I am of the opinion that with independence a racing certainty we have a number of priorities to contend with. First, there are British nationals – they must be our primary concern. Then, if we are requested by the governments of other nationalities to protect their citizens, we have a duty to do what we can for them. Next are the mixed races who have served the Raj well in running the railways and a host of other public services and utilities, as well as providing a much valued source of manpower for the armed forces. Finally, I believe that if there is a set-to between the Hindus and Muslims we would have to try and keep them apart until things cool down a bit."

The C-in-C replied, "I am, of course in command of both British and Indian forces. British units are fast running down and I doubt that within eighteen months we will be able to muster more than a couple of battalions, even with reinforcements. There is a rumour, we think seeded by subversive elements, that the Royal Air Force is to take over much of the army's role in India because they can get about the place much faster and use the air threat to great advantage, especially in the North West Frontier districts. Another false claim is that RAF personnel are to be kept on out here to service passenger aircraft of British Overseas Airways. There has already been a mutiny at the Allahabad maintenance base on the back of these rumours and the ringleaders of that little endeavour are now lined up to be disciplined."

The Viceroy lifted a black metal box onto the table and removed from it a manila folder. It was marked OPERATION MADHOUSE. "You see this?" he said. "It reveals what I propose to do if His Majesty's Government fails to believe that Mohammed Ali Jinnah means business when he threatens to destroy India if he is not given a separate Pakistan homeland. I won't disclose my plans for the time being, because if the document became public too soon I would have great difficulty in negotiating any reasonable form of settlement. However, I will tell you my primary objective would be the safe evacuation of British dependents and service personnel."

"That then means," the C-in-C replied, "we would have to rely on the Indian Army to hold the line. I must say, however, I would have some misgivings if Hindu troops were ordered to operate against their own brethren and the same goes for the Muslims. If we were to go a stage further and deploy them in cross-community operations, we could really set the sub-continent aflame; no-one will come out of it unscathed. I share your concern about the safety of British dependents and service personnel but many of them, especially the thousands of WOs and NCOs who give technical support to Indian units, would find themselves in danger if there was to be a repeat performance of the '57 mutiny. If they were to be withdrawn as a contingency measure it would create unrest and be interpreted as an indication of our political intentions. It would also seriously undermine the efficiency of affected units."

"Time is not on our side, and this is what I am going to do. One; send a telegram direct to the Prime Minister. I know this will bypass the India Office but we can't afford to indulge in the niceties of protocol. Two; I will strongly recommend that we split India into two as I have already outlined to you. Once they have decided who will get what, I will recommend that the princes and their estates shall be given the opportunity to decide their futures, either to go with the settlement or forfeit their possessions. I want you to draw up contingency plans to accommodate this strategy. When you have got the thing worked out, let me see it and we'll put forward an integrated military-political blueprint. I have one further concern and it is this: the French and the Dutch have also got colonial responsibilities in South East Asia. They have not really recovered from enemy occupation so they will be ripe for both internal troubles from nationalist activists and from outside interference brewed up by one or other of our erstwhile allies. We don't want the wind of their storms blowing in this direction. The last time we met you had in mind to set up an intelligence network to report on potential danger spots in the region. How is that working?"

"The operation is going well. The wartime Signal Intelligence Centre in Fort William, Calcutta is running the show. Chaps have been put in position in four locations; French Indo-China, Java, Malaya and one nearer home in Assam. They are all highly trained wireless operators and have been used to working behind enemy lines both out here and in Europe. A well experienced Intelligence Corps officer is in charge of the exercise and I am sure the whole enterprise will be worthwhile."

"Good show … anything useful come to light?"

"The chap in Assam has been sending us useful info about the INA. There are also a few Japs who made off into the jungle rather than surrender after we took Burma. I understand one or two high ranking Jap officers who are wanted to answer for wartime atrocities are also still at large. It is important that none of these characters get involved in any fight for Indian independence, so the sooner they are brought to book the better."

"Good enough Claude. Goodbye and keep in touch."

Chapter 4

Ten minutes to go before the 1900 hours wireless schedule. Harding had completed his 'opening up' drill: Signal Out – 12.50 M/cs, Signal In – 13.25 M/cs. He carried out final checks on his No. 53 Transmitter. It was capable of pushing 250 watts of power into a half-wave dipole aerial over a designated working range of five hundred miles. To reduce 'on air' time, he had tuned the output into a dummy, non-radiating load. The receiver, an American AR88, had also been pre-tuned by frequency meter ready for the incoming signal from Calcutta. Harding had opted for the AR88 for its selectivity, stability and reliability and in recognition of the fact that in wireless communications the quality of the receiver often outweighs that of the transmitter. He smoothed the paper of his message form and glanced at the wording; checked that it was brief and carried accurate information. Two freshly sharpened pencils lay to the right of the Morse key, ready to note time of receipt and to take down any fresh instructions from Calcutta. He placed his right hand on the Morse key, thumb and first two fingers resting lightly on the black Bakelite knob, and watched as the second hand of his watch moved up to the hour ... five, four, three, two, one, TIME:

The key contacts clicked to the even rhythm of his message as he sent:

AA (unknown station call sign), the internationally recognised call sign used when the sender was unaware of the receiver's identity. Harding had agreed with the Calcutta operators on the intelligence net that normal British Army wireless procedure would not be used. Call signs were an immediate giveaway to a wireless station's identity and relied heavily on cipher to maintain signal security.

Daily changing call signs, compulsory on tactical wireless circuits, were of little security value unless frequencies were also changed at the same time to confuse intercept stations and maintain secrecy.

He sent the call three times, then concentrated on picking up the reply through the crackle and hiss of atmospheric interference and the clutter of signals bouncing in from distant stations. The reply: AA K (send your message) came in at a strength five signal but was barely readable through the heavy interference.

Harding smiled as he recognised the style of the Calcutta operator, a good mate; they had worked to each other on many previous operations, never let a chap down. He belonged to the class of operators who could boast of working with a wet boot-lace for an aerial.

Satisfied that there were no errors in the message, Calcutta signalled R AR (received correct – out). Harding checked the total 'on air time' at sixty-five seconds over two frequencies. Not bad.

Undercover wireless operators worked to strict instructions to keep transmissions to short bursts of not more than two minutes. That rule, plus following the 'unknown station procedure' and sticking with evening operating schedules greatly reduced the risk of signals being picked up by unfriendly ears. Only in a life-threatening emergency would the Slidex code system be used and that was of limited security value, being quickly unravelled by competent codebreakers.

Happy that the message had been correctly sent, he put a match to his copy, ground the burnt paper to dust, switched the transmitter off and retuned the receiver to Radio SEAC Ceylon, the Forces broadcasting station for South East Asia Command. He timed it well; the voice of Mary Martin, seductive but very distant, came through his headphones. He switched in the loudspeaker and lay back in his chair to luxuriate in the tune and lyrics of 'Do it Again' … well, a chap could dream….

★★★

"Tell me Reeder, where exactly is area Charlie? I'd be grateful if you would be kind enough to show me." Captain Duncan Reeder unrolled an Indian Ordnance Survey map, laid it flat on the trestle table, which served as a desk, and anchored the corners with pebbles to hold it against the draught of the ceiling fan.

"I'll explain, Colonel. We agreed to give certain area locations alphabetic identity. It serves two purposes, security and speed of reference. The area given in Harding's signal is here, this one inch grid square on the Assam border. As you can see, it's some fifty miles south east of Imphal in country ideal for concealing the INA and near enough to road systems if they are minded to sneak home when the time is right for them. It's a safe bet that the air activity reported by Harding is connected to this airstrip here at Tamu."

Colonel Martin Grindley, late Indian Army cavalry read through Harding's signal:

241900F (.) INCR INA ACTIVITY AND AIR MOV CHARLIE (.)

"Well, that's pretty brief, what? Let's see what it sounds like in plain English … I expect it was sent on the twenty-fourth, that's today, at seven o'clock, right? Now, tell me what this letter F is about. Never could fathom out what these bloody signallers are up to half the time. Up on the frontier we relied on the flag, helio or lamp. Didn't hold with wireless."

Reeder looked hard at the colonel, trying to understand how he could attain the rank he held and remain ignorant of the value of wireless as a command and control weapon. He explained that the letter F suffix to the date-time group was the time zone indicator for East India, six hours ahead of Greenwich Mean Time. Grindley acknowledged his understanding with a lift of an eyebrow and waited for Reeder to unfold the information in the message.

"Harding reports that there is increased INA activity and some aircraft movements in this area." He pointed to a map square and continued. "This is area Charlie. We agreed to mark the grid squares with identifiable letters to save time in transmission and to maintain signal security. If you look, you will see Tamu airstrip is within the square Charlie, just inside the Burma border, and as I've already said, some fifty miles to the south east of Imphal, the nearest town of any importance. Outside the airstrip it's an area of pretty rough jungle with only a Jeep track giving ground access – an ideal place for deserters to hang out whilst they pluck up courage to strike out for their home villages back in India. I rather wonder if the two factors – INA and the flying activity – are linked in some way and centred on Tamu."

The colonel continued to stare at the map, uncertain as how to proceed with the intelligence analysis. He was only vaguely aware of the purpose of the Signal Intelligence Centre. The GHQ briefing which had ordered him to Calcutta made specific reference only to his role as a liaison officer with the object of detaining INA deserters in co-operation with a Chief Superintendent Maurice Sedley, Bengal Police Special Branch. All operational matters were to be left entirely to Captain Reeder. Grindley decided that he must make an effort to contribute to offering an explanation, if only for the sake of his rank and his presence on the ration strength.

"Funny business, assuming this Harding fellow has got his facts right. I've heard rumours of these INA *wallahs*. Let the rest of their countrymen down, bad business … deserve to be shot at dawn for the traitors they are. Worse than cowardice in the face of the enemy. I expect they'll get away with it for some trumped up political reasoning. Bloody politicians, ought to keep their noses out of military affairs … would have done some of 'em good to have been given a bellyful of action, that would have quietened 'em down a *thora.*"

Reeder chose to ignore the colonel's line of philosophy. "We are only floating the possibility of a link between the INA and air activity. I can't see aeroplanes flitting about the area and maybe landing at Tamu unless they are serving a need on the ground and the only suspect agency as far as I know is the INA."

"Hmm, right then, let's agree that the INA is involved with the air activity. That poses the next question – who has any aeroplanes in this part of the world and, better still, who can operate them?"

"Well, we can forget about the Japs. They are beaten and grounded. The Americans have now closed down all their installations in India, Burma and much of South East Asia, though I suppose they have still got their Pacific bases operating and perhaps some presence in French Indo-China and, of course, on the Japanese mainland."

"Ah, French Indo-China … what about the French? Or should I say The Vichy French or what's left of them. That lot surrendered to the Japs as soon as they appeared on the horizon back in '42. I expect they will be too busy trying to regain a foothold in that colony, just as the Dutch are trying to do in their pre-war colonies in Java and Sumatra. So, as far as the European powers are concerned the bets are off there."

"The only other power to consider is China. They received a tremendous amount of aircraft from the Americans during the war. OK, so America provided pilots as well, but many were manned by their own personnel. I don't know how many aircraft are still in their possession or even serviceable but they have a civil war blowing up. Some chap called Mao Tse-tung is leading a Communist uprising against the Chungking government and Generalissimo Chiang Kai-shek. Again, I can't see any China connection either. I suggest we report to GHQ and see if they can get some information from the Royal Air Force at the top level. If we start making local enquiries, it might create some suspicion and let the cat out of the bag."

"OK Reeder, you are in charge of ops, old boy. Better get on with it. I wonder if you might consider getting Harding to put his ear a bit closer to the ground. It can take a hell of a time to get GHQ moving, especially if they are to maintain a bit of secrecy about it and not go upsetting our late allies."

"Yes, of course, we are due for a wireless schedule with him on Monday. I'll get a signal off to him then. In the meantime we'll see who comes up with the answer first."

"If that's cleared up a bit, now, what about this Harding fellow, who is he exactly? Some sort of spy or agent as we used to call 'em up on the Frontier?"

"Nothing as glamorous as that, I'm happy to say. He's a sergeant in the Royal Signals who, together with half a dozen other specially qualified personnel, was sent here when our role changed from wireless intercept and decoding to that of an intelligence centre using undercover chaps on field intelligence, but being skilled wireless ops they can report info directly to us."

"I see … who is running the show up there with Harding and how many fellows are in the detachment?"

"Harding is running things and he is on his own."

"I would have thought that there would have been an officer in charge. Don't we have any to spare?"

"It's not a question of availability. There are oodles of officers hanging around with nothing to do except wait for their discharge to come up. The job that Harding is on, and of course the other chaps based in Malaya, French Indo-China and other places, requires special skills and experience so whether they are officers or other ranks makes no difference providing they are up to it."

"How do Harding's qualities measure up then?"

"For a start, he is a first-class wireless operator and fully capable of running and maintaining a station under the most difficult conditions. His special experience is a matter which Harding plays close to his chest, in common with others who have been deployed on secret operations. However, I can tell you that he was landed in occupied France three months before D-Day in support of a deception scheme to fool the Abwehr, German Intelligence, that the assault on Fortress Europe was planned to hit the beaches of the Pas de Calais. I hasten to add that I did not learn of this from Harding's lips, so I trust you will keep it confidential."

Grindley digested this interesting news before saying, "I see … never heard anything about that. I'm going to cut along now and get changed for dinner. See you for a pre-prandial, I expect."

★★★

Martin Grindley lay back on his steamer chair cooling off after a shower, a towel draped over his loins and sipping iced lime juice. The monsoon season was almost at an end and with it a relief from the prickly heat that burned like the cinders of hell into a chap's back. He gazed out over the white walls of Fort William to the distant tree sheltered villas of Tollygunge, the English oasis set well away from the stinking squalor of Calcutta and the dock areas.

Chapter 5

The sound of midnight striking from the bells of St John's Church in nearby Dalhousie was barely noticed by Gopal the *rickshaw wallah* as he pulled his, now empty, conveyance up the slope to Howrah Bridge. The little Bengali was muscle-aching weary after sixteen hours of backbreaking toil under a burning sun, lungs heaving to drag oxygen from the traffic polluted air, feet calloused and fissured from running over broken roads and his head pounding from the strain of hustling his way through congested streets. He was going home to a tumbledown shack in the festering slums of Anand Nagar, home to his Mila.

Gopal's mind pondered the day's events. Not that the day was any different from all his other days, the unbroken struggle to earn money for a bowl of rice to share with his Mila, the fight to save a few rupees to look after the young son whom Mila would bring into the world one day. So that he could provide for those two needs, he had to find money to pay the weekly hire for his *rickshaw* from Mr Chatterjee.

Mr Chatterjee was a very rich and very fat man. For the carrying of Mr Chatterjee from his rooms in Sudder Street to his writing stall outside the offices of the State of Bengal, Gopal's *rickshaw* had recently suffered a broken spring. When Gopal had tried to complain to a traffic policeman about the pot-holed roads and sunken tram rails he was told, "Calcutta Municipal and Tramways has no money to pay for repairs. I often get no pay, so bugger off, I tell you."

Gopal was still looking to pluck up the courage to approach Mr Chatterjee to make an honourable request for broken spring compensation to the important offices. He knew that Mr Chatterjee was a very clever fellow because the sign over his stall declared:

D K CHATTERJEE BA (failed) CALCUTTA UNIVERSITY

He was also a most shrewd fellow, having contracted to pay a small inducement on a weekly renewable principle to a certain official whereby he was guaranteed security of tenure for a five foot section of pavement adjacent to the side entrance of the state offices. This pitch was strategically located to ensure a steady stream of clients seeking help to thread a way through the confusing procedure of public administration. Mr Chatterjee was renowned for his expertness in writing very top-hole letters in a bold copperplate hand to form solicitations in the extravagant English esteemed by the Indian bureaucrat.

Gopal turned his thoughts to other matters. Young ladies he carried to the Hindu Academy in Upper School Street. They were always jolly and spoke kindly to him even though they were of a higher caste, unlike the ladies he carried for their daily shopping trips to market. They did not speak nicely to him and always carried a small *durree* to protect their sarees from the dusty seats. At midday he carried piled up *tiffin* cans to many office workers in Park Street for his curry stall friends who would also give him a drink of cane juice and a banana leaf of rice and *dhal*.

The evenings were often exciting for Gopal. He would summon up his strength for the most profitable time of his long day when he would carry British soldiers to the cinema and certain other places. They return to barracks all happy and often sing songs in soldier Urdu which Gopal understand:

> "Sixteen annas, one rupee
> Seventeen annas, one *backshee*
> O Deolali Sahib, O Deolali Sahib.
> For seven long years you bed my daughter,
> Now you go to Blighty, Sahib.
> May the boat that carries you home,
> Sink to the bottom of the *pani,* Sahib.
> O Deolali Sahib…."

British soldiers very good, give plenty *backsheesh* but sometimes if drinking too much *pagal-pani* they say, "Mr Churchill pay fare," then pretend to run away but they always give plenty money for ride. Last jobs for night taking sahibs and memsahibs home or to hotel after eating-dances at fine restaurants. They sometimes trying to do mischief thing in *rickshaw*. Mems not modest same like Mila.

Gopal had worked all day for the miserable sum of three rupees and ten annas which was nestling in a worn leather pouch hidden in the waist-folds of his sweat soaked *dhoti*. He had to find one rupee for *rickshaw* rent, give one rupee to Mila to pay for food and cow dung cooking fuel. The remainder would be secreted in the brass *chatti* to save for the day when he would be gifted with a son.

Within a few hundred yards of home, Gopal's thoughts switched to dwell on Mila. Almond shaped eyes almost as black as the glistening hair falling to her waist, firm young breasts swelling to maturity and almost ready for the day when she would no longer be a child-wife. Until that most blessed day when he could lay with her for the first time she would remain untouched....

★★★

Corporal Bailey checked his watch; almost midnight or 2359 hours in military time. Twelve hours to go, then it was goodbye to Red Road Transit Camp and on his way home. Home to his wife Stella. He wondered about the reception he would receive since he had learned from a neighbouring 'wellwisher' about her 'gallivanting' with some Canadians from a nearby airfield. It couldn't have been easy for her whilst he had been abroad for nearly four years. It was a blessing they had no children to worry about. She had a job on munitions and she had been saving his allowances and her earnings to put down on a house when he was demobbed. When he returned to the job which had been kept open for him at the Town Hall he knew everything would be alright.

The last night in the Calcutta transit camp and he had been

detailed for guard duty. As the first streaks of dawn appeared he went outside the guard tent to stretch his legs. The telephone rang.

"Red Road Transit Camp, Guard Commander speaking, sir."

"This is the Duty Officer, Calcutta District. There seems to be a bit of a flap on in town. You'd better alert the camp and get the Camp Commandant to give me a ring on Calcutta Mil 748. You might remind him to look up his copy of the contingency plan for riot and civil unrest. Got that?"

"OK sir. I'll enter the time of your call in the guard report for zero five-thirty."

Corporal Bailey ordered the duty bugler to call 'stand to' and gave instructions for the fire alarm to be sounded in urgent emphasis. After getting through to the Camp Commandant and relaying his message, he wrote up a summary of the event, taking great care to include all relevant detail. With only seven hours left before his scheduled departure on a homeward bound draft, he was not prepared to risk any failure in the proper discharge of his duties. He knew the army well. Panic situations set everyone on edge with the 'who did what, when and why' questions at any consequential debrief. Bailey was not the type to stick his neck out at this stage of the game.

Summoned to assembly points by bugle and fire alarm, half naked troops milled around exchanging cynical comment on the reason for being dragged from their *charpoys*:

"I smell no smoke, I see no fire, what the bloody hell's going on?"

"Time somebody set fire to this dump, the tents are falling apart ... I say let the place burn to the ground."

"Sandy's right, there's no sign of a fire in camp but if you take a *dekko* over there there's a right old blaze going on. Look."

Eyes focussed on the direction indicated to see plumes of heavy, black smoke drifting over the river almost blotting out the towering superstructure above Howrah Bridge.

A shouted, "Stand still you lot and listen for your names,"

brought any further moves to a halt. A permanent staff corporal produced a nominal roll and began to reel off lists of "last threes and surnames: Two nine nine Cooper, three eight seven Mason, four twenty Wainwright … Wainwright, anybody seen Wainwright?"

"Yes Corp, he went on draft yesterday. If you can hire a fast camel you will just about miss him as he embarks at Bombay."

"Very comical, I don't think. You lot will be laughing on the other side of your faces when you hear what the Sar'nt Major's got in store for you. Stand to attention, he's on his way now."

Washed, shaved and properly dressed in starched khaki drill with gleaming boots and polished brasses, he commanded instant and unwavering attention.

"Listen in, lads. There's some riotous behaviour going on in the bazaar."

Even in the largest cities of the sub-continent anything outside the camp or cantonment was always referred to as 'the bazaar'. "From early reports it seems as if it's going on in the slum area across the river and seems to be a localised affair between Hindus and Muslims. Now then, if these native geezers want to knock hell out of each other that's their business, it's up to the civil authorities to deal with it. However, if the commotion gets out of hand and British lives or property are threatened we have got to be prepared to act … that's why you have been put on alert. There are no British garrison troops in the area but there are some establishments which have to be protected, including District Headquarters, stores and workshops depots and the Military Hospital. The last mentioned is the responsibility of this camp, so an armed piquet of twenty rank and file with a sergeant in charge will parade in thirty minutes. The piquet will be issued with arms and fifty rounds each and will carry rations and water for ninety-six hours. Any questions?"

The sergeant-major glanced quickly over the ranks, anticipating the nuisance questions – none came. The men stood waiting for the next piece of unwelcome information.

"Right then, before you are dismissed I want to remind you

that anyone detailed for armed piquet duty is not entitled to take pot-shots at anyone causing a disturbance. You will be ordered to fire only on the authority of a senior officer at an ordered target. We don't want to worsen an already deteriorating political situation. Finally, there will be no troop movements until further orders. Dismiss."

Chapter 6

He tore the tail from his shirt to cover her face and to shield him from the censure in her eyes. Gopal had failed to save her. She had been beyond his reach as he had burrowed deep into the shelter of a garbage heap to protect his own life a few hours earlier.

He had been about to turn into the narrow lane that led to his dwelling when he saw the flames of many torches surging towards him. The slap, slap sound of barefoot runners seemed to come from all directions. Gopal was not aware of any religious festival, Hindu or Muslim or even Christian, which carried on through the night. When he heard the mob calling, "*Pakistan Zindabad, Pakistan Zindabad*," a burning fear hit his stomach.

When working in the jute fields of East Bengal, before venturing into the teeming city of Calcutta to earn enough to marry and raise a family, he had heard tales of street riots aimed at driving the British out of India and of demands made by the Muslim peoples to rule an independent state to be named Pakistan. It had also been rumoured that Mohammed Ali Jinnah, a Muslim leader in far off Delhi, had proclaimed that he would have India divided or he would have India destroyed.

Those tales and rumours, barely understood by Gopal, had surfaced from his memory as he ran to hide from the approaching terror. Little did he realize that he was to witness and play a part in the 'Muslim Day of Direct Action' planned for the 16th of August 1946 and in the 'Great Calcutta Killings' that were to follow.

Laying in his bolthole with eyes tight shut and hands covering his ears to blot out the repeated mantra, Gopal shook with fear. His bladder and bowels had emptied in shock and soiled his *dhoti* but he failed to notice any smell or discomfort against the stench of his refuge. If he had dared raise his head he would have seen scores of men running through the mean alleyways at a dogtrot pace, brandishing swords, daggers, iron bars and bill-hooks, some even carrying shovels. He would have seen dead and dying men and women, old and young alike, crippled beggars and tiny babies all lying in obscene postures on blood-reddening ground.

As the sun's heat penetrated the garbage heap and the noise of the night's terror receded, Gopal emerged into the awful scene of the night's butchery. The pitiful cries for help dribbling from the mouths of the barely alive mingled with the yelping of dog packs scrabbling for pieces of human flesh. Vultures flopped down to tear at the entrails of still-warm bodies. Kite-hawks, crows and unidentified carrion birds shared in the feast of flesh, returning time after time from delivering food to their nesting young.

Appeals for help went unanswered. The police and medical services remained out of sight, nervous of being caught up in any religiously inspired act of mass violence. The misery of being forced to live in the slums of Calcutta with its natural order of hunger, disease and early death owed little priority to dealing with any level of murderous outrage. There would be little outside help to aid the injured or comfort the dying. It would be left to the survivors of the night of killing to dispose of corpses in the best way they could. The poor had no dignity, not even in death.

★★★

He brushed away the cloud of hungry flies seeking to eat and deposit their eggs in her opened belly. He knew what had to be done for his poor Mila who lay crumpled in the dross from her cooking fire. Working quickly, he washed the blackening blood from her body and bound her wounds with bandages torn from an unbleached calico sheet. He untangled her knotted hair, brushed it, and laid it over her shoulders and her breasts. He dressed her tiny body in the soft pink *sari* she had worn on her wedding day and wrapped her in the remains of the torn sheet.

He placed her across the seat of his *rickshaw* and set off for the burning *ghats*. He took all the savings from his secret hideaway to buy wood and *ghee* for her funeral pyre and to buy a garland of yellow marigolds to lay over her heart.

There were many Hindu corpses to be disposed of after the night of killing and the burning *ghats* on the shores of the Hooghly were extra busy. The *dom raja* in charge of the proceedings was haggling with the crowds of mourners to get the best price for his wood and *ghee* from those who had arrived without fuel. The attendant *doms*, stripped to the waist, dripping sweat from the withering heat of the flames and with their bodies streaked with grey ash dust hurried to pile wood on the funeral pyres. As the remains of partly burned bodies were swept from the concrete plinths to make space for more, the *doms*, mourners and street children scrabbled to retrieve body ornaments or prise gold teeth from the jaws of fire-blackened skulls.

Gopal attended to Mila's cremation. He pushed the *doms* away and gently laid her body on the clean swept plinth, piled wood, poured *ghee* and touched the pyre with the flame of a torch. He stood at the place of honour at her head and with hands clasped in prayer and head bowed he chanted, "*Ram Ram, Ram Ram, Ram Ram,*" the Hindu invocation to divinity, until the wood turned to charcoal and her flesh was consumed by the flames.

He collected her charred remains and took them to the water's edge to be floated out to sea with countless other partly incinerated corpses. Now alone, he turned his back on that awful arena and hastened to the Temple of Kali, the Hindu goddess of destruction, where he called upon her to strengthen his arm to avenge the killing of Mila.

★★★

The stunned reaction of Hindus changed to an avenging momentum as they crept out of their places of refuge to hit the streets in the burning heat of revenge. Anyone hastily identified as a follower of Islam was slashed, beaten or ripped to pieces.

Victims lay where they fell. Some in the shafts of their *rickshaws*, some under loads of jute being hauled to the docks. Tram crews and taxi drivers, street vendors and messengers. Men and women, children and beggars. None were spared. Lorries and cars, shops and hovels were put to the torch, leaving columns of smoke to mingle with the rancid fumes of the burning *ghats*. The earlier mantra of *"Pakistan Zindabad"* now gave way to the Hindu call of *"Jai Hind"*.

By midday, corpses were lying bloated and putrefying under the furnace heat of the sun and swarming flies. Squealing rats nuzzled into the shambles left in the faecal sludge of open sewers. The streets were claimed by flocks of heavy grey vultures and snarling dog packs as the business life of Calcutta was brought to a standstill. Shops closed, public transport services were suspended. Fear spread to the prosperous residential areas where house servants deserted their posts and fled to the countryside to escape the terror.

By the evening of the second day of slaughter, Gopal lay exhausted in the broken remains of a street stall. A claw hammer, stained with blood and with strands of hair sticking to it, was in his hand. It held silent testimony to the debt he had collected on Mila's account. As he lay there, trying to make sense of the events of the last forty-eight hours, of the terror he had witnessed and the prospect of life without his Mila, he took little notice of a man who bent over him to place a small foil-wrapped pellet into his hand.

Chapter 7

Squadron Leader Mike Golding sat at a six-foot trestle table writing a letter. His wrist and forearm rested on a folded handkerchief to protect the pale blue airmail writing pad from the sweat oozing from his pores. His office was set up in the corner of the squadron stores tent. The smell of engine oil, hydraulic fluid and fabric dope combined to indicate the association with aeroplanes.

Aeroplanes had been central to Golding's service experience over three war zones. Following the carefree days of flying with his university air squadron, he had been commissioned into the RAF. Then, after operational training, he had been posted to the Desert Air Force to fly against Rommel's Africa Corps. A tour with Bomber Command flying Pathfinder missions over Germany was rewarded with the DFC and a posting to South East Asia in ground support operations against the Japanese. With the end of hostilities he was now engaged in closing down his squadron. They had informed him that the squadron was to go into 'suspended animation' or, as Golding put it, "we are for the bloody chop fellas – it's curtains for us." His beloved Mk XIX Mosquito fighter-bombers were even now being dismantled and stuffed into transit cases for shipment to some knacker's yard.

He lifted his pen and read:

> ... I hope this will be the last letter I'll be writing from Chittagong and I can tell you I'll be glad to get back home and shake off this damned prickly heat and sweat rash....

The urgent ringing of a field telephone broke his concentration.

"Hullo, Midge," (with the initials MG it was inevitable that Golding would carry the known name of Midget after the famous marque of sports car). "This is the adj. Can you get over here *ekh dum*, the CO wants to have a *bolo* with you about a job that's just come in."

He slipped the unfinished letter into a flight bag and reached for his cap, a touch of formality to complement his shorts and gym shoes, the standard form of working dress on the oven-hot airfield during the hours of daylight. Most of the station would be a-kip or sweating through a game of badminton or volley-ball – anything to escape the boredom of peacetime service on an airfield thousands of miles from home, pubs and cinemas.

Golding ducked under the flysheet of the station HQ tent to grab a mug of water, cooled in the large earthenware *chatti* standing on a frame by the adjutant's desk. It was very welcome refreshment after the five hundred yards walk across the airfield.

"What's the gen this time? Hope it was worth dragging me over here for and interrupting my word-flow." The station commander called them into his office, a canvas cubicle next to the orderly room.

"Welcome, Midge. How's the suspended animation programme going? I have a possible job here for you, so let's hope you've still got an airworthy aeroplane. Better have a *dekko* at this signal first." Golding read through the signal a couple of times and gave it back.

"I wish those bods at GHQ could make their minds up. First it's PUFO, then it's get your skates on. Sounds as if someone's got a bit of a flap on." The CO turned to an operational map hanging from a tent wall support pole and pointed to Tamu airfield.

"There's the target, and we are here, flying miles about two hundred, I estimate. We have no photo interpreter facilities here so you will have to plan on getting your pictures to RAF Dum Dum at Calcutta in the one trip. That's another two hundred and fifty miles and well inside Mosquito range. Do you know Tamu, Midge? From memory it's a typical Burma airfield, lots of hills and a tricky approach, mist can drop visibility to zero at the drop of a hat and it doesn't wait for the monsoon season. It can rain any time of the year up there, as well you know."

"Seems a simple enough op, but do we have any idea who these bods might be who are lurking about up there? If they are up to some mischief and they get the idea that we are spying on them, they could give us a warm welcome."

"Yes, we must consider the risk element in the flight plan. Tamu is approximately on the Chungking air route which kept the Chinese supplied during the war. I would be inclined to make your target run on a bearing that follows the same flight path. That means you will have to fly a dog-leg track to come in on a matching bearing. As for attracting unfriendly attention, I will authorise armed guns. I expect we still have a few bullets left in store."

"I take it that we have no idea who we are looking at. If GHQ is making this recce request it means that they are in the dark. One could ask: are they our own people? I suppose one could take the answer to be a firm no. If the brass don't know what's going on in their own backyard, it doesn't say much for the command structure. The only other people in the region with any flying capability are the Yanks, but they pulled out of India and Burma at the back end of last year."

The CO smiled. "Yes, I have good cause to remember the farewell bash they put on over at the Dacca airbase. Never could work out how they got hold of such generous supplies of Scotch when we were rationed to half a bottle per man per month. I suppose it could have been part of the Lend-Lease arrangement. Makes a chap wonder which side got the best of the bargain – 'Guns for whisky', to parody Hermann Goring's 'Guns for butter' rousing call … our finest tipple for their munitions. Right, where were we? Who can these bods up at Tamu be, and whose aeroplanes are they using?"

"Having ruled out our American allies, we are left with the Chinese and the Russians, the only two countries left with anything like an air capability. I think the Chinese have got too much going on in their own country with this Mao fellow leading a Commie rebellion against the Nationalists to bother with clandestine sorties into our territory. That leaves us with the Russians."

"Yes, it's common knowledge that they have a long standing interest in India, but they concentrated their efforts over the North West Frontier by stirring up trouble with the tribes. I know; I was up there in thirty-seven dropping bombs on the buggers from clapped out Wapitis. But I won't bore you with tales of my days as a Corporal Observer helping to guard an outpost of the Empire. No, there's no point in trying to speculate on possibilities. We can only pray that we don't stir up a political hornet's nest with this little exercise."

Golding studied the map at close range and made some notes of the terrain over which he would fly: rivers, mountain peaks, jungle and flat lands suitable for an emergency landing. The CO busied himself filling his pipe with Digger Flake from an airtight tin. Satisfied that the bowl was nicely packed he set about lighting up, a procedure that required skill and dexterity to avoid injury from particles of flaming phosphorus emitted from locally produced matches. He refrained from using a petrol lighter – "made the smoke taste like the exhaust fumes from a worn out engine."

Satisfied that the pipe had attained a nicely working temperature, he settled down to progress the current task.

"You are now going to fill me in on aircraft availability. I take it there are one or two still in working order. How long will it take to get something airworthy?"

"I'll push the fitters to drum up something fit to fly. There are four Mosquitoes left standing on their own legs. You might classify them as 'walking wounded' because they haven't had any routine maintenance carried out on them during the last couple of weeks and we know how this climate can play havoc with equipment, especially the electrics. I'm sure my Flight Sergeant fitter will lap up the idea of getting something ready to fly instead of stripping and packing."

"Good enough Midge, the brass will have to exercise a little patience. They know what the form is as well as we do. After all, they issued the suspended animation orders. Let the adj have a flight plan so he can arrange to get it cleared. I'll let Dum Dum know when to expect you."

Chapter 8

Harding lowered himself into a comfortable seat to enjoy the relaxed atmosphere of the Sergeant's Mess. All morning and most of the afternoon he had been busy with the weekly maintenance tasks on his wireless station. Halyards and guys adjusted on the aerial masts, an oil check and fuel top-up on the Coventry Climax generator. He relied on the generator for his power rather than on the uncertain voltage of the local civil electricity. The transmitter had been set up and tuned ready for his next schedule with Calcutta which was due on Monday evening. After satisfying himself on the serviceability of his wireless equipment, he had used the time before dinner to catch up on some letter writing. A letter to his parents to tell them of the uncertainty of his return home, an overdue reply to a mate serving with the RAF in Germany and a brief note to the secretary of his local cricket club to let him know that he would be happy to turn out if he was home in time for any of next season's games.

He looked at his watch. It was coming up to six-thirty – early dinner night to allow the chaps to join the recreational transport for the weekly cinema trip into town. The feature film was *Gilda* starring the luscious Rita Hayworth, a very tempting slice of Hollywood entertainment. Could women like her really exist outside the world of film and the long-legged, busty Varga pin-ups that adorned the walls above the soldiers' beds?

Harding was interrupted from his reverie by the enquiring tone of the mess waiter. "You not going pictures, Sergeant Sahib? Friday night all sergeants go to town on recreational truck. I know tonight very good film … *bahut acha bibi* … with very good titties." He demonstrated with hands cupped to his chest and eyes opened wide in lecherous wonderment.

"Not tonight thank you, early night in kip for me. Anyhow, less of the lewd thoughts, you old goat. Let's have a beer … I hear we have some Canadian Black Horse in the bar. Bring me one."

The waiter glided off to fulfil his mission, grinning widely that his awareness of the physical attributes of western females, as presented by Rita Hayworth, had been shared with the sergeant sahib.

Harding sat back to enjoy his ice-cold beer as he scanned the pages of a week-old copy of the *Daily Telegraph*. His thoughts ran through his possible plans for the coming weekend. Free of any duties … wireless equipment in good order … private mail up to date. Ha, yes … let's give it a go … now what did he do with that telephone number? Of course – map case, red lipstick. He gulped down his beer and went off to find his map case.

The girl on the military switchboard repeated the number:

"Shillong Civil twoo sev-en. I will call you back, sir."

"Speak up, Mr Harding. I put you through now."

A female voice not recognisable as Laura Erskine's came over the crackly line, "Erskine Estate. Who is that, please?"

"My name is Harding … Sergeant Harding. Er, may I please speak to Miss Erskine? I met her on the Shillong road last week and she gave me this telephone number. I was wondering if she got her wagon repaired OK."

"Oh, it's you, Mr Harding … yes, Laura told me all about your help when she was stuck on the Shillong road. It was noble of you to come to her rescue and I would like to thank you as well. I was becoming rather concerned and was considering sending someone out to look for her. Give me a moment and I'll go and get her for you. She's just in the study."

After a few moments' wait, Harding heard a different female voice. "Hello, this is Laura Erskine. Nice to hear from you. I was rather wondering when you would be ringing. How are you?"

"Quite well, thank you. I remembered where you had written

your telephone number so I thought I might give you a ring and accept the invitation you offered me ... is it still open?"

"Of course the invitation is still open. How about tomorrow if you aren't too busy? Perhaps you could make it by say twelve-thirty, in time for *tiffin,* then have a look around the estate and stay on for dinner. Aunt Julia would love to meet you."

"I take it that Aunt Julia was the lady who answered the telephone. Is she visiting or does she live with you?"

"She lives here with me, just two females running this estate. Anyhow, I'll tell you all about it tomorrow. See you then, 'bye."

Harding waited until the distant handset was replaced then blew hard into his mouthpiece and said in a raised voice, "TESTING, TESTING," to let the nosey telephone operator know that he was aware she had been eavesdropping. When he heard the line being disconnected, he knew that he had guessed right and that the camp grapevine would transmit the details of his telephone call to a wide audience.

★★★

Harding contemplated what to take as a 'thank you for having me' donation. Flowers were out ... he hardly knew the woman and anyhow they wouldn't last the journey in the climate, even if he could lay his hands on a suitable bouquet. Maybe a bottle of some sort would do? Under the impression that planters enjoyed a very convivial lifestyle, Harding thought they had probably got an ample supply of booze tucked away. Then he had a brilliant idea ... to go and see Ali the camp contractor, seeing as he had special purchasing arrangements to supply British forces. For whatever reason, all canteen, extra messing supplies and toilet necessities were catered for by approved local contractors because NAAFI didn't operate in India. An old army adage had it that the scarcest objects east of Suez were guardsmen and NAAFI sandwiches.

"Ali, you old sod, got anything new hidden away? I'm looking for a little something for a memsahib, nothing too grand … *tum malum?*"

"*Achcha*, Sergeant Sahib, Ali understand. Ali also know where memsahib for whom you wish to take present live. Very big tea plantation on Shillong road. If you wish to keep secret you must not be using telephone."

"Don't worry about secrets. I know where the information came from … can we get on with it?"

"Give Ali a few more moments to finish this business and I will look after you."

Ali was busy at his pay night post in the Rank and File Canteen receiving settlement from the soldiers for the unofficial credit he extended. His tally book held a page for each sundry debtor and was identified by such unlikely names as Joseph Stalin, Rob Roy or Flash Gordon. Freeman, Hardy and Willis held accounts on three successive pages. When all the debtors present in the canteen who could pay had paid, Ali closed his small ledger, slipped an elastic band round it as if to secure its confidentiality and slipped it into the waistband of his baggy trousers, the traditional garb of the Punjabi Mussalman. Ali was the current head of a family of contractors who had served the domestic needs of the British Army in India for over eighty years. It was rumoured that the founder of the business, having witnessed the spectacle of some of his countrymen being roped to gun muzzles and blasted into eternity for their part in the Indian Mutiny, had decided that service was a better option than sacrifice.

"You will take a coffee with me, Sergeant Sahib? Or if you would wish, something a little stronger, but alas I cannot join you in such a drink."

Harding smiled, recalling the tooth-crumbling power of Islam coffee; treacly thick, black as ebony and strong enough to fell a shire-horse. "Just a little if you please, and with a glass of *tunda pani*." As they drank Harding expanded on his requirements. "If I was back in England, I would probably try and cadge a few eggs or maybe a tin of Spam, gifts that would be appreciated with the current food shortages and with rationing still in force. But as this isn't England I wondered if you could help me."

Ali nodded his head and wrinkled his brow in concentration. Leaning forward to share his decision, he said, "I can show you nice ideas, please come with me."

They crossed the dimly illuminated camp, leaving behind the din of pay night celebrations and entered Ali's store compound. It was protected by a seven-foot fence of barbed wire and a fierce-looking Pathan *chowkidar*. Ali selected a key from the formidable bunch hanging from a chain beneath his shirt and released the hasp on a heavy, brass Aligarh padlock, allowing the steel reinforced door to swing back, giving entrance to a large cool storehouse. Jute sacks, wooden cases, crates and cardboard containers were neatly stacked on duckboards from floor to ceiling. He pulled back a woven straw mat to reveal a trap door let into the floor which he opened to reveal a stairway leading into a cellar. He lit a hurricane lamp and led the way down.

"Now, Sergeant Sahib, take a look round and see how I can solve your predicament. Perhaps a nice bottle of wine from Australia, or some vintage Champagne from France. I am told it is very good, but I cannot tell you from personal taste because the Koran orders no alcohol. Please look, I am in no hurry."

Harding gasped with surprise at the inventory of luxury goods bearing labels of international distinction. Cases of Highland malt, Cognac, various liqueurs, tins of Belgian chocolates, Dundee cake, asparagus, whole chickens, Parma ham, perfumes, soaps and bundles of Turkish and Egyptian towels.

"Where on earth did all this come from? It's the sort of stuff that hasn't been seen in years back home, at least not over the counter it hasn't. It's the sort of loot the Nazis pinched when they occupied a large slice of Europe."

Ali nodded his head with the sideways motion peculiar to natives of the sub-continent.

"One day soon when the British depart India as they surely will, there will be no contracting business for me with the British

Army. All this is what I call my insurance against that day. I have a British passport, so I can move to England or other Empire country, maybe Canada or Australia. But if that is too much difficult, I will try Kenya or Aden. You see, Sergeant Sahib, I have wide choice of places to go and all these goods you see here are my assets to begin new business in new country – goods can appreciate in value but money does not unless you lend to bank, which I do not trust or make private loan to people, who I trust much less. Now you know my secret, let me offer you any mortal thing you like for your social invitation."

"Well, you crafty old *wallah*, this is a surprise and no mistake. Never thought you had it in you to get yourself set up like this. Right, now I see you have some jars of Frejus peaches in brandy there. How about one of those? I tasted them once and they are a bit of OK. How much?"

"For you, Sergeant Sahib, there will be no charge. I make special gift."

"Nice of you to offer, but I'd rather pay. How about ten rupees? Does that seem a fair price?"

"If you insist, but that is more than one day pay for you." He gave a soft chuckle and said, "I am sure the memsahib will be worthy of your fine compliment. Here, take it."

Chapter 9

The noise of cold engines spluttering into life crackled across the airfield, breaking the dawn silence and launching nesting birds into a frenzy of flight. An inquisitive mongoose on the alert for his breakfast reared up with nose quivering at the alien sound and flying foxes returning to their habitats high up in a clump of deodars veered and lifted to avoid the air-carried vibrations.

Flight Sergeant Campbell and his fitters had worked non-stop for three days and two nights to get the Mosquito airworthy and accepted by Squadron Leader Golding and his navigator, Sergeant Jackson. The aircraft had been given a full system check and put through a schedule of 'bumps and circuits' in preparation for its reconnaissance mission.

When the twin Rolls-Royce Merlin engines had been run up through the rev counter checks, Golding gave the signal for the ground crew to move the starter trolley and pull the chocks away. He guided the aircraft round the PSP track to the enclosed range where he loosed off short bursts to clear the guns before take-off. Under operational conditions this exercise would have been carried out when airborne, but as this was a peacetime flight and a secret mission into the bargain, a chap had to be discreet.

A final check at the end of the runway, revs up to take-off level, then Golding released the brakes to allow the aircraft to lurch forward, propellers biting the air to gather speed into lift-off. After a low level circuit of the airfield, he eased back the control column and applied rudder to make a left banking turn and set course for his target.

Golding switched to intercom and called, "Right, Jacko, give me the course bearing, please." It was an uncomplicated flight plan which Sergeant Jackson had plotted on a piece of Ordnance Survey map and slotted into the clear plastic pocket above the knee of his flying overalls.

"According to the agreed flight plan, steer magnetic north for twenty-five minutes at our present ground speed of 150 mph when you reach an altitude of six thousand feet. When I give you the nod, turn right on magnetic 060 degrees. This will take us over target on a rough parallel to the old Chungking supply route. OK skipper?"

"Thanks, Jacko. What did the met briefing have to tell us about the weather?"

"We have a six knot wind from 240 degrees, air pressure at sea level is 1,100 millibars and visibility is good all the way, but be prepared for some turbulence over high geography."

"Roger. Let's settle down and enjoy the flight. Doubt if we'll ever get another chance to fly when this little job is done."

They left the flat waters of the Bay of Bengal to port and headed over the flood plains in the direction of Tripura, the most southerly district of Assam. The landscape of *padi* fields and jute crops set amongst clusters of thatched huts soon gave way to jungle clad hills and time for a course change.

As the flight progressed Jackson concentrated on his watch and counted down ready to warn his pilot to turn onto the new bearing. "Ready to change, skipper … three, two, one … now. 060 degrees."

"Roger, 060 degrees."

Golding put the Mosquito into a banking turn to starboard to line up his compass on the new flight path.

"What time over target, Jacko, and are we OK at this altitude to get some good pictures?"

"I estimate time over target at 0710 hours. If there are any bods hanging around on the airfield they will probably be still a-kip or too busy with breakfast to take much notice of us. I reckon the target to be about three thousand feet and as we are flying at six thousand feet above sea level, we should be at a reasonable height to do a fair job. That's providing there is no loss of visibility. As you know, you can never rely on the weather up in this region."

They flew over the Maripur river, crossing it at 45 degrees, experiencing some bounce as they hit the north-south mountain ranges with air currents abruptly changing in direction and strength.

"Thirty miles to go, skipper. Hold this course. I hope we get some indication when we reach the approach. The airfield construction engineers used to clear back the jungle to give a decent landing and take-off run, so let's hope nature hasn't worked too quickly to overgrow again."

"Let's hope you are right, Jacko. I'm going silent now. Leave the talking to you."

"Roger, skip. About six minutes to target. Steady. Keep to the west side of the runway. I'm starting up the camera … now."

Golding replied with a clipped "Wilco" and concentrated on keeping the aircraft level and on course. After less than fifty seconds they were over and clear of the target and heading on the same flight path until they were out of visual and sound range of the airfield, when Golding deemed it safe from ground observation to turn on track for Calcutta and RAF Station Dum Dum. They were under orders to hand in the exposed film pack to the Air Photographic Reconnaissance section at Dum Dum for developing and analysis.

With course corrections confirmed and set for the return flight Jackson asked Golding what he thought of the set-up on Tamu.

Golding's voice came over the intercom: "Not surprised Delhi was curious about this job. I wonder if they are going to be as astonished as us about the outcome. Apart from the fact that this allegedly abandoned airfield seems to be operational again with a Dakota sat on the tarmac, there is that bloody German Junkers 52 lurking in the dispersal area. I didn't have time to spot any markings on either aeroplane – did you see anything?"

"No, I didn't get a proper *dekko* at any markings except for what looked like CAT on the Dak. It will be interesting to see what the APR *wallahs* make of it. It has all the makings of a pretty serious business though; tents, and what looks like a few hundred drums of petrol stashed away on the edge of the jungle."

"Very shady goings-on, old lad. Wonder if we are going to get involved or will they leave it to the brown jobs to resolve? More in their line to do a ground recce to find out what the score is."

"Good enough … time to give Dum Dum a call. I estimate ten minutes to touch down."

Following the approach instruction of air traffic control, Golding brought the Mosquito in over the delta expanse of the leaden Hooghly, the river which acted as a sewer for the heavily populated rural plains into the sea and gave entry to cargo vessels to load the jute, hides and rice from the Calcutta *godowns*. The wide river was crudely dismissed as the arsehole of India with Calcutta right up it. With landing gear down and locked for touchdown, Golding applied full flap and adjusted the approach angle to follow a shallow glide path. The aircraft gave a slight shudder as it settled on the runway for the run in. He allowed the aircraft to slow down under its own reducing momentum without applying heavy brake as required on short jungle airstrips, then swung off the main runway to follow a reception Jeep along the perimeter track to the allocated slot on the dispersal apron. The twin Merlins gave a final roar then coughed to a standstill as the switches were cut. Pilot and navigator dropped onto the tarmac and moved out beyond the starboard wing to the waiting Jeep. A pretty young WAAF corporal in freshly pressed khaki-drill bush shirt and skirt greeted them.

"Good morning gentlemen, have a good trip? If you would let me have your film, please, and I'll take you off to flight ops mess for a late breakfast. The mess steward will take your flying overalls and get them *dhobied* for you. Should be ready in about an hour. We'll get your aircraft checked over and re-fuelled ready for your flight back to Chittagong … if there is anything else you require, please let me know."

She delivered the information with a competence not entirely compatible with her appearance: short brown hair, slightly windswept from driving in the open Jeep, a suggestion of mischief in her hazel eyes and a gentle smile curving her lips. As she stepped forward to take the film pack from Jackson he caught a whiff of citrus-fresh perfume, and a glimpse of brilliant white brassière edging from the vee of her open-necked shirt.

"This really is a nice welcome," Jackson said. "Thanks for the breakfast offer and the laundry arrangements. I don't think the skipper will need any fuel. Waste of time loading extra to take back with us because we are in the business of closing down and disposing of the aircraft. This is our final flight on this little beauty. We would be happy to take you back to Chittagong with us though, plenty of room for a pretty girl like you … are you going to tell me your name?"

"Officially I am Corporal Anderson. Socially, I prefer Joyce and I'd love to take up your offer, but I am on my way home, hopefully within the next week … sorry and all that but when it's time to go, it's time to go and I won't be sorry to get back to England."

"Come on Jacko, don't keep the girl hanging about. She's got her duty to attend to. Did I hear something about a late breakfast?" Golding and Jackson admired a glimpse of sun-bronzed thigh as she hitched up her skirt to climb into the Jeep and settle behind the steering wheel. "I think we both need a cold shower as well as breakfast – chocks away."

Chapter 10

"Good morning, Sergeant Sahib. Bed tea for you, drink now, very warm. Not doing duty today, Sahib, today Saturday."

Harding pulled the mosquito net back to be met with a close-up view of the shining, black face of Prem Lal, his Madrassi bearer. He took the enamel mug and gulped a mouthful of tea. It was lukewarm, very sweet, white with milk and tasted of chlorine after the mass medication of Indian water to protect the British soldier from the deadly cholera bacteria.

"Tell me, old sunshine, if India is as renowned for its tea as we are led to believe, why does it always taste of gnat's piss? Take it away and chuck it into the monsoon drain."

"You are always for ever telling me that, Sergeant Sahib. In turn I am always telling it to mess cook but he shout to me and say he is making bulk supply at one time and everybody like different flavour. He is unable to please all sahibs. But I tell you Sergeant Sahib that mess cook *wallah* is coming from Bombay side and they are not knowing about proper tea making. I tell him one more time for you."

"Save your breath and bring me my shaving water. I want you to get my grey flannels pressed and my best white shirt ironed and ready for eleven-thirty, *malum*? And I want a *pukka* shine on my brown shoes."

"I do all these things getting ready for you, and for your shoes, I give special polish – shining like a diamond."

"Stop boasting and get on with it. And don't forget – eleven-thirty on the dot."

Shouldering a haversack carefully packed with clean kit, the jar of Frejus peaches, and a pot of Beluga donated by Ali who had insisted on making a contribution on the grounds that he had been overpaid for the peaches, and with lowered eyelids had asserted that caviare held "properties of a very special nature," Harding set out for Erskine-Jalpai.

He had decided to make the trip on a hired bicycle as a welcome change from being bounced around in the Jeep and, apart from having to swerve often to avoid pot-holes and loose tarmac, he found the experience quiet enjoyable. When he reached the place where he had said goodbye to Laura a couple of weeks earlier, he turned on to the laterite-surfaced track which ran through some primary jungle then cleared abruptly into a vista of neatly lined tea plants. They stretched in ranks across the contoured terraces of north-facing slopes until meeting more jungle rising to the foothills of snow-clad mountain peaks. A sign at a track junction advised visitors to turn right to the tea sheds or left to the house. Harding turned left, and after riding through a belt of high trees, entered a wide approach drive surfaced in red gravel and flanked by well-cut lawns fronting a rambling stone bungalow. It was built in the English colonial style with a wide veranda standing some three feet clear of ground level and accessed by a wide flight of steps.

A black Labrador bounded up to greet Harding with vigorous enthusiasm, almost bringing him to the ground as he struggled to pull his bicycle onto the rear stand and respond to the dog's jubilation at his arrival.

"Steady on, Marcus, you silly old thing, that's no way to treat a guest … he seems to approve of you, though. I believe I am speaking to Mr Harding, am I not?"

Having succeeded in parking the bicycle and regaining his balance he looked up to see a woman descending the veranda steps. She was tall with dark hair plaited and pinned into a single coil above her neckline. Her hazel eyes appraised him through long lashes and her lips curved a smile of welcome. She was dressed for riding in a pale yellow silk blouse, with fawn jodhpurs strapped to highly polished George boots. When she closed to stretch out a hand, Harding detected the compelling scent of Chanel, a perfect choice for a beautiful woman.

"Good morning … er … ma'am. My name is Harding. I hope I am not intruding, but Mrs Erskine gave me her telephone number and I thought…."

"Of course you're not intruding. I am absolutely delighted to welcome Laura's gallant rescuer to Jalpai. You will be in need of some refreshment, so leave your things there. They will be taken care of."

A bearer stepped forward from the shade of the veranda to take Harding's haversack and wheel his bicycle round to the stable-block. She bade Harding take a seat by a table which held a jug of *nimbu-pani*, a bowl of ice cubes and some glasses.

She waited until he emptied his glass and said, "You may have gathered that I am Laura's aunt … by marriage, of course. My name is Julia Erskine and I hate being referred to as 'Aunt', or even worse, 'Auntie', so please call me Julia. So if you are content with that, then I will be. Now what shall we call you? I think Sergeant is much too formal and Mr is out of the question. Makes one sound like one is referring to a solicitor or something equally stuffy."

"Just call me Harding. That's how I've been known since I joined the army. A fellow gets used to the loss of a first name. Harding will do fine." He smiled at her and said, "Are you happy with that, er … Julia?"

"Entirely. When you are ready, Ramesh the bearer will show you where you can freshen up. Laura should be back soon. She is down at the tea sheds with Tommy Young, a neighbour. The electrical generator is playing up a bit and he has come over to help get the thing running properly."

When Harding returned to the veranda he noted that Julia had changed into a cotton skirt and loose shirt which revealed different parts of her figure. He thought that she would be in her mid to late thirties – a bit young to be an aunt, especially to Laura, whom he thought to be about his age, early twenties. She took the gifts, admiring the labels as she did so.

"This is absolutely lovely; French peaches and oh, the caviare. How very kind of you. I haven't seen anything like this for ages. Although we didn't have to put up with rationing like the people back home during the war, choices were often very limited when civilian food supplies had to take second place to the transport of troops and war materials. I won't be impertinent and ask where they came from, but thank you so much."

Further explanation was avoided with the arrival of Laura and her companion from the tea sheds. He was tall and rail-thin with a loose fitting bush jacket hanging over baggy shorts that almost met his wrinkled khaki stockings. Laura smiled at Harding and apologised for her absence.

"Nice to see you again. Sorry I wasn't here to greet you, but I'm sure Julia has been looking after you. This is Tommy Young … Tommy, I would like you to meet Mr Harding, my knight of the road. I expect Julia explained we have been having some generator trouble and Tommy gave up his Saturday morning to help us. He lives just up the road and is always prepared to come to the rescue when we have any technical problems."

Harding shook hands with Young. He had the calloused palm of a manual worker and spoke with a soft voice.

"Hullo, how are you? I've heard how you did a first-class job on Laura's wagon. Good thing you were in the vicinity at the time."

"It was no trouble … how did you get on with the generator, get it sorted out?"

"I think so. It's an ancient Parsons machine, pre-First War, I imagine and driven by an old car engine. Getting a bit tired now. Do you have any truck with machinery?"

"Well, yes, I suppose I do. Although I'm mainly involved with wireless sets, I often use generators when there is no mains supply available both for direct power and for charging batteries."

Julia broke in to announce that *tiffin* was ready and that Laura had gone off to freshen up.

★★★

"This line's bloody awful," said the duty officer at the C-in C's offices in New Delhi. "Who did you say you are? Speak slowly if you don't mind."

"I say again; this is Colonel Grindley. I spell GEORGE, ROGER, ITEM, NAN, DOG...."

"Yes, got it. Hullo Martin. This is Hugh, I'm duty officer. Look, try the green telephone ... might be a better circuit. I'll get my people at this end to patch you through. Give me five minutes."

Grindley went through to access the green telephone system. It was located in the restricted area adjacent to the cipher office. To gain access, he was required to sign in and confirm his identity even though he was attached to the intelligence centre. This precaution irked Grindley, who was more used to the informal procedures of Indian Army infantry regiments than the strict security of higher levels of command and control. "Stupid buggers must think I'm a bloody spy," he mumbled to himself as he flourished his signature across two spaces of the visitor's book.

"Hullo Martin, back again ... now, what's the form, old boy?"

"I must speak directly to the C-in-C. It's most secret and for his ears only. We seem to have unearthed a real bag o' worms at this end."

"Sorry old boy, I'm afraid he's off station for the weekend. Gone to a farewell parade for a homeward bound battalion, then he's staying on for a bit of a *ram-sami*. Not due back until sometime on Monday – might be able to raise him on the telephone but can't pass any classified stuff."

"OK. I have a package of int material for him. I'll get it off by special courier, by air if I can arrange it, or if the worst comes to the worst, by courtesy of Indian Railways."

"Sorry I can't be of more help. Make certain it's addressed to him personally and marked in some way to identify it without marking it with your unit. Can you see to that?"

"Yes ... now let's see. I'll mark it KINGSMAN. Yes, that's it, look out for a package with that name on it and make certain the boss gets it ASAP."

Chapter 11

After a curry *tiffin,* served with rice and mango chutney and washed down with a glass of iced coffee, Harding felt very comfortable and slightly drowsy. If he had been back at camp he would most likely have gone to bed for a couple of hours. After all, Saturday afternoon was for being 'in bed or out of barracks' as old soldiers often insist. He came back from his reverie to hear the voice of Julia.

"Perhaps you are wondering how two women came to be running a tea plantation in this far-flung corner of the British Empire … I'm sure you are dying to find out."

Harding lifted his head to face Julia. "If you would like to tell me I'd be happy to listen … I must admit it did cross my mind after first meeting your niece on the Shillong road a couple of weeks ago. She didn't say a lot except that she lived on a tea estate with her aunt."

"I don't suppose she thought it necessary to go into any further detail about herself. Judging from the mood she was in when she eventually reached home, I'm surprised she even told you her name. She can get a bit petulant at times, especially when things happen over which she has no control."

"Yes, she was in a bit of a paddy when I found her by the roadside with a non-runner and no immediate assistance forthcoming. Tricky situation. I was glad to have been of some help. Those roads are no place for anyone to be stranded for long. It was much safer during the war with lots of troops always on the move. There are a few villains about now. It's rumoured that there are even a few Jap deserters lurking around who fled into the jungle rather than surrender."

"Well, I hope none of those characters come prowling around

here. Although we rely on an old *chowkidar* who sleeps on the veranda for some protection, he is only armed with a *lathi*. But he has Marcus for company and he can get very annoyed with intruders." When the old dog heard his name he scrambled from the shade of the veranda. "Let's go and see how Laura and Tommy are getting on with the generator. They said it was almost fixed when they came back for *tiffin*."

As they walked Julia continued the conversation. "My husband Carter Erskine died just over a year ago. I was much younger than him. We met in England in the last summer before the war when he was on leave from India and near the end of his stay we married by special licence. We didn't have any children but Carter brought his nephew out to learn the ropes with a view to taking over the running of the business when he retired. So with Mark's future and the future of the estate assured, everything seemed to be OK."

"How did Laura become involved?"

"She was stationed at Comilla with HQ Fourteenth Army. That's where she met Mark. He was serving with the Assam Rifles on special attachment to the headquarters. He knew that Carter was keen on him to marry and produce an heir and he brought her here on a short leave. Sadly, Carter died shortly after they were married. Mark went missing on the very last operation of the war; Operation Zipper, I believe it was called. Laura obtained early release and special permission to remain in India to help run this place."

"You seem to cope pretty well. Do you have any skilled supervision to help with the cultivation and processing, for instance?"

"We have a sort of manager. He was originally taken on by Carter to keep an eye on the labour force and as he showed some promise he was given responsibility to oversee the more routine tasks of planting out and pruning. During the war he had to expand his duties until finally, with Mark away and the loss of my husband, he now does just about everything with the exception of running the accounts and marketing."

Julia led Harding into the generator shed where Laura and Tommy, both sitting on upturned tea chests, were wiping their hands on cotton waste.

Laura smiled a welcome and said, "Just in time to see this bloody thing perform or burst into flames. Would you like to have the honour, Mr Harding? You coaxed the engine on my wagon back into life, as I recall."

Harding took up the challenge. He grabbed the starting handle and gave the engine a couple of turns then held it back against compression. On the third attempt it backfired, spluttered uncertainly then settled down to a steady beat, bringing a modest glow to a light bulb hanging on a flex from the roof. Tommy explained the system: an old Austin 7 engine coupled to a Parsons generator which supplied either the tea sheds or the bungalow through a changeover switch. It did not have the capacity to feed both circuits at the same time so it worked on a rota system: sheds by day, domestic by night and weekends – a heavy load for a clapped-out system.

Laura took up the story. She pulled back a tarpaulin that had been covering a new generator. It was a brand new 27.5 kVA Meadows, mounted on a concrete plinth and secured with heavy spring-washered bolts.

"Mark was planning to get this installed but the war got in the way. He was unable to get any suitable help locally so it was just left. There is a box with some switches and other electric kit which I suppose is part of the job, but I don't know what else would be needed to get the machine running."

Harding looked over the generator. The 'hours run' meter showed that it had only done some twenty hours, barely sufficient to run it in. He found that the exhaust was connected to the open air and a fuel storage tank on a raised platform had been installed behind the shed and piped into the shed. The other three watched him in silence as he completed his survey.

Harding concluded, "If I could have a sight of the installation and operating handbook, I can get the system running – assuming, of course, there are no faults that might show up in the process. If you can get a supply of diesel fuel I would be happy to have a go."

Tommy said, "Now that things are more or less back to normal, road tanker deliveries are OK, and, don't forget, thousands of gallons a week are required to run sawmills and many heavy vehicles are now running on diesel. If you like, I can give you a hand to get the generator set up. I'm not much use with electrics, but I can be of some help I expect."

"Well, do we give it a try?" asked Harding, turning to the ladies.

Julia said, "If it's not too much trouble. I'm sure we would be very grateful to you. It would be lovely to have a reliable source of power for the business and the house."

"That's settled then. I'll pick up some tools and whatever else may be needed to complete the job and try and get over tomorrow morning. Is that alright with you, Mr Young?"

Tommy looked a bit sheepish. "Sorry old chap, 'fraid I can't make it tomorrow, got something on … as it happens I should be on my way now. Might be able to fit it in later in the week. See how it goes, hey?"

As Tommy Young said his goodbyes the two women exchanged knowing glances and smiled at Harding who smiled back. If there was a secret joke he was too polite to enquire.

Chapter 12

The rain forests of high Assam were home to Tommy Young. After coming down from Cambridge University and three years with the Indian Military Engineering Service, he had found a job with the Forestry Department. Although that department of the Indian administration was not as socially favoured as the high-born Civil Service, the life suited him very well. There was minimum contact with his peers, no social commitments to honour, and maximum privacy to live his life in his own way.

He lived in a shabby bungalow. The few people who had seen it considered it little better than a game hide or even a native hut. The floor was of beaten earth, the walls of paper-thin woven rattan and the roof was thatched with rice straw. A trestle table served for dining and writing, a couple of wooden chairs and a club chair with faded blue covers completed the seating arrangements. A deodar bookcase contained a collection of mildewed paper-backs and a bamboo hat-stand supported a collection of umbrellas, walking sticks and a double barrelled 12-bore shotgun. Bedroom privacy was achieved through a threadbare chenille curtain slung from the roof to screen a hemp strung *charpoy* and an *almirah* which contained a few odds and ends of clothing.

The miserable dwelling was protected by a broken down wall and a rampant hedge of prickly pear to discourage inquisitive animals and visitors. The fruit of the prickly pear was safe to eat but it had the sinister effect of producing blood-red urine.

A small shack attached to the bungalow housed Tommy's bearer, an old fellow who answered to the name of Jock. He had acquired the privilege, and right, to adopt that style of address after many years of camp-follower service with successive Highland regiments on the North West Frontier.

Jock emerged from his shack in response to his master's arrival and his immediate need for a bottle and a *lungi* to cover his nakedness after he had stripped off his shirt, shorts and stockings which he flung under the table. He didn't have a laundry bag. After a couple of slugs of whisky to rid his nostrils of the ever-present smell of lamp-oil, he settled down to read his once a week copy of the *Times of India* which carried news of the British element in the sub-continent including social events, departures for home and political comment. Two pages and a few drinks later she came to him.

The heavy, cloying scent of California Poppy signalled her presence. Tommy Young insisted she always wear it when calling on him. He couldn't put up with the rancid smell of coconut oil, a favourite hair dressing with native women. He had bought a bottle of the perfume on a rare trip to Shillong which had triggered her desire for more Western luxuries with a set of 'weekies' at the top of her shopping list. Young's discreet enquiries resulted in him learning that 'weekies' were a set of seven pairs of knickers, one pair dedicated to each day of the week, ranging from white on Sunday to black for Saturday night. He showed no preference for knickers of any colour.

A couple of bottles of Johnnie Walker Black Label and Lucy made the weekend for Tommy Young. He couldn't see the sense in complicating matters by transforming her into a Westernised tart. If he yielded to her yearning for knickers, who knew where it would lead? Perhaps nylons or even high heeled sandals. A chap couldn't be too careful. Bare legs, bare feet and bare arse – Tommy was perfectly happy to make do with local customs.

Chapter 13

Laura invited Harding to accompany her to the tea sheds to see how production was running after the morning's power loss. As she was explaining the withering stage, where freshly picked leaves and buds were spread on trays to dry at the beginning of the process, a little Indian made a noiseless approach to them. He was dressed in gleaming white trousers and shirt. His black hair was plastered down with lavender perfumed brilliantine. He smiled a greeting to display a set of small teeth stained red with betel-nut juice.

"Good afternoon, Missy Memsahib. Everything is OK. I am coming to see withering shed even though it is outside my working time. I did not know you were bringing a visitor."

Laura and Harding both suspected that he was lying. The news of Harding's presence at Erskine-Jalpai would have been quickly signalled all round the estate within minutes of his arrival.

"There is no reason why you should know that I was showing a visitor around. Mr Harding is a friend and is interested in tea growing … this is Narayan Rao. He is now the estate manager and lives at the native quarters. He comes from the Nilgiri Hills, the tea growing area in South India. He is well experienced in tea cultivation and has been a great help in running the show in recent months."

Harding was not impressed by the man. His blood-shot eyes matched his red-stained teeth and his garlic-laden breath compounded with the smell of his hair dressing to produce a very disagreeable body scent. The sight, smell and smarmy apologetic voice of the fellow put him in the 'little shit' category.

When Laura invited Narayan Rao to relate the legend of tea drinking, he smiled with glee.

"Certainly, Missy Memsahib. One day a long, long time ago, the Lord Buddha was doing meditation in the shade of a peepul tree. He was very tired and weary and was being overcome by the desire to sleep. He was not allowed to sleep when doing the meditation so, in order to stay awake, he plucked off his eyelids and flung them to the ground. At the spot where the Lord Buddha's eyelids fell, the very first tea plant sprang up. I have to say to you that this is a story believed by uneducated people but I am knowing quite well that tea first come from China. Is that not the case, Missy Memsahib?"

"Yes, I am more inclined to accept that than the yarn about Buddha. The accepted explanation is that drinking plain water in many parts of China was a dangerous practice because it was swarming with so-called invisible devils. I suppose we would refer to the invisible devils as typhoid or cholera microbes, so they learned to kill them off by boiling the water first. This made the water taste flat and uninteresting so they took to flavouring it by adding herbs of which tea was the most desirable."

"I think I know which version I believe," Harding said. "Now, what about the rest of the set-up? I suppose there's more to it than what I have seen so far."

Laura continued, "Yes indeed, but remember it's all fairly new to me, not having been brought up in the tea industry. It can be a bit labour intensive at certain times of the year, so we hire in labour when we need it … a bit like market gardening back home I suppose, but we do keep a small permanent labour force. They root cuttings in pots then transfer them to the nursery beds when they are about twenty inches high. After twelve to eighteen months, depending on the weather pattern, they are planted out on to the growing slopes. Tea grows quite successfully at altitudes up to seven thousand feet. The highest plantations produce the finest teas but at the cost of a lower yield, hence the high prices paid for the most exclusive varieties."

"How does your product stand in comparison with other varieties?"

"As I have admitted, I am a beginner at this business but I

understand that as we are at about two thousand feet we produce a good quality tea from well selected stock which gives a reasonable yield. It is highly regarded as a breakfast beverage and carries a characteristic malty aroma. We drink it at any time, of course, and when we get back to the house we shall be having some with our afternoon tea. You can then judge for yourself."

"That sounds a very English idea. I look forward to it and I'll look upon tea with added interest in the future, especially if it's Assam and, who knows, maybe from this very plantation."

"Shall we move on? Perhaps you would like to explain the next bit, Mr Rao."

The manager exuded a smile of pride at the form of address and hurried to say, "My great honour, Missy Memsahib. Through here in this place we put the withered pickings through this nasty looking machine that breaks the veins and releases the enzymes. Then they go under heavy rollers to make smaller. After this we leave to ferment and dry out until they become dark brown and ready for grading before packing into chests for shipping to the auction houses of Calcutta and London. If that is all, and I am not required further, I will please be excused."

"Not just yet, I'd like to take a look in the packing shed if you please, seeing that you have the key."

Narayan Rao shuffled his feet and mumbled. "Not ready for inspection today, maybe we continue at another time when it is not my time off, I take my leave now … goodbye."

"Not so fast," said Laura, gripping his arm. "I said I wished to look in the packing shed and I want you to be there too. This isn't a formal inspection and as you are more familiar with things than I am, I would like you to be present. Understand?"

She led the way into the packing shed where empty tea chests were stacked from floor to ceiling. A few smaller sample chests were scattered on a bench alongside a weighing machine. It was very clear to Harding that she was displeased at the sight of the sample chests on the bench. She exploded in a show of anger.

"I was under the impression that these samples had been sent off days ago. No wonder you didn't want me to see this place. Just tell me what the hell has been going on?"

Narayan Rao backed away and focussed his eyes on the floor.

"I am very sorry. I have many things to do now that Erskine-Sahib is away and unable to take charge. I am sad for this mistake and I will make certain the problem is rectified in next few days."

"You're absolutely right. You will get these samples away even if you have to work all night and if you can't I'll get someone in who can. If we don't get a move on we'll be missing the best buyers at the Calcutta auctions. Come on, Mr Harding. Let's get back to the house. I expect Julia will be waiting to serve tea."

As they walked back, Laura said apologetically, "I shouldn't have lost my temper with that fellow but they can be so bloody annoying at times. They make out that everything is perfect with nothing to worry about when the exact opposite is true. I only stick with it for Julia's sake and try to hold the fort until Mark turns up. I still don't know what happened to him. No eyewitness reports or anything to indicate what happened." She glanced at Harding as if he might offer a clue as to what could have taken place.

"Julia mentioned that he had gone missing on the very last British operation of the war," Harding said.

"Yes, I just couldn't believe it. We thought that everything was all over and we could get back to normality then wallop, this had to happen … Operation Zipper, you must have heard of it."

Oh yes, thought Harding, I've heard of it. I was in Force 136, a special formation put together to carry out sabotage and deep penetration reconnaissance operations against the Japs in South East Asia. They were trained and organised to mount Zipper, the invasion of Malaya, but things went horribly wrong. To start with, the landings took place one week after the Japanese Emperor had ordered all fighting to cease and three days before the Japs made their formal surrender to Lord Mountbatten, the Supreme Commander in South East Asia. It was never explained why the operation went ahead under those circumstances unless, as some cynics suggested, it was to let the dogs run after months of intense training. Whatever the official reason, it turned out to be a complete fiasco. Poor reconnaissance and indifferent mapping had guided landing craft to hit the beaches in the wrong place. They grounded on offshore sandbars, forcing troops to disembark and scramble on to lighters to make the initial assault. When tanks and support transport on the run in became waterlogged and stranded short of the beach-head, the local Japanese commander came to the rescue and ordered his recovery vehicles to drag them clear of the tide-line.

As Harding explained his understanding of the operation he became confused. There had been no exchange of fire, no prisoners taken, no battle casualties and therefore no bodies to count. How had Mark Erskine come to be posted as missing?

★★★

A slight drop in temperature and a late afternoon breeze that stirred the banks of brilliantly coloured rhododendrons aroused Harding from sleep. He had remained on the veranda, stretched out on a steamer chair, completely relaxed with thoughts far removed from the routines of army life.

As his thoughts floated he tried to picture how things were back home. Being some seven hours behind local time, he guessed his mother would be doing her weekend shopping. Trying to obtain a little extra to produce a decent Sunday dinner and waiting in line for the meagre ration. He imagined his father in the garden, cutting a few late vegetables to help out or doing some maintenance on the Hillman that had been laid up since 1939.

He did not hear the near silent approach of Ramesh.

"Please, Mr Harding-Sahib, I have to show you to the guest room where, if you so wish there is bath for you. Julia-Mem say for me to get shirt and trouser from haversack for pressing and please to join the ladies in the library at maybe seven-thirty for drinks before dinner ... *thik-hai* Sahib."

"Yes, thank you Ramesh. Ladies – library. Seven-thirty. Got that."

After his bath, having taken in the magnificent splendour of marble slab tiles and gleaming copper plumbing with a plentiful supply of hot water, fine English soap and soft white bath sheets, Harding paralleled the experience to the standard army bathing arrangements of lukewarm water, carbolic soap and *dhobi*-hardened towels. With some thirty minutes to go for the library rendezvous he decided to take a stroll through the gardens. He halted in the open area of the lawn to view the night sky after the sun had moved on to leave an absolutely black backdrop to the thousands of stars. The familiar navigational aids of the Plough and the North Star, invaluable to the traveller, were quickly identified. As was Orion, the hunter giant of Greek mythology, set light years distant in the southern hemisphere. Orion was his favourite constellation. He traced the figure outline through the markers placed on the outstretched arms, astride legs, three prominent stars tracking his belt and the nebula indicating his sword. When Harding found himself in unfamiliar territory he made a special point of searching out Orion in confirmation of its presence and the unchanging relationship of man with the universe.

★★★

She looked beautiful. He recalled when he first met her; stranded on the road with a broken down station wagon under the fierce heat of the mid-afternoon Indian sun, hair soaked in sweat, face streaked with engine grime. In recent hours he had seen her in working clothes struggling to make sense of a faulty generator … but now…. She wore a short dress of dark green, her corn coloured hair was tied back with a green velvet bow. Her legs, now revealed, were long and slender. She looked cool and in control, with her presence enhanced by a soft light perfume. Before Harding could find the right words of greeting she spoke.

"I trust you enjoyed your rest. You seemed ready for it after cycling out here under the blazing sun and then being force-marched round the estate ... I expect you'll be ready for dinner now. Julia has been in conference with the cook so I think we can count on something a bit special. I know she always enjoys entertaining guests and that she will be looking forward to dining with you. Just imagine, a lone sergeant sharing dinner with a couple of widows." She gave a light laugh. "I might just as well be a damned widow. I don't much care for this state of marital limbo. Come on, let's see if Julia has turned up yet in the library."

The library was lit by bracket-mounted candles which reflected a warm glow from panelled walls. A heavy oak reference table stood in the centre of the floor. Recent copies of *Country Life* and *Tatler* lay on the table. Floor to ceiling shelves held a variety of books in unmatched bindings and of differing sizes. It was obviously a working library, unlike those literary collections of showy displays arranged for decorative effect.

Gesturing to the shelves, Julia said, "Rather a collection there. Carter loved books and would read almost anything he could lay his hands on. Do you read much, Mr Harding?"

"Yes I do, I enjoy a detective novel or a murder mystery ... something by Edgar Wallace or even Agatha Christie. Come to think of it, Agatha's murders were often committed in libraries. They must have a special attraction for that sort of thing."

The arrival of Ramesh to announce dinner ended that vein of conversation.

"Dinner now ready for you, Memsabib."

Led by Ramesh, Harding escorted the ladies to the dining room and, in turn, held their chairs until both were seated. Ramesh presented a tray on which lay three crisp, white table napkins. The dinner began with iced consommé, followed by Chicken Marengo which, explained Julia, had been invented by Napoleon's chef, and was completed with a raspberry water ice. Heavy silver cutlery, sparkling glasses and a centre arrangement of red roses added to the excellence of the occasion. Conversation, assisted by fine wine and a warming brandy, flowed easily, taking Harding's thoughts far beyond his reasons for being in this part of India.

"That meal," said Harding, "was really great … and the chicken, far superior to the grey stringy offering we sometimes see in the mess. It reminded me of the chicken we used to eat at home before the war."

Laura looked across the table at Harding. "Do you think you will be going back home in the near future? Ghandi and Nehru seem to be making noises about getting the British out of India and people are doing a lot of muttering about it. Even some of our estate labourers are saying it's time we left them to rule themselves. I hope we don't face another mutiny. That must have been absolutely horrid, especially for the women and children."

Harding thought carefully before replying. "I only know what I read in the newspapers or what I pick up on the radio. We never get any official information from the army about what's going on. The powers that be must think we don't care or we don't need to know about the political situation. The only official thing we have been told is about a new income tax system which is being extended to the services – something called 'pay as you earn' as I recall. Most of the blokes are looking forward to getting home for demob and picking up where they left off when they were called up."

"What will you be going home to?" Julia asked. "Do you have any career plans … university, for instance?"

"Don't know about university. It was never on the agenda for anyone in my circle of acquaintances, so I haven't given it any thought. There is a scheme, I understand, where members of the forces can sit an entrance exam that would guarantee admission to university, providing they pass of course. There will be a cost to be met, so unless there are funds in the family or a chap can get a part time job to help out it's a bit of a long shot."

Harding declined a second drink when Ramesh offered the bottle of brandy. "Thank you, but no. I have to consider riding straight on my way back to camp. The roads have some pretty reckless drivers by day; I would probably find myself and my bike under some truck wheels if I didn't keep my wits about me in the dark."

Julia asked him to find some dance music on the Murphy radiogram that stood in a corner of the drawing room. This area had been cleared of the obligatory tiger skins, now skirting the edge of the polished wood floor. He managed to pick up a short wave broadcast that gave some half decent reception and asked Julia if she would like to dance with him.

She danced close, moulding her slim figure to him as they moved to the slow rhythm of the music. Julia danced well and never sat out any of the numbers at the Planter's Club social evenings. She would select dress patterns from *Vogue* for these events and from fine materials bought from the bazaar would get the visiting *derzi* to run them up on his hand-cranked Singer where he would sit all day working on the veranda. He was skilled at producing dresses to Julia's exacting requirements, worthy of any Western couturier, which she wore to superb advantage. But that was before Carter's untimely death. Since taking on responsibility for the estate, the dances and other social events had been replaced in her diary with the demanding calendar of tea cultivation: planting, gathering, processing, marketing and financial issues. Time had to be put aside to deal with the problems of the estate workers and their families – childbirth, domestic arguments, sickness and education of the children.

As she danced she directed her thoughts on Harding. She put his age at about twenty-two, some fifteen years younger than her. She wondered if she held any attraction for him. He was handsome enough, tall, well built and confident but rather restrained in manner. She closed up to him even more to test his response and held her cheek close to his shoulder, but she felt him tighten his posture in resistance. She felt that he was afraid of misreading her intentions and making a fool of himself. Maybe he had some ideas about an affair with Laura. After all she was more of an age match to him…. Her thoughts were cut when the music ended and she heard Laura say, "Come on, you two, time to break it up and give a girl a chance."

Laura came easily into his arms as the music went into the relaxed tempo of a slow foxtrot. She did not dance with the formal skill of Julia and Harding held her at a distance as they moved through the steps. He did not wish to appear as if he was making a play for her. After all, she was still a married woman even if the loss of her husband was unconfirmed. Slow down Harding old lad, can't risk getting involved with a female with the uncertainty of army life to consider and although either woman was very desirable he judged it to be an 'out of bounds' area.

As the distant radio station faded into the atmosphere, bringing to an end the short wave broadcast, Julia ordered coffee for her guest. They sat talking until Harding, glancing at his watch said, "I think it's time I took off. I don't want to be caught creeping back into camp with the dawn – might set the chaps speculating about my recreational life."

"If you must," Julia said. "It has been a most enjoyable day and if you can spare the time please come and visit us again."

They saw Harding to the veranda steps where he said, "Thank you, you have been wonderful hostesses and it has been a very lovely day. I'll give you a ring during the next few days to arrange to come over to see if I can get the new generator running. Goodnight and thanks again."

Chapter 14

As Harding emerged from the estate track onto the Shillong road, the sound of worn gears and a grinding transmission shaft alerted him to the approach of a lorry. It was driving on sidelights only, a hazardous undertaking on unmarked roads in absolute darkness. He dismounted from his bicycle and hurried the machine into the safety of the roadside scrub until the lorry had passed him. But it did not pass. It halted with the sidelights switched off, waited a few minutes then drove into the estate.

He did not recall Julia or Laura mentioning anything about late night transport entering or leaving the estate, not that it was any of his business, but perhaps a word of warning to take care travelling on the unlit estate tracks if lorry movements were expected might have been in order. Either they wished to keep any information regarding late night visitors under wraps or they were unaware of such a possibility. Remembering the estate manager's reaction to Laura's annoyance and his lame reply, Harding wondered if the visit was anything to do with him. He decided to go back to see if the women were in any danger.

He propped his bicycle against the base of a banyan tree and set off on a diagonal route to pick up the marks of smooth tyres made by the lorry along the estate track and down to the tea sheds. He slipped into the undergrowth and made his way parallel to the track, all senses alert to the danger posed by any lookout that had been posted.

He halted at the sound of a breaking twig and lay prone, controlling his breathing by taking in long draughts of air and allowing his lungs to deflate slowly to reduce possible signs of his presence. The creak of an axle spring and the scrape of a match being struck betrayed the immediacy of an unknown individual. The pungent smell of *bidi* smoke accompanied by the hawking and spitting of a phlegm-laden throat told Harding two things: the fellow was an Indian and that he was taking no precautions to avoid detection. He moved closer to the sound source and lay flat on the ground to silhouette the outline of the lorry against the charcoal grey sky. He saw it was an old Chevrolet, possibly a three-tonner, with an ornate, open sided cab typical of the general purpose lorry used on Indian roads for the carrying of goods or overloaded with passengers where the railways offered no service. Satisfied that the fellow in the lorry posed no problem, he moved back into the undergrowth to make his way nearer to the tea sheds to see what was going on.

The screaming whine of mosquitoes seeking to settle on his exposed face and hands was a nuisance, as indeed were the green flashing lights given off by clouds of fireflies that dazzled his vision as he crawled towards his objective. He halted every few yards to listen for the sound of any movement before continuing. When he picked up the smell of engine oil and the lingering smell of petrol exhaust fumes, he knew he was near the generator shed. It was then that he heard the sound of voices, sometimes raised in annoyance, coming from the direction of the packing shed. He crawled forward as silently as he knew how, testing the ground ahead before placing his weight on it, until he saw a faint light coming from the louvres of a shutter. As he moved nearer to gain a view of the interior through the restricted slats of the shutter he saw Narayan Rao. He was stuffing a calico-wrapped package, about the size of a house brick, into a tea chest. The side of the chest was stencilled with the name of the consignee: ASSAM BENGAL TRADING COMPANY CALCUTTA. Narayan Rao could be heard pleading, "Please to hurry sir, Missy Erskine asking about samples being late and I could not say why I am delaying until this package come. She was with English man from army. He seem greatly interested in tea business."

The reply was delivered sharply in a clear English accent. "Look here, Rao, you'll do as you're bloody well told. I'll take care of any problems with missy or this army fellow you talk about, and if you don't watch it I'll take care of you too."

Narayan Rao continued to complain in a whingeing voice, "I pray to God that this caper is dangerous for me, if I come to grief and am getting sack I cannot look after my family, please Sahib…."

"Shut up you fool, this is between you and me. Get these samples away double quick. I want them on the Calcutta Mail by tomorrow night even if you have to walk to the bloody railhead to get them there. *Malum*?"

Harding heard the sound of hammering as the tea chest was nailed down and the rattle of a lamp glass as the light was extinguished. He crept behind a pile of broken tea chests to watch Narayan Rao, accompanied by the visitor, emerge from the packing shed. The manager hurried off to the worker's lines, the latter made his way up the track to the waiting lorry. When Harding heard the sound of the lorry start up and drive away he left his cover and went into the packing shed. After a search he found a box of matches and re-lit the hurricane lamp to examine the sample chest which had been left on the bench. A red spot above the stencilled 'BENGAL' attracted his attention.

There was no red spot on any of the other sample chests.

Chapter 15

Two days later Field Marshall Sir Claude Auchinlech, the Commander-in-Chief of all forces in India, British and Indian alike, sat with the Viceroy, Field Marshall Sir Archibald Wavell, in the study at the Viceregal Lodge, New Delhi. Auchinlech waited whilst the Viceroy studied the KINGSMAN report rushed up to GHQ from the Signal Intelligence Centre, Calcutta. When the Viceroy had finished reading he made a few notes in the margins of the report and read through it again.

It was laid out in Staff Duties format with clear headings, few verbs, standard military abbreviations and stamped TOP SECRET in red ink.

From   Sig Int Calcutta
To   C-in-C India Command
Subject   INA Assam/Burma
1. Information
    (a) Incr INA activity in subject area.
    (b) A/c mov map sheet 97
2. Nature of Situation
    (a) Activity centred abandoned airstrip Tamu MR
    050397.
    (b) Air recce reveals:
        (i)   Qty one Dakota a/c bearing CAT identity.
        (ii) Qty one Junkers 52 a/c no identity.
        (iii) Bulk fuel dump.
        (iv) Rhombic ae array firing NW.
        (v)   Tented accn area.

3. Interim Objective.

Suggest ground recce to confirm user identity and activity.

4. Courses Open.

(a) Keep under observation.

(b) Mount op to neutralise activity.

5. Conclusion.

Unlikely authorised use of airstrip. Recommend course of action at para 4 (a) above be followed. Pse advise.

The Viceroy handed the report back to his C-in-C and studied the air recce photographs through a desk-mounted magnifying glass. When satisfied that he had absorbed the detail, he held his comments until he made an analysis of the situation.

"I am very pleased you brought this report to my attention, Claude. I think that you're having the same concerns as me, insofar as there is some nationalist activity going on. As I see it we have the INA, albeit in a much depleted form. Then there is this camp set-up and what appears to be a bulk fuel dump. Finally we have a German transport 'plane and an unknown Dakota bearing the identity CAT which has never been heard of previously. I think you should signal Calcutta and get them to mount a ground recce before we take any further action."

"Good, I'll get a signal off as soon as I get back to my HQ. With your agreement, I'd prefer to keep this business away from the political intelligence people for the time being."

The Viceroy nodded. "Considering the highly charged political situation and the civil unrest which keeps breaking out, I am inclined to accept your proposal and keep it within the Service Intelligence domain. Unlike MI6, they don't have any complicated double agent juggling to manage to divert their efforts and I'm sure we can rely on your int people to keep the job uncluttered."

Both men were battle-hardened. After serving in the First World War, where Wavell lost his left eye to a German shell splinter fighting with Black Watch, they had progressed in their respective careers through the lean years of the nineteen-thirties to command desert armies in the Middle East Campaign. In 1941, with a force of two British Divisions, Wavell routed an Italian army of ten divisions capturing 400 tanks, 1,200 guns and 130,000 prisoners. The latter had been calculated by a bright young staff officer to cover an area of 25 acres; 5 acres of officers and 20 acres of other ranks. Shortly after this brilliant success, when civilian morale following the Dunkirk debacle and the shock of heavy naval losses had been at its lowest ebb, he was promoted to Field Marshall by Churchill and appointed to the post of C-in-C India. His command was extended to include responsibility for Malaya and the island fortress of Singapore plus the defence of the Dutch East Indies. Although he had British, Indian, Australian and Dutch formations under command, it was a below-strength force and unable to prevent the Japanese conquest of South East Asia. He reverted to his role as C-in-C India until 1943 when he was appointed Viceroy in succession to Lord Linlithgow.

When Wavell was moved to India in 1941 after his successful Middle East campaign, Auchinlech, who had served long periods in India before the war and following a number of appointments in the European and Home Commands, was sent to take over from him as Middle East Commander. After a series of successes and defeats in the to-and-fro desert battles and resisting pressure from Churchill to launch a premature offensive against the Axis forces, he was sent back to India as C-in-C to replace Wavell.

They had both tasted success and defeat in battle and skirmishes with political bosses when ordered to carry out impossible tasks, sometimes being expected to act in direct contravention of their military training, strategy and plain commonsense. Both men were acutely aware of each other's problems and responsibilities in the delicate and thankless duties of maintaining political stability and public order in a sub-continent torn by deep religious factions.

After the horrific Calcutta riots of August, in which British troops were eventually called in to quell the madness of inter-racial butchery, the predominantly Hindu Congress and the Muslin League agreed to form an interim government. The Muslim League had no intention of co-operating with Congress and soon boycotted the constituent assembly, leaving the Viceroy helpless. During one of their fruitless discussions, Gandhi, adept at making devious statements, exasperated the generally placid Wavell into asking him to stop his lawyer's talk and use plain English because as a simple soldier he was confused by the legalistic arguments being put forward.

Chapter 16

During the two days Harding had taken to complete the installation of the new generator at Erskine-Jalpai, he saw little of Julia and Laura. Julia was having, according to Laura, "a woman's trouble" and needed a few days' rest. Laura was busy supervising the many activities associated with tea growing and apart from sharing an occasional cup of tea with her, Harding had been left to get on with his work.

He calculated that only two phases of the three-phase output were required to power the existing circuits; one, the blue phase was wired to the tea sheds; the second phase, green, was wired to the bungalow; and the third, red, was fed into a resistance field to equalise the load. Harding constructed the resistance field, which he located in a safe area at the back of the generator shed, from fencing wire laid over waist-high angle-iron pickets and protected from earth by ceramic insulators. To avoid accidental contact with the potentially lethal system, he enclosed it with a barbed wire apron fence and displayed a DANGER HIGH VOLTAGE sign on it. At night, the resistance field glowed purple-red in an unwritten warning.

Chapter 17

Harding sent R AR and switched the transmitter off. He re-tuned his receiver to Radio SEAC, Ceylon. As the close harmony voices of the Andrews Sisters fought with the crackling of rising atmospherics riding in with electrical storms brewed up in the jungle valleys filled his headphones, he read through the latest signal from Calcutta:

011845F (.) YOUR 241900F (.) EXECUTE GND RECCE (.) REPORT SOONEST (.)

He destroyed the signal and sat a while to consider the order and its implications. "Must be something more important than a few INA *wallahs* left to rot in the jungle. Wonder if it has something to do with the odd aeroplane my Naga contact told me about." Harding decided to tune his receiver across the higher frequencies to try to pick up the BBC Overseas Service in the hope that they may have got hold of a news agency report. Past experience told him that one could learn more from the news agencies than was often available from official sources. Harding was in the dark about the RAF recce flight and the interest being shown at the top level in Delhi. He concluded that if Calcutta thought he could cope with a ground recce then it couldn't be a matter of great intelligence value. After all, what could a chap operating alone dig up that could normally demand the weight of a fully armed reconnaissance patrol with supply back-up?

★★★

He escaped from the mess after supper and the piss-up session that was getting under way to work through the night on his recce plan. He drafted and discarded as unworkable a number of ideas that could provide the answers demanded by Calcutta. As the sun began to rise and burn away the morning mist, he put down his pencil to review his preferred scheme framed on the standard military operations precept of:

Information Intention Method Administration Intercommunication.

Harding's information and intention were clear: To produce an intelligence report on suspected Indian National Army activities at and in the area of an abandoned airfield up on the Assam/Burma border. He could dispense with the intercommunication heading – he didn't have any access to support resources. He was therefore left only with the two vital factors of method and administration; movement and survival to consider in depth.

Under the method heading he broke down the operation into three phases:

One – Move to objective. Travel by road to get within walking range of airfield, say two miles, park Jeep in camouflaged hide and advance on foot.

Two – Establish an observation point that will afford a good field of view and be easy to withdraw from in an emergency. Be prepared to remain in position for a maximum of three days or until satisfied with the quality of intelligence recorded.

Three – Record facts by photograph and notes.

Four – Report … mark time on this in anticipation of wangling a few days in Calcutta to deliver report by hand. No secure means of transmitting classified information.

The administration precept raised three vital essentials: rations, medical aid and weapons. Rations together with water would dictate the distance he could travel on foot both to and from the observation point and the length of time he could remain on watch. The simplest solution would be to carry about five days' supply of American 'K' Rations. They were neatly presented in three waxed cardboard packages – breakfast, dinner and supper. In addition to meat, biscuits, dehydrated vegetable and cereal, the ever considerate US Department of Defense also included a supply of cigarettes, matches, candy and even toilet paper. From past experience, Harding, in common with most of his contemporaries, found the American diet too rich and spicy and much preferred the plainer British issue Compo rations to provide a more acceptable form of nourishment in the field. He decided to rely on individual cans of corned beef, a few two-ounce tins of salmon, a supply of hard-tack biscuits and a kedgeree of rice and whatever protein the mess cook could conjure up which could be eaten cold and should remain edible for at least two or three days. Water, as always in field conditions overseas, was of primary importance. According to War Office ration scales, sixteen gallons per man per day was the aspired amount for all purposes. At a weight of a hundred and sixty pounds plus containers to satisfy just one day's consumption, that target was far in excess of his carrying capacity and was ruled out of the question. Instead, Harding concentrated on calculating the minimum need to satisfy thirst and body liquid loss through sweat if he was to avoid heat exhaustion. He decided that he would have to rely on one and a half gallons at a weight of eighteen pounds including containers, and by including a supply of sterilising tablets to make safe any jungle water he might come across, he would have to make do with that.

For medical aid he listed a supply of Mepacrine anti-malaria tablets, salt tablets, field dressings, a tourniquet, two ampoules of morphine, sulphonamide powder, insect repellent and foot powder.

As an extra precaution he decided to pack a mosquito net. He had no wish to risk a bite from the virulent Anophelese mosquito that infested the Kalewa valley, an area of deep wet jungle close to Tamu airfield. During the Burma campaign, men fighting in that area who had failed, forgotten or because of enemy action, were unable to take full precautions against receiving a bite from that lethal insect, had succumbed to shivering bouts of fever in the evening, to be found dead the following morning from cerebral malaria. Harding was not prepared to take any chances of collecting a dose of that condition.

With personal protection at the forefront of his mind, he decided to rely on his .38 standard issue pistol and the customary 24 rounds plus a .303 jungle carbine with 20 rounds of 30 grain ballestite cartridges. These were of similar appearance to blank ammunition but were normally used to provide the propellant charge to hurl a grenade from a rifle fitted with a projector cup. With sufficient power to launch a No. 36 grenade some seventy five yards, the muzzle blast from the ballestite cartridge was capable of delivering a terrible wound in close quarter, jungle combat, scoring easily over aimed rounds.

Harding rounded off his inventory with binoculars, his privately owned camera, a 6.3 Voigtlander Bessa, notebook and pencils, a prismatic compass, a one-inch map of the area, a machete and an entrenching tool.

He worked through the remainder of the day to assemble his kit and secure it on an Everest lightweight pack frame. With a total start load of about forty-five pounds including arms and ammunition, he would quickly reduce the burden as he consumed rations and water. After making a final equipment check he decided to carry a blanket and a monsoon cape to give some protection against falling night temperatures and the possibility of a sudden downpour during his prolonged watch. He ate a generous supper, showered and turned in early … on active service always eat when you can, bathe when you can and sleep when you can, because you never know if you'll ever get another opportunity – that's good soldiering.

★★★

"Good morning, Sergeant Sahib, bed tea for you. You go up country today, I got extra kit ready for you, shirt and trouser…."

"Who said anything about going up country, you nosey old sod? I certainly didn't."

"You order Prem Lal get ready extra kit, you collect other kit together and make Jeep ready for long travel. Prem Lal know and understand these things and you tell me early call before sun get up."

"OK buggerlugs, I give in. Yes, I am going away for about five or six days and I want you to keep an eye on things until I return. Keep everything *pukka* and in good order and don't forget I want to see some clean kit ready for me – I'll be needing it. Yes, and I'll be looking forward to sleeping on some fresh, clean sheets. *Malum*?"

Chapter 18

"Signal from Assam, came in last night. Here you are, have a look at this, sir."

Captain Reeder looked hard at Colonel Grindley and continued, "We are under starter's orders now and no mistake. Hell of a job to ask of a chap, hope he makes out alright."

"Well, if your Sergeant Harding is as bright and reliable as you think we don't have too much to worry about. I don't know about you but I had to issue orders under active service conditions when I was damned sure some of my men would be killed or wounded. As commissioned officers that's what we are trained for and paid to do: Give orders and make certain they are obeyed."

"Yes, true enough, but this is peacetime with no formal war activity going on. There may well be an internal security problem brewing up which is really the responsibility of the civil authorities acting under orders from the politicians."

"Our brief ordered by the C-in-C himself is to keep the situation under observation and that is what we are doing by sending Harding along to view the ground. If he reports that there is a danger of armed activity then it will be out of our hands – don't you think?"

"I have a feeling that someone up there is in the business of stoking up political unrest to get us out of the country. Wavell is trying to get some sort of power sharing agreement ironed out between the Hindus and Muslims so that we can leave some kind of stable government behind. Although Nehru and the Congress Party appear to be in favour, old Jinnah and his Muslims don't want to know. Remember how the Day of Action ended up a few weeks ago when Jinnah got his heavy gang carving up the Hindus? When they retaliated it just proved how things could turn out when we depart. Burma is in a bit of a froth as well since Mountbatten installed Aung San to head an unelected government. Not one of his Lordship's best moves during his time as Supreme Commander in South East Asia. We have only to read the intelligence reports to know that there are nationalist movements springing up in the old colonial territories of France in Indo-China and the Dutch in Java. If things turn nasty we can't expect any sympathy from the Americans. They are not in favour of our presence in this part of the world. Did you know that within days of the Japs packing in, President Truman cut off our Lend-Lease arrangement but kept it going with Russia?"

"You are surely not suggesting that our wartime allies are mixed up with this Tamu business, are you? Perhaps in liaison with the Russians? That is a stupid idea Duncan. I shouldn't spread that bit of nonsense about if I were you."

"Of course not. Neither the Russians nor the Americans could be officially involved. But remember sir, the RAF recce spotted a couple of transport aircraft on the tarmac at Tamu, and who has an air transport capability in this part of the world? The Americans, us and the Chinese, and with a Communist revolution getting under way in China I can't see them being involved. So that leaves our people, which can be counted out, and our American friends."

"We are in the bloody dark as usual, old boy. Let us wait and see what Harding comes up with. I see the sun is over the yardarm; time for a peg or two before changing for dinner. Coming?"

Chapter 19

Blood-red light from the dawn sun streaked the grey, cotton wool mist as Harding turned onto the Imphal road. Ahead lay three hours' driving. If time allowed he planned to take on a meal at the Chinese restaurant he frequently used in Imphal, then aimed to push on to get within marching range of his objective before bedding down for the night. He knew he was taking a risk to enter the jungle alone by day but to travel in darkness would be stupid and dangerous. Apart from night-prowling animals, swamp and ground broken by gullies presented hidden hazards.

As the morning progressed he had to remain alert to avoid a snarl up with other road users. Bullock carts, hand-carts, overloaded lorries and buses with passengers hanging perilously to roofs and open windows scrambled for a share of the highway. Scrawny cows, of divine status to the Hindus and stunted by underfeeding, were given space consideration denied to the poorer travellers trudging the broken tarmac with their tattered umbrellas raised against the spiralling heat of the sun.

He accelerated to take advantage of a clearing stretch of road, passing the Erskine-Jalpai estate that had now become a new centre of interest to him. Since setting up the new generator there had been no contact with the two ladies living there. He allowed his mind to reflect on the very pleasant day and evening he had spent with them … a couple of extremely attractive females; especially Laura, the pretty young wife of an absent husband. And Julia, the more openly sensual woman … and probably dying for a brief affair….

His thoughts switched to consider Narayan Rao, that little shit of an estate manager. He was certainly up to no good. Went a bit furtive when Laura challenged him about the tea samples; and then the late-night visitor, he seemed to have more than a passing interest in the samples. Harding tried to dismiss the episode from his mind … not his business, didn't want to get mixed up in any sort of caper with civvies even if they are English – never know where it might end up.

After he had been on the road for about three hours and with the sun now high in the mid-morning sky, he pulled into the shade of some roadside trees to do a POL check on the Jeep. With the task completed he decided to make a brew of tea to clear the dust from his throat. He washed the sticky, salt laden sweat from his face, arms and hands with some of his precious water taken from a canvas *chagul* that hung on the side of the windscreen. The container, being porous, worked on the evaporation principle to keep the water cool, a useful device against the overpowering heat.

Imphal, a town some fifty miles on the Indian side of the Burma border had suffered a prolonged siege in the summer of 1944. Japanese forces under the command of General Mutaguchi had been halted there after a determined advance to invade and take India from the British. Relief forces under General Slim had broken through and by the autumn had pushed the Japanese 15th Army back to the river Chindwin, having lost an estimated sixty five thousand troops through battle casualties and disease. Two years after that engagement, Imphal still carried traces of the extensive damage suffered during the fierce battles but the Happy Moon Eating House had survived intact.

Harding parked his Jeep in full view of the open door and opted to sit at a table from where he could keep an eye on the vehicle and its load. An unattended vehicle was a tempting prize for the young thieves who prowled the side streets.

Mr Ong, the eating house proprietor emerged from the kitchen through a beaded fly screen to greet his customer.

"Welcome Mr Harding, I no' see you for maybe two, three weeks. What can I get for you? Over sixty choices from my menu, all proper Chinese edibles cooked for you by my wife."

Harding looked up from the map he was studying and said, "Good day to you too. Get me a cold beer and have another ready to follow that. I want to get the taste of dust out of my throat, and remember I want a clean glass, not one of your fly-blown beakers, savvy?"

"Not worry, I look after my good customers." He barked an order in Cantonese to an assistant lurking behind the fly screen and joined Harding at his table.

"Business not very good since war finish and British soldiers go home. You go home soon, Mr Harding?" Harding did not reply. He preferred not to discuss service matters with civilians – never could tell what use they would make of idle talk. "Your beer here now. This is Tiger Beer coming long way from Singapore. Hope you like, much better than Indian beer from Murree."

Harding took a long draught of the ice-cold beer and wiped his lips.

"Not bad, not bad at all. From Singapore you say, that's a hell of a distance. How did you manage to get it here?"

Ong leaned forward and whispered, "There is new import trading company at Tamu just over border in Burma. I sell them supplies … food and other things, you know." At this disclosure he leaned forward, winked and tapped the side of his nose with his forefinger. "They bring me things from Singapore and Malaya and sometimes good frozen meat from Australia. You no tell people this information. I like keep business affairs secret, you hunnerstan?"

Harding maintained the conspiratorial air and replied in a low voice, "Won't breathe a word to a soul, Mr Ong, none of my business…. Let's have another bottle of Tiger and organise an omelette while you're at it. Make sure it doesn't taste of garlic this time."

Of course the omelette, a pallid looking submission made with eggs from scrawny dust fed chickens did taste of garlic. Like curry, it tainted most fare dished up in Asian eating houses. He dredged the omelette with black pepper and gritty salt and prepared to make the most of the last cooked meal he would have until he returned from his recce task.

"You no ready go yet, Mr Harding? Another beer maybe, or you like take rest for afternoon with one of my girls? Clean girl, clean bed." Whenever Harding dropped in to the Happy Moon the old Chinaman offered the services of a girl from the attached massage parlour cum pleasure annexe. "Very good for healthy young man to have girl every day and no trouble if he plant baby." Harding had heard that girl babies fathered by Europeans could be sold at puberty for a very worthwhile sum, especially if fair-skinned with hair to match…. "Look, I show you nice girl, very beautiful … give much pleasure." Ong called out in English, "Come meet my friend, he good man, very strong for you."

The bead curtain rattled as it was brushed aside to reveal a tall Chinese girl. She was wearing a cheongsam of Thai silk, high collared to her slender neck and split to the hip to flash her scarlet lace knickers. She sauntered up to Harding's table.

"I introduce her to you. She is called Jasmine, daughter of high officer in army of Chiang Kai-shek. She is so much special beautiful girl. Her father executed because he made deal with Communist rebels to save many peasant lives in Manchuria after Japanese lose war. She come to me and work to make money then go to United States for new life. She bring much happiness to you. I make special price for you, Mr Harding."

He agreed with Ong that she was very nice but he had to move on to reach his destination before last light. "Perhaps another time, old lad."

"You always tell me another time. I keep clean girls, proud boast my establishment no clap. Inspect every day. Any girl give client infection she go plenty quick. Chop-chop." With that he gave the table a karate blow in emphasis of his trading policy. Crockery and glasses jumped and clattered as Jasmine withdrew with a gentle smile on her pale golden face.

As Harding stood to make his departure, Mr Ong laid a hand on his arm and with his secretive look said in a low voice, "You my friend, Mr Harding. I tell you there are bad men here since British Army leave Imphal at end of war. They come late at night to deal in *afayung* with local traders who sell to workers on tea plantations and forestry camps."

"What are you on about? What is this *afayung* stuff you say they are flogging?"

"I tell you this is very bad joss ... dope, you hunnerstan?" He gave a dry chuckle. "Very funny thing, Mr Harding. British in India grow opium and sell to China long ago. Now India bring in from other places in Asia."

"Goodbye, Mr Ong, no time to hang about, got to get a move on."

★★★

As Harding drove away from the Chinese restaurant, through the lean-to outskirts of Imphal to continue his journey, Captain Reeder in Calcutta was reading a signal just handed to him by the operator working the Malaya wireless link. It was a report detailing the arrival and departure of a Dakota aircraft on a grass airstrip at Batu Pahat in Johore, the most southerly state in Malaya. The aircraft was carrying the identification: CAT. It had loaded one passenger and taken off within ten minutes of touchdown.

★★★

A rutted track leading into the jungle gave Harding a start point for his trek up to Tamu. After he had driven about a hundred yards he halted and went back to obliterate the tyre marks left in the soft red earth. He cut a sweeper of bracken and twigs to remove all traces of a recent vehicle entry, taking care to carry out the operation without being seen by any passing traffic, which he avoided by dropping into the undergrowth when he heard any signs of movement.

The going was fairly good for the first few hundred yards. He was following a track used by the timber cutting gangs of the

Indian Forestry Department, but as the stands of teak had been economically exploited the operations had been abandoned, bringing the vehicle-wide track to an end. He continued to force the Jeep along but, with the engine revving high in low gear ratio on four wheel drive, he was compelled to make frequent stops to allow the engine to cool down as it reached near boiling point. After spring-bottoming over a succession of boulder strewn water courses and losing traction in deep mud banks that threatened to leave him stranded, he set about searching for a secure location to laager the Jeep for the duration of his recce. An escarpment with a rock overhang and an abundance of trailing vines gave him the ideal spot. He manoeuvred the Jeep into a position close up to the rock face and jammed chocks under all four wheels to support the handbrake, which, in common with the majority of Jeeps, was pretty ineffective. Happy that the vehicle would not move even if a sudden downpour shifted the unstable ground, he rigged a camouflage net over the vines and thatched the cover with creepers and ferns to construct a well concealed hideaway that was safe from view and sheltered from the elements.

With map, sun and compass he established his position in relation to his objective and calculated that he had about two thousand yards in a straight-line march. With natural obstacles adding to non-effective route distance he estimated he was liable to have something like a two and a half mile tramp ahead of him. Under flat country conditions that would take about forty minutes – even allowing for the burden of a forty-five pound load – but with something like a trek of about two and a half miles in jungle he would be fortunate to do it in less than eight hours with frequent rest halts. With less than one hour to last light he decided to delay his march until the following morning. The jungle was a hazardous environment in daylight. Only a fool or a desperate man would take it on in the dark.

He fixed up a fairly comfortable bed by rearranging the canvas covered seats of the Jeep into a linear mattress stretching from front to rear which, if he slept with knees bent, would just about accommodate his six-foot body. He pared a bundle of bamboo shavings and laced it with petrol to get a fire going and a brew of tea boiling. Before turning in he made up the fire with damp brushwood and green branches to deter night prowling animals and put up a protective smoke barrier against flying piss-beetles and mosquitoes. Of the two, piss-beetles caused the most immediate discomfort by shooting a blistering irritant onto the skin but malaria carrying mosquitoes were the more dangerous in the long term. With his mind concentrating on both menaces he crept under his mosquito net, making sure it was tucked in and offered no point of entry to any insect. As a final provision he loaded his carbine with a couple of 30 grain ballestites, applied the safety catch and secured it to his wrist with a lanyard ready for instant use.

Although he was worn out after the tiring journey by road and track he spent a very restless night after being awakened at intervals by the hoarse croaking of bullfrogs and the occasional rasping call of a nearby panther advertising its presence and availability.

By 5am he had had enough. He scrambled from his makeshift bed, fed the smouldering fire, made a brew and stirred a couple of hard-tack biscuits into some hot water to form a very welcome porridge. After a wash and shave he reviewed the situation and considered how he would complete the next part of his plan, which was to reach his objective two thousand yards distant through difficult terrain. He was aware that if a jungle patrol might make about four miles in a day he would be hard put to it to manage two. Harding would be responsible for clearing his own track, often hacking at tangled growth with his machete, maintaining the true course by frequently checking and recording bearing changes, counting his paces to calculate distance covered and remain alert for the presence of a potential enemy and hidden dangers from unexploded ordnance or booby traps left to degrade in wartime battle areas.

The Japs had been especially cunning in the improvisation and planting of fiendish booby traps known as *pangyi*. They were made from short bamboo stakes cut to a needle point, fire hardened and driven into the ground with the business end concealed in loose vegetation and angled to achieve efficient penetration, even through a metal-studded boot sole, into the victim's foot. Barbed splinters prevented clean extraction and accelerated a gangrenous condition resulting in a hastily amputated limb or an agonising death if the casualty could not be evacuated to a forward field hospital. *Pangyi* were sometimes clustered in off-track positions to catch troops, who, suspicious of being caught on regular tracks, would mistakenly believe they could escape the threat and take avoiding action by following a parallel route. Anti-personnel mines, encased in wood to escape clearance by audio mine detectors also posed another life-threatening hazard. With man-made threats postscripted to natural dangers and uncertainties, Harding felt he had extensive care inventory to worry him. All this on top of the essential reason for his lone presence in the jungle, which, according to an edict issued by the late General Orde Wingate, the Chindit Commander stated that 'No patrol is to consider the jungle impenetrable until it has penetrated it.'

Chapter 20

Viceregal Secretariat
New Delhi, 9 September 1946

TOP SECRET

For eyes of C-in-C only

1. India Office London passed KINGSMAN report to Foreign Office due to international political implications.

2. Have ordered MacNair to Calcutta as my personal representative.

Archibald Wavell

★★★

To make absolutely certain that he had correctly plotted his start point, Harding checked again with map and compass before extending a pencil line through his position to give him a base reference bearing to magnetic north. With this line established, he drew a line on a bearing of 30 degrees magnetic from his start point to take him to his target area of Tamu and noted the reciprocal of a 210 degrees bearing for the return journey. After identifying a couple of natural features visible from his start point to help him find the precise location of the Jeep on his return, he cleared the ground in the immediate area of his traces and made final preparations for departure.

He immobilised the Jeep by removing the rotor arm and ignition coil, which he stowed in his pack, then stuffed a plug of mud into the exhaust to prevent the engine being started, even if a potential thief was clever enough to overcome the lack of a rotor arm and ignition coil. The camouflage net and protective thatched foliage were carefully rearranged and checked to ensure that, even at the close range of about five paces, it was well concealed. After hoisting the Everest pack frame with its forty-five pound load so that it sat high on his back, Harding adjusted the web straps to maintain an optimum support position and tightened the waist belt to avoid the heavy weight dragging it up to his chest, constricting his lungs and bruising his ribs. A final check to ensure that his carbine was loaded, this time with four rounds of ballestite, his pistol fully loaded with six rounds of .38 and secured to his belt with a lanyard. With compass and map case hung round his neck and the razor-sharp machete thonged to his wrist, all key safety measures in place to prevent the loss of vital survival and navigation equipment, he set out on his solo recce patrol following his planned bearing of 30 degrees magnetic and counting the paces of distance covered.

After each block of one hundred paces he made a mark with wax crayon on the Perspex cover of his map case, which, by applying the formula of 'one pace taken in the jungle equals roughly two thirds of a yard on hard ground,' an approximation of true distance covered could be calculated. With natural features obscured by the high tree canopy, bearing and distance travelled were the only navigational devices available to Harding. Water courses, although generally running north-south from the Himalayas to the low lying plains, were of little help in trying to fix a map position due to their constantly changing route as a result of high rainfall producing soil erosion which altered the direction of flow very different from that indicated on the map.

As the sun's heat soared and evaporated overnight condensation, it created a swirling waist-high ground mist. This screened trailing plant stems and rotting debris which forced Harding to lift his feet clear of the jungle floor in order to avoid taking a fall. This made increased demands on his energy and forced him to take a rest halt after some forty minutes when the heat and humidity began to tax his stamina. He took about five minutes to regain his breath, gulping in large amounts of the warm moist-laden air that carried little oxygen.

Harding dumped his pack and removed his sweat-soaked shirt to get what little air there was circulating around his body. Although his feet were running with sweat he dare not risk removing his boots for fear of being caught unawares by a potential enemy. Anyhow, he had no spare water with which to wash his feet, neither did he have sufficient pairs of clean socks to allow the luxury of a change at every halt. After massaging his neck and shoulder muscles to relieve the ache brought on by the heavy pack, he took a sip of water to wash the thickening saliva from his mouth and throat and to help him swallow a salt tablet, a necessary safeguard against the threat of heat exhaustion. Again, to conserve his precious supply of water, he resisted the desire to wash the drying sweat from his face and neck. Instead, he wrung out the sweatband that was tied to his forehead to wipe his skin, not as effective as a good rinse, but it was a small step to help prevent raw sores from his sweat-salt.

Harding knew the dangers of underestimating the fatigue of jungle travel and he thought that he had put together a carefully considered plan. But he had not reckoned on his comparative unfitness for the task. Apart from the physical demands, one had to establish a state of mind that would allow the traveller to cope with the hazards, both real and imagined, of working alone in the unfriendly jungle.

When his twitching muscles and heavy heartbeat had settled down he concentrated on working out a position fix. From his pace record he calculated that he had covered about four hundred and ninety yards. After deducting an estimated fifty yards for minor diversions to avoid fallen trees, patches of swampy ground and the rise and fall of the terrain, he had something like a quarter of a mile to his credit in the space of forty minutes. Not too bad, but if he was to reach his target before last light he had no time to waste hanging about on extended rest periods.

Feeling confident that he was on the correct line of march, he donned his shirt, shouldered his pack, checked that loose items of equipment were secured to his body and began the next stage of his trek.

His clothing was soon blackened with sweat which soaked into his trouser and shirt seams, making them saw-edged to chafe crotch and armpits with every stride and arm movement. The latter being especially uncomfortable when his right arm, holding his machete, continually arced to cut tangled vegetation which arrested his progress.

Frequent checks on time and distance showed that his rate of progress was slowing down. When he stumbled into a dense stand of high bamboo he hastily retraced his path to get clear of the hazardous growth. He was afraid to risk the danger of attempting to beat a track through the close stems which brought forward view almost down to zero. He cast a track to left and right of the obstruction and reached the unwelcome decision that he would be forced to follow a new bearing of 120 degrees magnetic for a distance as yet unknown until he was clear and then able to decide on a new direction that would guide him to his objective.

He followed the amended course for about an hour with frequent rest stops until he was confident that he had escaped the bamboo menace and could concentrate on working out his new route plan. Harding slipped off his heavy pack and lay down with his feet raised above his head until the throbbing of blood in his legs subsided. He followed that with arm and upper-body exercises until the pain eased from his knotted muscles and aching bones. Then, with his head propped on his pack, he fell into an exhausted sleep.

The sound of water dribbling over a rocky stream-bed awakened him. He scrambled to his feet and checked his watch to find that he had been asleep for less than thirty minutes. After taking a few paces in the direction of the sound that had disturbed him, he found a watering hole which, judging from the amount and variety of animal prints on the muddy banks, was well used by the local wild life. The prints ranged from the enormous indentations left by elephants through to the tiny hoof marks of mouse deer. The thought of wild beasts being on the loose had not so far given Harding any cause for concern. He had been too deeply involved in combating the discomforts of the Assam jungle to worry about meeting any hungry man-eaters. He recalled from his survival training at the Ranchi Jungle Warfare School that elephants, although inclined to be a bit ponderous and often unpredictable should be avoided, but if retreat was inevitable at the threat of being chased by an angry specimen, the pursued should 'run downhill'. Harding assumed that such advice was delivered to instil confidence in a chap and owed more to theory than reality.

The thought of replenishing his partly expended water supply was a sensible move, provided he could stomach the idea of taking it from an animal's watering hole that carried the penetrating sour stink of big cat's urine. Confident that his water sterilising kit could take care of any water-borne bacteria, he made up his mind to take advantage of the opportunity and top up an empty water bottle. He found a point upstream where there was little evidence of animal use and, by carefully filtering the water through his sweat rag into a mess tin, he removed all the solid matter to produce a fairly clear yield into which he dissolved a couple of sterilising tablets. Now, with his water ration fully restored, and having bathed the sweat-sore parts of his body, he felt ready to push on. He shouldered his pack and plunged into the jungle again on a new bearing to head almost due north and make for a position from where he could resume his original track of 30 degrees magnetic.

Within ten minutes of his last halt, Harding emerged from the green gloom of the jungle into an area of tropical savannah: thin sandy soil with sparse vegetation of brush and thorn. He took advantage of the treeless terrain to set his map by bisecting the angle of a prominent hill feature with the position of the sun. According to his best calculation he was now just about back on course for Tamu but with something like twelve hundred yards still to go. The bamboo diversion had cost him time and distance that he could ill afford and the chances of reaching his goal before last light were rather remote. Reluctantly he came to the conclusion that he would be compelled to set up a bivouac and continue his march the following morning. An unattractive prospect, so he decided to risk making a brew: some welcome compensation after a frustrating day.

He moved back into the jungle and selected some rising ground on which to set up his overnight bivouac. Harding scraped a level base with his entrenching tool and laid bracken to form a crude mattress under an A-frame of green bamboo to support his mosquito net. His brew of black tea, boiled over his hexamine fuelled stove, gave him some encouragement to tackle his kedgeree of, by this time, slimy grey rice and stray fibres of corned beef. It had not travelled well, but Harding was not in the business of expending his stamina on carrying worthless supplies and he forced down the unappetising meal.

After the strain of the day's march, with the repetitive pace counting, the vital demands of accurate compass reading and the continual need for drinking water as he cut his way through tangled clumps of dense undergrowth, Harding fell into a deep sleep within a few seconds of settling down on his bracken mattress.

He awoke with an alarmed suddenness to hear the rustling of leaves close by and a burst of sound as something ran off yelping into the darkness. He guessed that it was probably a hungry jackal foraging for an evening meal and posed no threat to him, at least as long as he remained alive. The remainder of the night was spent taking fitful dozes, unable to sleep for the incessant screaming of mosquitoes trying to home in through the net for a taste of blood, and the nearby intermittent croaking of bull-frogs. Although tempted to emerge from the safety of his net and make a brew, he resisted the idea knowing that he would be an immediate target for the mosquitoes and any other night-flying insects that happened to be around. When the morning sun at last made a welcome appearance, bringing an abrupt end to the night sounds of the jungle and driving the mosquitoes back to their breeding grounds in the foul pools of stagnant swamp-water, Harding quickly brewed a mug of tea and ate a couple of hard-tack biscuits. He was intent on conserving the cans of corned beef and salmon until he was absolutely on the edge of hunger, when he hoped the tasty rations would renew his strength and raise his spirits if his morale hit zero. He quickly removed all signs of his overnight stay, repacked his kit and took off with the firm intention of reaching his objective before last light.

He had made about two hundred counted paces when he came across a track which curved in from the left to follow his own route. It appeared to be fairly well used and Harding guessed that it was probably an inter-village path used by the few indigenous forest dwellers who were venturing back into their traditional areas now that the war was finished and it was safe to live there once more. He needed no encouragement to use the path; it was just about in line with his planned bearing and would make the going much easier. After two hours and several rest stops he decided it was time to take some food and a drink of his precious water. The biscuits were softening with the humidity and he could see some mildew spores forming on them. But he scraped the green spots away and quickly ate them, washed down with lukewarm water from his second water bottle. He had drunk the water he had collected the previous day and was pleased that his crudely attempted purification process had worked and that he was suffering no ill effects.

At the unnerving sound of approaching voices he grabbed his kit and slid into the undergrowth to take up a position from where he could observe the track through a screen of long grass and ground-trailing vines. He brought his carbine up to his shoulder, thumbed the safety-catch and waited with stomach-churning alertness, ready to take on whoever might pose a threat.

Harding knew he had chosen the wrong side of the track for a concealed position when he felt water soaking through his clothing; he was lying belly-flat on soft, wet ground and was unable to move away until the danger had blown over. He had a lateral field of vision of not more than a couple of yards with a corresponding vertical view. It was sufficient for him to establish that he was watching a forage party of the INA, led by a man wearing the three-chevron armband of a *havildar* and carrying a Lee-Enfield rifle slung over his shoulder. His uniform was a mixture of Indian Army khaki-drill and the Japanese issue of drab olive-green, with a coolie hat perched on his head. His boots were broken from the welt and held to the uppers with sisal twine. A sorry looking individual who had once been a proud, well turned out soldier of the Indian Army, but had been bullied into joining the treacherous freedom army of Subhas Chandra Bose to follow him in the fight to rid India of the Imperialist British. The sorry specimen was followed by three pairs of men; each pair was carrying a load of dead and dying chickens crammed into a net secured to a bamboo pole.

Harding was taken aback to see a dozen or so girls wearing the traditional Burmese sarong being led by a beautiful Chinese girl dressed in a black *samfoo*. He recognised the Chinese girl as Jasmine, the young lady from Mr Ong's establishment back in Imphal. She called out for the remainder of the party to wait for her as she dived into the bushes close to where Harding was hidden. The party slowed down but did not halt, with the *haviladar* shouting "*Jaldi karo*," hurry up. Harding froze, both in fear of being given away and from embarrassment at being witness to a woman's private needs as she relieved herself. As she stood to pull up her pants she saw Harding and opened her mouth to let out a scream. He threw himself on her, pinned her to the ground and with his machete held across her throat urged her to keep quiet.

All she saw was an unshaven man covered in wet mud, with red-rimmed eyes and a sweat-blackened bandana tied around his forehead. With his mouth close to her face she smelled his thirst-soured breath and turned her head to avoid it. But as she moved she recognised the British soldier to whom she had been made available by Mr Ong two days before. She lowered her eyelids then raised them slowly to indicate that she was no longer afraid and relaxed her body in his powerful grip. When Harding lifted his hand from her mouth she took a few sharp breaths to clear her lungs and said, "What you do here like this? I thought you were *dacoit* to kill me."

"No time for any explanation. What are you doing with those people?" Harding replied.

"We are being taken to Tamu for celebration. Please, I must hurry, let me go now."

He dare not risk keeping her any longer for fear of the escort returning to look for her and discover him. He knew that he would have to let her go and warned, "I am on a very important task. You must not give me away or there will be big trouble from the government. Savvy?"

She got to her feet and nodded her head vigorously to show that she understood. Then, she kissed him hard on the mouth before running off to catch up with the party of girls and her INA escort.

Harding stayed where he was until he was certain that it was safe to go on. As he waited he considered the information that Jasmine had given him. First, she was going to Tamu and second, there was going to be a celebration. Two questions required to be answered. Just who was at Tamu and what celebrations were to take place? He could not reconcile the idea of a destitute bunch of Indian Army renegades taking up residence at an abandoned airfield with the arranging of a celebration that required the company of some ladies of pleasure and a chicken buffet. For one thing they would not be able to meet the costs and what the hell did they have to celebrate anyway? He had envisaged the INA remnants to be living off the land or seeking shelter from villagers sympathetic to the independence cause after they had been defeated and left to rot in the jungle. Their officers had either been arrested and sent to Delhi to face trial, or had gone on the run seeking to preserve their own skins until the Raj had been banished from the sub-continent and they could return to their homes and a hero's welcome.

After a wait of about ten minutes he collected his kit together and was about to shoulder his pack when he saw a daub of black slime in the fold of his left elbow. He failed to shift it when he tried to brush it away. When he saw the thing slowly expanding he realised with deep revulsion that it was a leech, firmly attached and enjoying a blood-meal at his expense. He dropped his pack and loose items of equipment, tore off his shirt, boots, trousers and cotton drawers and glanced quickly over his body. He found half a dozen ranged over his neck, chest, arms and abdomen. He was unable to see his back but by running his hands over his skin he felt some relief that they were only attached to the front of his body where he had been laid in the seeping mud. Harding recalled the standard method of removing the disgusting creatures was treat them to the end of a lit cigarette. It was dangerous to pull them off because of the possibility of their tiny teeth being left embedded in the flesh to fester and turn septic. A lit cigarette was a non-starter; he did not smoke. He could of course leave them until they had their fill when they would drop off voluntarily or … try some salt. He remembered his father giving garden slugs a sprinkle, when they responded to that treatment by curling up to die. He did not have any salt but he did carry an ample supply of salt tablets. He found they were soggy from the moisture they had absorbed from the humid air, but they were easy to crush into a damp powder that he carefully applied to the first of the blood-sucking bladders. It quickly contracted and releasing its hold, dropped off. He repeated the treatment to the rest of them. After carefully checking the seams of his clothing he felt confident that he had got rid of the pests and that he didn't have any lurking in any body crevices. He remembered, with a smile, a story he had heard that West African troops serving in Burma would disobey any orders to enter the jungle unless they had been issued with French letters. They secured the sheaths to their penises with insulating tape to prevent leeches gaining access and, so they believed, render them impotent. It had been an amusing source of speculation as to why they demanded a constant supply of contraceptives when the accepted opportunity to employ them was so remote.

He applied some sulphonamide powder to the lesions left by the leeches and hurriedly dressed, taking care to roll down his shirt sleeves and seal the cuffs with surgical tape to reduce the chances of the odd leech slipping in from any wet undergrowth which he might brush against. After checking that his trouser legs were tucked into his socks, with his puttees tightly wrapped around his ankles he slung his pack over his shoulders, secured his loose items of equipment and began walking.

A check on his position indicated that he had about five hundred yards to go to be within sight of his objective. The track followed by the INA party lined up neatly with his confirmed compass bearing. He decided that if he took the risk and followed it he could make his objective by last light and find himself a suitable lying up point from where he could observe and record the maximum amount of intelligence. With an achieved pace count of six hundred behind him he halted for a breather and to take a drink of his diminishing water supply. He knew he would have to find somewhere to fill up his water bottles before he could make the return trek. The idea of purloining some fresh water from the INA appeared to be the best, and maybe the only option available to him. The more he thought of it, the more compelling it became, but how feasible remained to be seen.

Thirst temporarily abated, Harding left the track that he felt sure would take him right onto an occupied area of the airstrip and made his way through a stretch of tangled undergrowth to bring him out into a safe area. He knew that most tactical airfields had the operational and administrative functions located clear of the approach and take-off flight paths and set up on one of the long sides of the runway. With this typical picture in mind, he aimed for, what he judged to be, one of the runway ends. He came out of the green semi-darkness of the jungle into a belt of low bush that bordered the runway. He dropped to his knees and crawled forward to gain a view of the set-up. It was much as he had thought it to be, with the runway constructed on a general north/south alignment with a collection of dilapidated bashas, old tents and a long wooden shed with a corrugated metal roof clustered about fifty yards from the east side of the runway. A four-section stores marquee stood behind a crude barbed-wire fence and an armed guard.

An open-air cookhouse equipped with *tandoori* ovens, sawyer stoves and petrol hydro-burners was in full blast. Cooks, engulfed in clouds of steam and the blue fumes rising from hot fat, stripped down to drawers and food-soiled undervests, were chopping, pouring and stirring in sweat-streaked preparation of the evening meal. The smell of boiling rice and *dhal* mingled with the acrid smoke of *ghee*, heated almost to the threshold of combustion.

At the northern end of the runway and opposite the admin area on the loading/unloading apron was a parked aeroplane with the tail backed into the bush and partially hidden from air observation by an overhanging tree canopy. Harding made a positive identification of it as a Junkers 52, the easily recognisable three-engined German troop and general cargo carrier operated by the Luftwaffe. It was difficult from his position to read any markings on the wings or fuselage that would assist in confirming to which organisation it belonged.

A couple of men, whom he took to be aircrew, were stretched out on camp beds in front of a two-man bivouac pitched on bare earth under the port wing. They were too far away for Harding to make a firm identification of their regional nationality, but he thought they could be Europeans as they appeared to have made sleeping arrangements remote from the Asians across at the admin area. Twenty yards from the Junkers 52 was a pair of Indian draught elephants chain-hobbled to a tree and feeding from huge swathes of grass being brought to them by a *mahout* from the adjacent undergrowth. From a cursory examination of his recce target, Harding felt he had seen enough to fill a half dozen pages of his notebook; it was now time to establish an observation point from where he could record the 'who, what and when' of his intelligence report and assess the extent of the activities at the airfield. It was darkening rapidly as Harding circled the airfield aiming for a position on the east side of the runway which appeared to be deserted and would give him a good field of view to cover the main area of usage.

★★★

Duncan Reeder stood beyond the thick outer wall of Fort William. The night sky of Calcutta was overhung with the street lights and neon signs of Chowhringhee and the central metropolis of the sprawling city. He always considered Calcutta to be at peace with itself during the hours of darkness; unlike the straining, sweating struggle of its poorest inhabitants to earn a meagre living through the burning heat and humidity of the day. His thoughts centred on Sergeant Harding whom he judged would now be well advanced on his recce somewhere in the North India jungle and wondered how he was standing up to the extreme conditions imposed by his difficult task. Reeder was always sensitive to the dangers to which field intelligence personnel were exposed. He knew from wartime experience that, on many occasions, information being transmitted from a clandestine wireless station working within enemy territory would be brought to an abrupt end when the operator had been forced to close down and withdraw to safety in fear of discovery. Sometimes never to open up again….

Although some parts of the picture were coming together it was still much too early to form a substantial intelligence brief. So far, he had Harding's preliminary report of INA activity and aircraft movements, then he had the RAF recce photographs followed by a report from Malaya of a Dakota bearing the CAT markings making a brief stop at Batu Pahat.

Who the hell is CAT? If it's a new commercial airline, who owns it? Where is it based? Is there a link with the Tamu report and therefore a connection with Operation KINGSMAN? A number of questions to be answered – hopefully Harding will provide some answers and when this MacNair fellow, now on his way from

Delhi as the Viceroy's representative, arrives he may have some light to throw on the problem. Hell of a lot going on. Interesting to see where it will lead.

Reeder left the comparative evening cool of the *maidan*, an expansive grassed area to the east of the grand colonial buildings and the bustling commercial centre of Calcutta, and re-entered the breathless confines of the fort. He called at the operations room to see if there was any word from Harding but he was met with a negative response. Nothing since the signal to inform Calcutta of his impending recce patrol. Reeder wondered at what point they should send in an armed patrol to lift him out – if it went in too early it would give the game away and alert the INA to transfer their operations, whatever they may be, to another area. He made a mental note to give Harding another couple of days then review the situation.

Chapter 21

After reaching a position some one hundred yards short of the dispersal area and diagonally opposite the admin area, Harding found a suitable spot to set up his observation point. He stumbled across a huge tree that had in the past suffered a lightning strike, ripping it from the ground and exposing its tangled root system; a ready-made laying up point, offering first-class cover and easy to withdraw from into the jungle if he was in danger of being discovered.

He found a clump of bamboo and selected some stems to form a laying-up platform, which he cut to length with his machete. He covered the bamboo frame with interlaced canes and ferns and finally laid his groundsheet over the rough structure. Aware that even outside the rainy season a heat generated storm could blow up with little warning, he secured his monsoon cape to some overhanging roots which he camouflaged with trailing vines that had attached themselves to the fallen tree. He completed his task by fastening his mosquito net to the underside of the monsoon cape to make his hide safe from night flying insects.

When he was satisfied, he took himself off into the jungle to clean himself and put together a meal of sorts. He stripped naked and with a half mess tin of water dabbed the dirt and sweat from his armpits, crotch and feet. After a dusting of talc he climbed into some clean underpants, trousers and shirt. The dirty clothing, which had been on his back for three days, was rolled into a tight bundle and secured to the outside of his pack. He felt he had earned the right to fill up with a tasty meal before settling down for the night and a small can of salmon seemed an appropriate choice.

He smiled ruefully at the familiar John West label which displayed a full colour illustration of an attractive serving suggestion complete with thinly sliced cucumber, lettuce and tomato.

"How delightful."

He opened the can to find that the heat had robbed the contents of its juicy firmness. He ate the fishy sludge with a couple of hard-tack biscuits washed down with half a mug of lukewarm water as it was far too risky to make a brew. After burying the empty can and attending to his natural comfort needs in a hole scraped in the earth with his entrenching tool, he returned to his prepared hide.

It was completely dark with the admin area lit by a few high-pressure paraffin lamps but they provided insufficient light to see anything worth recording, even with binoculars. With his mind working on how he was going to gain more worthwhile intelligence he fell into an exhausted sleep.

When he awoke he checked his watch. It was just after midnight and the airfield was bathed in bright moonlight. He had been asleep for over five hours and was stiff and sore from the effects of his jungle hike. He crept out from his shelter and did a few exercises in the deep shadows to ease his seized up muscles and aching back. His mouth was sand-dry but he could afford to take no more water from his dwindling supply. Unless he could find a clean water source he knew he would be in trouble during the daylight hours when the full heat of the sun would be on him from morning to late afternoon. He made up his mind to take a closer look at the admin area and try to filch some water. He clipped two empty water carriers to his belt and set forth on his foraging trip.

Harding planned on following a route through the edge of the jungle and make a detour to approach the parked Junkers 52 from behind the tail plane and take a closer look in the hope that he could pick up some information on its identity and crew. The original operating agency of the aeroplane was clearly seen under patches of dark green paint hastily applied to the high tail fin, wings and fuselage over the swastika and open cross insignia of the Luftwaffe. He crawled nearer to the bivouac to make certain the crew were in there and not sleeping in the aeroplane, before clambering up the short aluminium ladder into the fuselage. He crawled forward to edge through an opening in the canvas curtain to gain access to the flight deck to look for maps or perhaps a flight plan that would help identify the new operator of the machine. There were no maps or charts to be seen but he did find a maintenance log slotted into a seat pocket. The dated record of servicing and repairs confirmed that it had been in regular service with the Germans until April 1945. Subsequent entries were written in the Cyrillic alphabet used by the Slavonic countries of Eastern Europe.

Once back in the shelter of the jungle he paused to regain his breath after the tension of the previous few minutes. He was tempted to get back to his hide, pack up and get away fast to report this significant piece of intelligence. But he had to get his hands on some water first and that meant carrying on with his night prowl over to the admin area.

He moved as quickly as he dared, taking care not to create a noise that would alert the sleeping camp. As he moved to the rear of the stores tent he went close to the wooden shed he had seen on his initial scan of the airfield. Now that he was out of the jungle cover he was forced to adopt a ground-hugging cat crawl to avoid going into high silhouette from the moonlight. It was then that he caught his foot on some cable leading from a shuttered opening and snaking to a clearing beyond the admin area. Stopping, Harding followed the path of the cable with his eyes, and could see the four high masts of a transmitter aerial with the cable running to it. The masts were positioned in the characteristic diamond formation demanded by a rhombic antenna. He saw that the cable was feeding the south-east end of the diamond to give a radiating direction to the north-west … Moscow?

Why did a trading company working at an abandoned airfield find it necessary to erect a high frequency, long-range antenna, which, depending on the transmitter output, was capable of working world-wide distances? The answer to that question plus that of the parked Junkers 52 would have to be found by a better informed authority. Harding's task was to ferret out intelligence; it was then up to Calcutta to sift his report and analyse his findings.

Whatever the purpose of the antenna might be, Harding made certain it was going to be out of use for a while. He found a piece of loose rock and scraped the cable against it until he had removed the insulating sheath and broken through the copper wire conductor. To give the damage an appearance of hungry animal behaviour he left some teeth marks on the broken ends of the cable and moved away.

As he crawled past the cookhouse area he almost slipped into a garbage pit full to the brim with empty cans, packing material and food waste with rats, bandicoots and cockroaches scampering over the mess. Harding shivered in disgust. If that was a sample of the way the INA ran a camp they had certainly forgotten the basic rules of field hygiene.

When he reached the stores marquee he stopped and listened carefully for sounds of the armed guard. When he heard the sound of coughing and the toe-nail-curling hawking of phlegm followed by the creak of *charpoy* ropes under strain, he knew that the guard was awake but taking things easy – on his back. He crawled under the makeshift barbed-wire fence and by unfastening a lacing cord from two bottom eyelets of a wall join he slid into the marquee. He lay still until he was satisfied there were no bodies, sleeping or awake. Then, aided by shafts of moonlight he made a swift appraisal of the interior.

Some jute sacks in an untidy pile lay propped against a roof pole. They held rice and lentils and seemed to present an easy food source for a number of rats which had found their way into the store. Harding was thankful that neither commodity was on his shopping list. However, some black painted jerricans, the standard colour of British service water containers, were quite definitely on his shopping list. After ensuring the water tasted reasonably fresh and carried traces of chlorine, he quickly filled both his water bottles and deciding he was in danger of overstaying his welcome, hurried back to his hide. He settled down for a sleep just as dawn broke orange-red, casting long shadows over the runway.

★★★

The rumble of heavy chains being dragged over the ground jerked Harding awake. He carefully parted some hanging camouflage to watch the pair of elephants swaying along the edge of the runway towards the south-westerly end. He prayed that the elephants were not endowed with the scent responses shared by most indigenous creatures, aware that his now objectionable body smell was an absolute giveaway, even to the *mahout* perched on the neck of the nearest animal. He kept his fingers crossed and hoped. When they had disappeared from sight, Harding crept from the hide and withdrew to his admin area back in the jungle to try to eat some food. He regretted having eaten the rice which had left him with recurring bowel discomfort and threatened him with a dose of the squitters. But he chewed a couple of hard-tack biscuits and took a few sips of water to keep something in his stomach to stave off hunger pains. His eyes were burning through lack of sleep.

He was alerted to the sound of an aeroplane that came in low over the airfield from his right. It lifted into a climbing 180 degree turn to complete a full circuit and return for a landing attempt. He could see men come out from their sleeping quarters to watch the landing, which was accomplished to the squeal of tyres hitting the ground and smoke plumes blown back from the scorched rubber. The aircraft braked to a halt with both engines switched off and waited. By leaning forward and looking hard left, Harding could just see the two elephants being driven into position to have their chains coupled to the undercarriage to haul the now dead load back to the dispersal area. As the aircraft was being dragged up the runway a short aluminium ladder was swung from the fuselage and two men dropped to the ground to walk the length of the runway towards the admin area.

The pair passed within thirty yards of Harding giving him a

good sight of them. They were both of oriental appearance. One, a slight fellow with a wispy beard, was dressed in Chinese peasant-style black trousers and a loose-fitting shirt. An American pattern web belt and holster carried a pistol secured cowboy fashion below his right arm. His companion was of a much heavier stature, dressed in jungle green shirt and trousers with a peaked fatigue cap badged with four red stars. A Sten gun slung over a shoulder completed his turnout.

When the pair were out of earshot Harding noted the detailed appearance of both men in his notebook and waited for the elephant powered aircraft to pass his field of vision. It was a Dakota and carried the identification CAT. He focussed his binoculars to reveal its original US markings of a star and white bands on the fuselage and wings that had been painted over. Through the open side window of the flight deck he could see the head and shoulders of a white man wearing an olive green shirt and a black baseball cap. A half-smoked cigar was clamped between his teeth. He quickly set his camera and took some shots of the procession before the Dakota passed beyond range and turned into the dispersal area where it parked alongside the Junkers.

The two passengers who had walked up the runway were now being greeted by a tall white man. He had dark hair and a full beard and was wearing a golf pullover and suede desert boots. After handshakes, the white man, accompanied by an armed INA escort and a coolie, hurried across to the Dakota to return with a couple of heavy looking haversacks. It seemed to Harding that the haversack contents were of value since the armed escort and the white fellow closed up on the coolie and his burden until they entered the wooden hut from where the aerial feeder led that Harding had cut during the night.

He wondered if the damaged feeder had been discovered. It soon would be when they tried to tune the transmitter for their next schedule whenever that might be – not good practice to attempt loading into a zero impedance. He had a quiet grin to himself.

During the remainder of the morning Harding maintained a close watch, but except for the normal activities associated with a field camp and the occasional appearance of Jasmine escorting her female charges to and from a hessian screened ablution and latrine facility, there was nothing of note to record.

He decided to wait until the camp had settled down for the afternoon kip session before retiring to his admin area for some food. He had water and a can of corned beef on the menu, hardly a mouth-watering attraction, but he was damned hungry and anything remotely edible would be welcome.

A movement on the far side of the runway made Harding reach for his binoculars. When he brought them into focus he saw a man wearing the saffron robe of a Buddhist monk followed by a boy staggering under the weight of a bedding roll head load. The monk belied the usual appearance of a holy man. He marched with a purposeful stride and as the robe parted with each step the gleam of highly polished knee boots was displayed. Harding aimed his camera to capture the monk on film and then made some descriptive notes of the pair. The monk was met with handshakes all round before he was ushered into a tent by the tall white man.

As the cookhouse area was cleared after the *tiffin* meal break and kites and heavy black crows dropped down from their perches high in the trees to scavenge for food scraps, Harding withdrew from his hide to open a can of corned beef and make the best of his mildewed hard-tack biscuits. Like the salmon, the contents of the can were in a lumpy liquid form and would have benefited from heating up but it was a risk he was afraid to take. Instead he just swallowed the stuff to try and appease his unremitting hunger before crawling back to his hide and continuing his vigil.

Increased activity and movement in the accommodation area alerted Harding when a group, including the two men who had landed in the Dakota, the Buddhist monk and a man in Burmese style dress joined the tall white man in an hour-long discussion in front of the wooden shed. Harding was too distant to hear what was being discussed and resolved to move nearer in order to get some close-up photograph shots. Carrying only his machete for personal protection he slipped back into the fringes of the jungle and following a route parallel to that of his night recce, made for the edge of the fuel dump where, at a range of about fifty yards, he took a dozen shots of the group as the meeting broke up and they drifted off to their respective billets.

When Harding took up his observation position back at the hide he saw some tables being set out with Tilley lamps for lighting and some seating for the VIP five. Some mats and cushions were spread out on the ground to left and right of the tables and a small Indian band equipped with *sitars,* flutes and small drums squatted to one side, leaving the mats and cushions on the other side to whoever else was to join the *ram-sami.* When the band struck up with a screeching, discordant tune, Jasmine and the girls took up position alongside a serving table which was being laid out with trays, tureens of food and bottles.

As the sun disappeared behind streaks of crimson cloud, the VIPs took their seats to be waited on by the girl hostesses who poured drinks and presented food to their guests. The occasion became more and more noisy as the evening proceeded until one or two of the VIPs slid away from the table, to be, Harding presumed, offered further entertainment by the *filles de joi* in the privacy of their billets. Jasmine stayed on with the tall white man until he retired, unaccompanied, to the wooden shed.

Harding relaxed as silence fell on the airfield. His attempts to piece together the significance of the events of the day made little sense. Instead, he concentrated on committing the results of the night's activities to memory and writing them up the following morning. He checked that all loose items of kit, weapons, binoculars and water bottles were within easy reach, pulled the mosquito net into the edges of his crude sleeping platform and settled down for a few hours. Even the whine of mosquitoes and the crashing of heavy flying insects were ignored as the effects of the jungle march and the body weariness of humping a kit load over formidable country took their toll to draw him into a deep, dreamless sleep.

★★★

Captain Reeder completed his daily intelligence brief and re-read it before passing it through for typing:

Nothing yet to report from Harding. The agent in Malaya reports large quantities of arms and ammunition supplied to the Malayan Anti-Japanese Army remain unaccounted for and are a cause for concern to the military authorities there. The French are facing resistance from the local population in Indo-China and the Americans are being unco-operative in offering help to the French forces who are trying to re-assert their rule in that region. A local activist named as Soekarno is creating trouble for the Dutch in Java by employing Japanese troops, who are awaiting repatriation, to harass Dutch nationals.

Chapter 22

He stared at the big green eye hovering above his face. It moved away slowly as he levered himself up into a sitting position to take whatever action was needed to deal with the presence. It had disappeared. He lay for a while puzzling as to what it may have been. He lifted his wrist to see the time: so, there was a green eye after all – the luminous dial of his army issue Ebel watch. It was two-fifteen. He had slept solidly for almost two hours.

Harding was cold and his clothing, clammy from absorbed sweat, stuck to his back and thighs. Except for the rustle of trees and the occasional sharp cry of small mammals caught in the jaws of night hunting predators, all was quiet. His thoughts turned to the idea of a hot bath, fresh clean sheets, a soft mattress and many hours of undisturbed sleep. He recalled the body needs of a sleep/awake ratio pattern that affirmed twelve hours of normal sleep is the minimum requirement to recover from forty-eight waking hours. And that because sleeplessness is cumulative he reckoned he was due a sleep recovery period of...? When his thoughts turned to the extent of what had been accomplished already, on his own, with no outside assistance or emergency back-up on call, a shiver of panic ran through him. For the first time since setting out on the recce he felt trapped in a plight of his own making and the wisdom of taking on such a demanding task. His orders from Calcutta had been to carry out a ground recce and report. Did they believe that he could drive up to the airfield, park somewhere and pick up some information readily available to any innocent passer-by? Had he, by planning to approach his target from the jungle, taken on more than his training and experience could grapple with? His thought processes devolved to the possibility of sustaining an injury or sickness, both misfortunes highly likely in his present circumstance. When in charge of men he had always looked to their safety and well-being and now he didn't even have the prop of responsibility and leadership when the need to inspire and encourage subordinates overrides private fear.

Without the rations and water to support another full day watching the airfield and then make the difficult journey back to his Jeep, he decided to make preparations for a first light departure. He felt satisfied that he had sufficient notes and photographs to satisfy the Calcutta people and that little more was to be gained by hanging on and possibly being overtaken by some mishap which would compromise his expended efforts and make the gathered intelligence worthless.

By first light he had dismantled his hide and tidied his admin area, with all waste buried and overlaid with vegetation. After a final check to ensure all his kit was complete and properly secured he moved off to get clear of the area before the activities of the day began.

He followed the track which the INA foraging party and Jasmine and her charges had taken and instead of breaking through the jungle at the point where he had taken cover from them, he kept to the better route. It was not clear to Harding where it would lead, but having made up his mind to do the return march in one day he was stuck with it. He made frequent checks on distance and direction and by early afternoon emerged from the jungle onto a road at a point he estimated to be about eight hundred yards from the timber trail he had driven up on the first day of his mission.

By mid-afternoon he had located his Jeep. Fast growing creepers trailing over the hide had made the vehicle even more effectively concealed than when Harding had left it four days earlier. He was hungry and very thirsty, having almost drained the last of his water at the midday halt. The reserve of water left in the *chagal* had evaporated, leaving the canvas dried hard and empty. He began to feel a cramp in his stomach – sure signs that he was in for a bout of heat exhaustion brought on by dehydration and lack of salt. He had taken no salt tablets for over twenty-four hours due to rationing his water intake and now he was paying for his neglect. With no food or water available to him he decided to try and make it back to Imphal and Mr Ong's restaurant.

He removed the hardened mud plug from the Jeep's exhaust, replaced the rotor arm and ignition coil, and after a few pushes on the starter switch the engine fired and quickly settled down to a steady throb. He hid his pistol, carbine, ammunition, notes and exposed film inside the false floor bolted under the rear seat and stacked his pack, equipment and camouflage net on top.

Night had fallen before he reached the Imphal road and although it was a relief to be driving without the sun beating down on him, he was feeling feverish and nauseous and starting to lose contact with his surroundings. He tried to concentrate hard on his driving but on two occasions he narrowly avoided colliding with unlit bullock carts. On the verge of collapse he drove off the road, stalled the engine and passed out.

Harding knew nothing of the next forty-eight hours. Fatigue, lack of sleep, food and water had caught up with him. He at last made a partial recovery to faintly hear a soft voice somewhere in the distance encouraging him to open his eyes. But before he could summon the strength to obey he slumped back into a stupor. During the following hours he endured alternate bouts of shivering and fever. As the wakeful periods became longer he thought he could feel a warm body close to him but he dismissed the thoughts as hallucinations. The sound of movement and the feel of his body being gently rolled over to free the sheet he was laid on brought him back to reality. When he smelled the soft incense perfume of burning joss-stick, lit to deter mosquitoes, he guessed that he must have somehow made it back to Mr Ong's establishment.

He guessed correctly. He was lying naked on a clean white sheet in a tiny cubicle of a room with Jasmine bending over him. When she saw he was awake she wiped his face and forehead with cool rosewater and called out a name. Her call was answered by a

Burmese girl who scurried in giggling at the sight of the naked sergeant sahib and passed a bowl and spoon to Jasmine.

Jasmine spoke softly to him. "Come, please, this will make you well." She spooned warm arrowroot gruel into his parched mouth until his stomach rebelled and he started to retch and dribble the thin liquid onto his chest. She cleaned the vomit from his skin and tried to answer the questions she believed he was trying to ask.

"You soon better, not worry about possessions, everything OK. Pack things safe under bed, motor car in Mr Ong's compound. We find you on road. I drive motor car to this place. I think you have sickness from leech."

Harding responded with a weak smile and fell asleep.

Chapter 23

Constable Suresh Ram of the Bengal Police did not like doing the all-night duty at Kushtia Railway Junction. There was too much racial difficulty. Congress *wallahs* coming down from Calcutta to make troubles with robbery and interference to Muslim League peoples who then do retaliation. Always these happenings at the railway station. Railway station always centre for political troubles in India.

The station clock mounted above the First Class booking office was standing at 6am and time for Suresh Ram to go off duty. Except for some *loos wallahs* intent on stealing from the company coal yard and a cow deciding to die at the end of the 'up' platform, it had been a quiet night. He watched until the Assam Night Mail cleared the station 'down' signal and the red lamps on the guard's van had faded into the distance and went to unchain his bicycle from the 'Hindus Only' faucet where it had been secured all night. The minor incidents report could wait until after breakfast when he would go to sign off and collect his month's pay.

He wheeled his bicycle onto the side of the railway line, the accepted footpath for pedestrians in rural India, and headed for his home in the Police Lines. As he crunched his way over the track ballast he considered the domestic problems weighing heavily on his mind.

Having been cursed with a family of two daughters and an over-ambitious spouse, the matter of suitable dowries to match the needs of suitor families was a vexed question that left Suresh Ram in a situation of grave difficulty. His police pay was barely sufficient to feed and clothe his family, and with Meera, his youngest and most beautiful daughter now at the centre of sensitive marriage negotiations with Moti Das, the son of a well-to-do seed merchant residing at Mymensingh, he was almost at the end of his wits with worry. With only three weeks left before the marriage ceremony he was in daily touch with his gods to help with his problem.

The date of the marriage had been set by the *prohit* Tunda Basu, a crafty wedding arranger. Under no circumstances would the *prohit* extend the date to give more time for Suresh Ram to englut the shortfall in Meera's dowry. The *prohit* insisted that he had set the date according to the carefully studied horoscopes of both bride and bridegroom and if they were to enjoy a happy and fruitful life together then the stars, the gods and the supreme regard to Tunda Basu's rupee flow were not to be denied. Suresh Ram knew all too well that the itchy-palmed fellow had taken into account other impending weddings and in order to have the pleasure of arranging them all, had fixed dates and times according to his calendar. In addition to charging a horoscope fee he also arranged wedding breakfasts and the musicians to provide entertainment which brought him substantial commission. After all, the prospective in-laws insisted that because the good police constable was to be relieved of providing for his daughter after she was married off, it was only fair that the girl arrive at the nuptial chamber with more than a few trinkets and jangling bracelets.

When Suresh Ram spotted a small tea chest partly concealed by some bushes at the base of the station approach signal post, he stopped to take a closer look. He thought it could not have been there long. The local people were very poor and even an empty tea chest would be a valuable find to be carried home and brought into service as a table or storage cupboard. He turned the chest over to find that it was sealed and therefore full of tea. The name: ERSKINE-JALPAI was stencilled in black paint across the lid, together with the name of the consignee, ASSAM BENGAL TRADING COMPANY, CALCUTTA with a red painted dot the size of a one rupee coin above 'BENGAL'. A hand printed cardboard label affixed to the side read: ASSAM BENGAL TRADING Co, East Howrah Godowns, Calcutta.

Ram knew what he should do according to Police Regulations and Standing Orders. His duty was to take the goods in charge and deliver them to the police station, enter the incident in the First Report Book and write up a description of the goods in the Lost and Found Register. Alternatively, as the goods were discovered on the line and therefore on railway property they could be held to be the responsibility of the railway company. He leaned his bicycle against the signal post and considered the facts: the Police Service and the Railway Company were both bureaucratic organisations, each would insist upon having a say in the disposal of the property. The constable knew that this matter could take months, even years to settle. Indeed, it could well be submitted to higher authority or even the district magistrate before a conclusion could be reached.

With all facts carefully considered, the fact of his daughter's wedding dowry was uppermost in his mind. He could save officialdom much trouble and expense if he kept the find for himself. If, as seemed highly possible, the tea chest had fallen from the Assam Night Mail, it stood to reason that it was full of high quality tea from the high plantations of Assam and would fetch a good price in the bazaar, unlike the dark green dust that passed for tea in the poor country districts.

He balanced the chest on the carrier of his bicycle and continued his journey home. The dawn redness would soon be disappearing in the full light of day and Ram did not wish anyone to see his prize. He had just reached the level crossing to turn onto his home road when he noticed the rear tyre had deflated.

"Good morning Constable, having some trouble?"

Ram lifted his gaze from the disabled bicycle to see Sub-Inspector Jenkins standing before him. Ram's heart sank.

"Sir, I have to make the report that I discovered this box by the approach signal post as I was going off duty and I am taking it to the police station."

The Sub-Inspector waited until he was sure the constable's

explanation was the best on offer and said, "You have passed the road to the police station, bloody donkey. Now tell me what intentions you have." Although Sub-Inspector Jenkins was of Anglo-Indian parentage he adopted the mannerisms and posture of a *pukka-sahib*, but his English was still delivered in the sing-song, flowery style of a *babu*.

Having recovered some composure and with his thinking process back in a state of control Ram gushed, "I tell you, sir, I am going home to change into clean uniform before presenting my good self at the police station with the goods."

"You will come with me now at this very minute to the police station. Then I will make all necessary arrangements to deal with the business after I have decided how to proceed. *Malum*?"

As Constable Ram wheeled his bicycle, rear wheel rim bumping over the stony ground, he set his mind to work on how he could outwit the Sub-Inspector. There were always rumours going the rounds in Indian communities about people and their doings. The higher the rank and standing of the person at the heart of the rumour, the greater the degree of interest it raised. And Ram had heard many allegations of the Sub-Inspector's private doings that might be raised in order to gain ascendancy over his superior officer and the disposal of the expensive Assam tea. It had often been observed that Sub-Inspector Jenkins had a frail side to his character. Although barely forty years old, Mrs Jenkins had, since many years ago, lost the bloom of youthful promise and never joined her husband in any social intercourse, not even to entertain family at her home. She much preferred to follow the ways of her Indian forebears in housekeeping, dietary and social practice. The intimate affairs of her relationship with her husband were largely speculative ... could it be that the Sub-Inspector had been at 'the other side of the railway track' on a visit to the private emporium of pleasure operated by the *bibi* Lakshmi?

Constable Ram was about to raise the question of the Sub-Inspector's moral rectitude and the price of discretion when the chest slipped from the bicycle carrier, bounced once and ended up in a monsoon ditch. The chest split, spilling tea into the less wholesome contents of the ditch and evaporating Constable Ram's dowry aspirations.

The Sub-Inspector swiped the errant constable on the head with his swagger stick and screamed, "You senseless pinhead, don't just stand there, bloody do something now, I tell you."

Constable Ram propped his bicycle against a dried up deodar tree, surveyed the tattered inner-tube which protruded, umbilical-like, from the slack tyre and looked down into the ditch.

"I am thinking, Inspectorji, that this is big trouble. What shall we say to owner of the tea and the Railway Company? I am telling you, sir, I am most worried at this event."

"Never mind all that, we cannot leave evidence lying about. Get on your belly and retrieve the chest."

When Constable Ram crouched to reach into the ditch to salvage the broken tea chest, his groping hand made contact with a package the size of a house brick. He brought it to the surface. It was wrapped in calico and sealed with surgical tape. In a state of wonder he handed it to the Sub-Inspector who handled it with care. He knew that Congress *wallahs* were active in the area and were not averse to planting bombs wherever they thought it would cause the most trouble.

He handed it back to the constable. "You can get rid of this and say no word of this to anyone, *malum*?"

Chapter 24

To be an honorary member of Calcutta District Officer's Mess was a convenient arrangement for both the mess and Maurice Sedley. The former profited from the monthly mess fee and bar profit, whilst the latter found it an oasis of comfort, conviviality and the opportunity to exchange sensitive information with Army Intelligence. Although Maurice Sedley held the rank of Chief Superintendent in the Bengal Police, he chose, for professional reasons, to be known as Mr Sedley of the Indian Civil Service. He worked from an upstairs office in Lal Bazaar Street, a small alleyway near Police Headquarters. Few people, including officers at senior levels in the police hierarchy, knew what his duties entailed. He ran a spy network through a system of agents, some Hindu, some Muslim, some Anglo-Indian and even some British. They all had one thing in common: they were loyal to him. He harvested his agents from corrupt business houses, crime syndicates and runaway debtors. They served his purposes very well.

Maurice Sedley did not own a car, and never made use of an official one. Cars bore number plates and could be readily identified. He always used public transport for local travel: trams, buses, taxis, *rickshaws* and *tongas*. He could not even be identified with a family – he did not have one, at least not that anyone in Calcutta was aware of.

Having arranged to meet Colonel Grindley at 9pm he stepped from his hired *tonga* at fifteen minutes to the hour at the Victoria Memorial. He paid the driver and waited until the conveyance had clattered off in search of another fare before completing his journey into the fort. He arrived at the mess entrance at two minutes to the hour where he was greeted by a uniformed waiter with bowed head and a respectful *"Namaste."*

After exchanging weather talk and agreeing that with the monsoon season now at an end, the summer madness of riot, killing, rape and arson would subside, Grindley ordered a pot of coffee and a couple of large pegs of single malt.

Grindley had known Sedley for only a couple of months and although they had met on several occasions he found the man difficult to fathom. On the surface he was polite, well mannered and was fluent in Urdu and Bengali. He spoke in the manner of a blind man moving his eyes from left to right as if reading Braille and consequently never looked one in the eye during conversation. He looked like hundreds of white men domiciled in the East who were in the shipping or commodities business; white suit, black shoes and a yellowed, parchment-like complexion, dried out with the tropical sun and bouts of fever.

The nature of Sedley's visit was quickly explained. "I have been given, by one of my contacts, a small pellet of opium. It appears that a certain *rickshaw wallah* who had got himself mixed up in the August riots gave it to my chappie. The *rickshaw wallah* insisted it was given him by some person or persons unknown."

"So ... what's that got to do with anything that my organisation is involved with? I would have thought the possession of dope was a police matter."

"Very true, but this is not the local stuff. This sample came from either Siam or Indo-China. At least, that's what the forensic people tell me and that puts a different aspect on the matter."

"You mean there's a bit of smuggling going on? A case for the Customs and Excise Department, I would have thought."

"If, as you suggest, there might be some smuggling, then there's a cause for greater concern. In order to smuggle dope one has to have adequate capital to buy up sufficient quantities to make the job worthwhile, pay people to carry it and bribe officials to turn a blind eye. This means that someone pretty big is behind it. There's no evidence that any of the pre-war crooks who specialised in international crime have returned to this part of the world."

"Then, if there aren't any gangsters about to deal in dope for profit, and your informant tells you it is apparently being given away, the profit motive can be ruled out. Can there be a more sinister interest at work here?"

"Well, just listen to this. Late this afternoon I received a message from one of my up-country contacts. It seems that some constable stationed at Kushtia was caught trying to sell a package of opium to a local *zemindar*. Under interrogation he confessed to having found it on the railway line in a tea chest and was hoping to sell it to pay for his daughter's dowry. His Sub-Inspector is suspended from duty awaiting disciplinary action because he was involved in the find, but thinking the package might contain a bomb he funked it and ordered the constable to get shut. The tea chest was in transit from Assam to Calcutta and if the dope found in it proves to be from the same source as the *rickshaw wallah's*, there's a good chance that we can open up a wider investigation."

Grindley called for a waiter to bring more malt and told him to chalk it up on Mr Sedley's bar chit. Then he asked, "All very interesting, but what has this got to do with my operation? Remember, our arrangement is to effect the arrest and disposal of the INA traitors, not to smoke out dope runners."

"You have a fellow working in Assam and the dope at Kushtia was found in a sample of tea consigned from the Erskine-Jalpai estate to the Assam Bengal Trading Company here in Cal. It would be helpful if you could ask your fellow in Assam if he could give me some information about the estate – yer know … where it is, who owns it, how large it is, anything to help us put together a link in the supply chain."

"I'll have to put this to Reeder, the Ops Officer. It's up to him to task his field operators and this job sounds a bit outside their training and experience. However, I'll give it a whirl and see what can be done. As a matter of interest, how does this dope affect anyone who takes it? Does it send 'em a bit *jungli* and bloodthirsty or something?"

"Just the opposite in fact, it's supposed to be a soporific – pleasant dreams an' that sort of thing. It's derived from the opium poppy and some is still grown in parts of Bihar for local use. The authorities take no notice and if the locals enjoy smoking a pellet or two with the rot-gut liquor they brew up, so what. If it stops them getting het up about their miserable existence and getting a bit restless it's all to the good. It's my theory that somebody is doling this stuff out as a reward for going on the rampage. The riots in August were not spontaneous – they rarely are. Agitators, recruited by political activists, spread rumours of religious killings which fire up fears and hatred between Hindus and Muslims that are always simmering just below the surface. These zealots are then rewarded for their efforts with opium which satisfies their addiction and leaves them some to distribute to the poor sods caught up in the violence. Then, when the next riot gets started up there are more willing stooges ready to kill and maim for their share of the dope and the happy dream afterwards!"

With the conversation over, Sedley made his way out of the mess, leaving Grindley to ponder this new turn of events.

★★★

Harding's mind was churning with the experiences and observations met with during the nine days he had spent on the Tamu intelligence gathering mission. The forty-eight hours he had spent being nursed by Jasmine had been something of a write-off, leaving only a hazy recollection of her presence and ministrations. She had done well by getting him fit to travel back to his Shillong camp and seeing that all his clothes had been washed to get rid of the jungle filth and stink they had picked up. He had been relieved to find that the notes and film he had shot at Tamu, together with his arms and ammunition, had remained untouched and with that information he set about drafting a tidy report that would make sense to the Calcutta people.

After a full half day of writing and covering three full pages of foolscap, he decided it was too much to send in clear by wireless and as there was some exposed film to be processed, he had the perfect excuse to wangle a few days in Calcutta.

Chapter 25

Red-shirted railway coolies stood guard over the piles of First and Second Class passenger luggage which stood like islands in the swell of humanity surging over the 'Up' platform at Parbatipur Junction. They were waiting to board the 9pm North Bengal Night Mail to Calcutta, a noisy and smoke filled journey of two hundred and fifty miles through the stifling Indian night.

Parbatipur stood at the junction of the metre gauge railway that ran down from the hill station of Darjeeling and from the Bramaputra Ferry link to Assam and the high jungles of Burma. In contrast to the rural halts and village stations, the major terminals and junctions which marked the beginning, end or line changes on the railway system swarmed with fare-paying or roof-riding passengers throughout every hour of the day and night. In addition to dealing with passenger traffic, the Indian railway stations offered places of assembly: somewhere for the homeless to eat, sleep and wash and for hawkers to ply their trade in selling violently coloured cold drinks, milky tea, sticky confectionery and complete meals of curry and rice dishes. Holy men and beggars, many with mutilated bodies, vied with each other to cadge a few annas from the better off passengers. If the Indian Civil Service was central to the running of the vast sub-continent, the railways embraced the communication system vital to its existence.

With almost an hour to the expected departure time, the train of mixed class passenger and baggage cars stood in an off-platform siding waiting to be coupled to the locomotive which was being coaled and watered over at the engine sheds. Coolie women with baskets of coal perched on their heads teetered up steep bamboo ladders to tip their loads into the black dust clouds that rolled up from the slowly filling tender. When one of the women lost her footing and spilled her load in the meagre light cast by dim oil lamps, she was cursed at by the tallyman who entered a penalty against her paltry wages. Even the weak and pregnant toiled hour after hour in the burning sun by day and the sweltering heat of night to load tenders or clean out fireboxes when the locomotives dropped their dross-choked furnaces at the end of a stint.

The locomotive, now coupled up to its train of dun-coloured coaches, nosed into the platform to the accompaniment of clanking valve gears, loose connecting-rods and the roaring of exhaust steam ejected from dripping cylinders. Before it came to a buffer-rattling halt, waiting passengers surged forward, heaving and shouting, pushing into coaches and jamming doorways to claim a space in the suffocating Third Class Unreserved. Tin trunks, baskets, bed rolls, cotton-wrapped bundles and children were passed overhead to be claimed by their owners. Luggage coolies reached up to windows and doors to claim reward for their services from clients almost hidden under the struggling mass.

The impatience and near panic extended to the vendors who raced to and fro urging travellers to buy food and refreshment for the all-night journey ahead. Even the mendicants, some barely able to crawl, dragged their bodies to the platform edge, and with their begging tins rattling on the ground wailed, *"Baksheesh, baksheesh,* I can wait no longer."

In the quiet of the refreshment rooms, Sergeant Harding folded his copy of the day's *Times of India* and, seeing the platform almost clear of frantic travellers, nodded to his hired coolie who head-loaded the kit box and bedding roll and trotted it along the platform to Second Class Coach 'D', Two Berth Sleeper Coupe No.3. The coupe welcomed him with the lingering smell of countless curry meals, consumed over many years of passenger service, a stench of stale urine and the sharp presence of Jeyes Fluid liberally applied to the 'hole-in-the-floor' lavatory facility. As Harding reached over the lower berth to open the louvred shutters and allow the outside air to filter in, a couple of dark red, antennae-waving cockroaches scurried off to seek shelter behind the bat-wing lavatory doors. Harding saw that a so far unidentified travelling companion had made up a bed on the upper berth and an army issue valise had been stowed in an overhead luggage net. With some minutes to go before the off, he stepped down to the platform to buy a sack of ice to sit in the inward opening door space which, once the train got under way, would draw cooled air into the coupe and bring a little relief to the occupants.

In a First Class, Single Berth Sleeping Compartment of Coach 'F', Laura Erskine sat at the open window. She was staring into the thinning crowd on the platform when she focussed her gaze on the British soldier clad in jungle green moving slowly towards her. She saw that he was wearing the black chevrons of a sergeant and as he drew closer, she recognised him.

"Good evening, Sergeant Harding. Waiting for a train?"

He looked up to the window and smiled. "Just waiting for this thing to start, Mrs Erskine. Are you bound for Cal too?"

"Yes I am … got to keep the business going. I've arranged to see our agent and discuss some contracts, say hullo to the bank people, squeeze in a bit of shopping and maybe catch up on the latest offerings from Hollywood. How about you?"

"On a duty visit but I hope to find a bit of civilised entertainment as well."

A vigorous clanging of the station bell and a blast on the locomotive whistle in reply signalled the imminent departure of the train.

"I'd better get back to my coupe. Look … I'm sharing with another chap, you are welcome to come and join us for a while. I don't think he'll mind, it's a bit early to turn in. I'll get the guard to lock up your compartment – keep everything safe for you, OK?"

"Thanks. It will certainly help the long journey to pass," said Laura. Arrangements were quickly made to secure Laura's belongings. They both stepped out of the train to run together down the platform hand in hand, jumped into the coupe, splashing through a water puddle trickling from the melting ice, and the train began to roll. A Sikh, stripped to vest and cotton drawers turned in surprise at the sudden arrival. All three stood silent. Then, as if on cue, they burst into laughter. The Sikh hastily grabbed trousers and bush jacket to present a more composed appearance and introduced himself as Subedar Rasil Singh of the Bombay Sappers and Miners. The subedar, modest by culture but well practised in British form, apologised for his state of undress as he swiftly buttoned his jacket and said in faultless English, "Are we to be honoured with the lady's company on our night journey?"

Harding quickly explained. "Only for a part of the journey ... I'm sorry to have dropped in like we did. Please forgive me. May I please introduce the lady – Mrs Erskine. I repair wagons for her – or rather I did on one occasion in Assam a few weeks ago. We met just before the departure bell rang. My name is Harding, Royal Signals. It seems we are sharing the coupe reservation."

The subedar smiled, shook hands and said, "I hope we all have a pleasant journey and may I say welcome to our modest accommodation, Memsahib. I am very happy to meet you. Perhaps you would both like to join me for a small night cap ... you take spirit I assume?"

Harding turned to Laura with eyebrows raised in unspoken query.

She hesitated before answering. "That's a splendid offer. Thank you, perhaps with a little water?"

Laura and Harding shared a bench seat by the window and Rasil Singh perched on a small pull-down seat near the wash basin. After Harding and Rasil Singh produced tin mugs, a stone jar of Rosa, a locally distilled rum alleged to cost about one rupee a gallon, was uncorked and measured out. Rasil Singh prevailed upon them to wait until he opened a can of peaches and shared it amongst the mugs. Satisfied that he had produced a carefully prepared drink, Rasil Singh raised his mug and said, "I drink to the health of a beautiful English lady and a British soldier – may you both enjoy great happiness."

Rasil Singh told Harding and Laura that he was going to the Officer Cadet Training Unit at Dhera Dun, where, after a short course, he would be awarded a King's Commission in the Indian Army.

In a puzzled voice Laura said, "But I was under the impression that you are already an officer judging by the pips on your bush jacket."

"Yes, I suppose I am in a way, but only a VCO: a Viceroy's Commissioned Officer. I have rank command in the Indian Army but only over Indian troops. I am not senior to any British Other Ranks I come into contact with when on duty. I am expected to address Sergeant Harding as Sir and he would refer to me as Sahib ... a bit back to front, you will agree, but that is how things are in the protocol of the Raj. The Indian railways are a classic example that illustrates how things are ordered, with First Class available only to Europeans and wealthy Indians. British Other Ranks and we VCOs travel Second Class whilst army drafts and Indians go Third Class Unreserved, and the poor who cannot afford to pay fare sneak travel on roofs or by clinging to running boards and buffers."

Harding listened with interest to Rasil Singh's oral critique. In common with most British soldiers, his interest in India, its culture and politics was limited to what was revealed in newspapers or that which directly affected him. So far as he was concerned, India was an overseas land that had formed a base from where a war had been fought and won. The idea that he was involved in preserving British rule, even to the extent of fighting independence movements, did not enter his head.

"You are not in the services are you, Mrs Erskine? The WAC Is, or anything like that? If you will pardon my assumption, you do not seem to be of a permanent residence in this country."

She smiled and held her tin mug for another drink. "This is rather nice ... just a little, please. Well, I was in the services. It was where I met my husband. He was running a tea plantation with his uncle until he volunteered for war service. He went missing on the last operation of the Japanese war ... perhaps you remember, it was

Operation Zipper. I was given early release in this country to help my husband's aunt, by now a widow, to help run the estate. I don't yet know if we shall stay on when the British hand over to an Indian administration. My real home, and that of Aunt Julia, is in England, of course."

Rasil Singh smiled in understanding at the uncertainty of the future of the British in a free India and said, "I also do not know what the future may hold for India. I believe that we should run our own affairs and with the days of European colonialism numbered all over the East, that day may come sooner than we think. But there is going to be a lot of trouble before India can enjoy a settled future, what with the Hindus and Muslims both demanding a free and independent state and the Indian princes sat in the middle not knowing how they will come out of it. I'm sorry to say this, but British prestige was dealt a severe blow when the Japanese overran Singapore, Malaya, Burma and crossed into North East India – things will never be the same again for you in this part of the world."

Harding did not take up the changed theme of the conversation and directed his interest to the slowing down of the train as the broken rhythm of the wheels crossing track points signalled their arrival at Naogaon, sixty miles on from their start point at Parbatipur. Laura said it was time for her to return to her compartment and thanked Rasil Singh for his hospitality.

As Harding escorted Laura back to her compartment he told her how much he had enjoyed her company and said, "If you have a spare evening in Cal, perhaps I could take you for a meal or maybe a trip to the cinema. That is, if you don't mind being seen in the company of a sergeant," he added with a broad grin.

"That is a super idea … that is, if you don't mind being seen out with a widow."

They exchanged their Calcutta contact telephone numbers and, as he held her forearm to help her access the compartment, she bent her head to kiss him on the cheek.

"Thanks again for making the journey so pleasant," she

murmured. "Hope the subedar doesn't snore and keep you awake all night. Look forward to seeing you in Cal – say in a couple of days' time, after I've got my business done."

"OK, see you then … goodnight."

★★★

Harding spent a restless night. His lines of thought switching from Laura to Tamu and the set-up there: unidentified aircraft, fuel dump, foreign aviators, visitors of some significance, a long-range high efficiency wireless aerial, elephants and a fairly well established camp. He wondered if, when he had delivered his recce report, he would be sent back to Assam and whether he would be able to see Laura again after Calcutta. She had laughingly declared herself to be a widow. Had she been officially informed of her husband's death? If she had, she didn't seem particularly affected by it. His shifting reflections scrambled for primacy of status in the numerous wakeful moments during the hot, damp night.

The lurching of coaches on their bogies and the clanking of buffers as vacuum operated brakes were banged into action roused Harding from one of his brief naps. He leaned up on an elbow to peer through a window space. There was no sign of a station, only the dull brown earth at the jungle's edge and the sight of villagers emerging from their hovels shrouded in cotton shawls with *lotahs* of water clutched to them hurrying to their defecation grounds.

After several shrieks on the locomotive whistle, the train moved on from its temporary halt to draw in alongside the 'Up' platform at Kushtia Junction. Harding checked the time: two hours to Calcutta, another two hours of rising temperature in the airless coupe. The subedar slept on. He had had enough. He swung out of his berth and ducked into the tepid shower which shared space with the latrine, taking care to hang on to his soap with one hand in case it slid from his grasp to end up down the hole in the floor. He sat by the window opening until his body dried off, and with still one hour to go, dressed in a fresh uniform and packed his kit ready

134

for the railway coolies' baggage stampede at Sealdah Station, the very welcome end of the line. With a final sigh of exhaust steam, the wearied locomotive brought the train to a juddering halt and disgorged its passenger load to join the swarming population of an already overburdened city.

Harding had barely wished his overnight travelling companion a safe onward journey and a successful outcome to his commissioning course before a coolie, armband number 622, dragged his kit from the coupe, hoisted it onto his head and trotted off down the platform to the taxi lines. After seeing his kit safely stowed on board the ancient Minerva taxi, he ordered the driver to take him to Fort William. As Harding eased himself into the cab, he noted that the Sikh driver was accompanied by a fellow Sikh escort armed with a *kirpan*, the small razor-edged sword. It was explained to him that, being concerned for the safety of his passengers in these dangerous days of political and religious rioting, visible weapons were always carried and held at the ready.

It was about three miles from Sealdah Station to Fort William, the solid military engineered construction which stood on the *maidan*. The taxi driver with hand on klaxon to blast obstructions from his path, buffeted his way over roads almost at grid-lock with bullock carts, bicycle and manually propelled *rickshaws*, *tongas*, over-laden lorries and handcarts fighting the timetable oriented public transport vehicles for way space. People spilling over from crowded pavements added to the noise and confusion as emaciated cows moved unhampered from refuse pile to refuse pile seeking to fill their shrunken bellies. Pedestrians stepped over clusters of poverty-afflicted untouchables who slept, washed under street taps and ate whatever food they could scrounge, wherever they happened to be at the time. Babies, barely able to crawl, wept and held their hands to their mouths in silent petition for something to quell their hunger. Flies hovered over open sewers and animal droppings to settle on eyes, lips and the raw, festering sores of the mutilated limbs exposed by beggars to elevate their need. Some beggars rocked their way along on legless bodies, rattling empty cans on the sun-heated flagstones to attract attention to their plight. Pain and suffering were not unique to those miserable beings. It extended to other creatures caught up in the misery of life in India as Harding saw when the taxi edged its way into Red Road, passing the sprawling Transit Camp to reach Fort William. A huge water buffalo, its tail severed at the root, was playing host to a black crow sat on its hindquarters and pecking deep into the animal's spine. A pair of crows hopped about impatiently on the grass waiting their turn at the living meal. Harding had heard little enthusiasm from other British soldiers about life in India and to him, Calcutta seemed to contain everything that was wrong with the place … extravagant wealth and poverty, romance and squalor, crawling heat and a city with a surfeit of religious taboos. Most people appeared to have a child-like irresponsibility to managing their condition of living adversity, but would without warning explode into a frenzy of appalling physical brutality and slaughter.

★★★

Captain Reeder glanced quickly through Harding's log of the Tamu reconnaissance mission. It was in original form and having been roughly handled at times was in a sorry state and barely readable. Harding had written it up in chronological order commencing at Day 1, with his arrival at his mission start point in the jungle. Reeder gave the report back to Harding and suggested he get it typed out and submitted soonest, adding, "This is amazing stuff. I'll get the films developed and enlarged and see if we can identify any of the characters you spotted up there. I will set up a debriefing group for 1100 hours tomorrow. That should give you sufficient time to freshen up your report and give you a decent night's sleep. I should warn you that you are likely to be closely questioned by one or two interested parties from on high so be prepared for anything they throw at you."

Harding found some space in an empty office and worked through to a final draft by the early hours of the following morning.

He delivered it in a sealed envelope to Captain Reeder's room in the Officer's Mess with a note asking him to "please arrange copies as required," and headed off for a long overdue sleep.

Chapter 26

"Morning, Reeder. Our fellow from Assam got in alright? Produced his report yet?"

"Morning, Colonel. Yes, I have a copy here for you. I've set up a debriefing session for 1100 hours. Could last well into the afternoon, so I've arranged with the Mess Sergeant to send some sandwiches and drinks over and we can have *tiffin* on the job. That OK?"

"That sounds fine ... give me a few minutes to study his report then I'll go through it with you."

Grindley signed for the secret document on an AFA16 and settled down to read:

Day 1	1730	Arr march SP. 2,000 yards from Tamu MR 013215.
		Est base camp and secured Jeep.
Day 2	0700	Left base camp on bearing 30 deg magnetic. Taking rest halts at about 45 minute intervals.
	1315	Changed line of march to 120 deg magnetic to bypass extensive bamboo area.
	1545	Cleared bamboo area. Replenished water supply & treated it with WSP.
	1630	Entered area of light bush. Calculate 1,200 yards from Tamu. Est bivouac.
Day 3	0700	Left overnight bivouac. Taking frequent rest halts.
	1100	Making better time on well used path.

		Seems to head in my general line of march.
	1445	Observed INA forage party 2 NCOs and 6 men plus 12 women incl 1 from Chinese Restaurant, Imphal. Picked up a number of leeches.
	1700	Arr airfield Tamu. Runway laid out N/S approx. Identified diesel powered gen. Adm area E side of runway, tents, bashas and huts, cookhouse area etc. Junkers 52 a/c. Pr draught elephants. Set up obs pt.
Day 4	0010	Awoke after short sleep. Recce to adm area for water. Boarded Junkers a/c, ex Luftwaffe then Russian entries in log after Apr 45. Rhombic ae tx firing NW, feeder dis. Bulk fuel dump:- 100 Oct, MT 74 and Derv.
	0900	Dakota CAT landed 2 pass (see attd report). Towed to dispersal by elephants. A/c tac signs painted out.
	1240	Buddhist monk arr on foot. (See attd report).
	1300	Native Burmese arr on foot. (See attd report).
	1600	All arrivals plus tall white man hold meeting. (See photos).
	1900	Dinner party. Ended approx 2300 hrs.
Day 5	0600	Broke camp. Left Tamu.
Day 9	1830	Arr back at Shillong.

Colonel Grindley looked at the notes he had scribbled as he read Harding's report.

"Well, Reeder, seems his recce was a worthwhile operation but there are a few blanks to fill in. Four days to get back to Shillong? Give him say, a day, to hoof it back to his Jeep, then another day to drive back to Shillong … so what the hell was he doing for the other two days which he doesn't account for? Wonder if he spent a couple of days with some popsie on a bit of R and R?"

"No idea, sir. It's confirmed that his first wireless contact with us was on the evening of day nine, so clearly he has made an accurate log of his timings. Expect he will fill us in on the whole story when he produces his description reports and we get the photographs of the visitors he shot. Hope they will be ready for the debriefing group at 1100 hours."

"Did he mention anything to you that doesn't seem to be written in his log?"

"Yes he did, but it was only regarding a halt he made at Imphal on his way up to Tamu. He got into conversation with a Mr Ong, the owner of a Chinese eating house there, who hinted to Harding that he had suspicions about some opium smuggling going on, and that it might be connected with a trading company that's been operating at Tamu on the old airfield."

"I would have thought that anything connected with Tamu should have been included in Harding's report … if he mentioned this to you why on earth didn't he record it?"

"He said he was not prepared to put his name to hearsay information, especially something as slimy as dope smuggling."

Grindley raised an eyebrow in feigned disbelief and outlined the subject of the discussion he had held with Chief Superintendent Sedley and his request for assistance in tracing the source of an opium discovery at Kushtia and added, "Perhaps we can ask Harding to have a look into this Erskine-Jalpai connection when he returns up country; can't see it'll do any harm. Sedley says he can take care of any snooping that needs to be done in Bengal but he has no wish to get involved with the Assam police."

"I have some disquiet about this business on two counts," responded Reeder. "First, the presence of an ex-Luftwaffe aeroplane that bears signs in its logbook of being under Russian operational orders and second, this get-together of a disparate group of people. These two points alone suggest very sensitive international political implications. If you add in the possibility of dope smuggling then we are intruding directly into civil police territory. Harding's training and experience is outside the realm of political intelligence or criminal investigation and he would be well within his rights to question the validity of orders to operate in either capacity."

"Look here, Reeder. I don't give a damn whether your Sergeant Harding might consider any order lawful or otherwise. If you don't issue the order to him then I most certainly will. I don't know what sort of set-up you have in the British Army but in the Indian Army, subordinates carry out orders given them and do as they are told without question."

"With due respect, Colonel, I have to say that explains why many of them turned on their superior officers and comrades to fight alongside the Japs as the INA did. I could hardly see British troops in such a role. In my experience we hold discipline in the British Army through mutual respect and the unspoken understanding that all ranks carry out their duties to the best of their training and ability. I am one hundred percent behind Harding and he has already done far more than we are entitled to expect. However, I'm certain that if I put it to him that the Erskine-Jalpai estate is a possible link in a dope running racket and that it would be helpful if he could keep an ear to the ground, he would give it a whirl. Will that do for you?"

The Colonel grunted an indistinct reply and slammed out of the office.

Reeder sighed deeply, shook his head in a token of despair, and began to study Harding's report to digest the detail in preparation for the debriefing group.

★★★

They sat at three sides of two trestle tables lined up in a square formation and covered with a grey army blanket. A large-scale map of the Assam/Burma border area hung on the fourth side. The clammy air was being gently agitated in the to-and-fro motion of a split bamboo *punkah* driven by an extended linkage of shafts and belting from a steam powered engine installed in Queen Victoria's reign. It brought little relief to the sweating discomfort of the men who occupied the room.

Harding had been motioned by Colonel Grindley to a seat near the wall map. He had briskly opened up the meeting with a "Good morning gentlemen" and a round of appointment identifications commencing with himself.

"To those who don't know me, my name is Lieutenant Colonel Martin Grindley, Indian Army, now attached to G Int, GHQ Delhi. I was posted here to liaise with this Signal Intelligence Centre in connection with the apprehension and disposal of Indian National Army personnel who are still hiding out somewhere in the northern jungles. It now seems the original brief of this unit has suddenly changed to something a bit deeper as we are about to discover. Now, in clockwise order from the right let me introduce Chief Superintendent Maurice Sedley of the Bengal Police. He has been involved in assisting us in disposing of captured INA personnel and as he will explain later, in dealing with something a little more serious which has come to light. Next we have Flight Lieutenant Mason of the Royal Air Force. He is in charge of a special intelligence set-up covering Malaya and part of French Indo-China. Then we have Major Kendall, the Brigade Major of 73 British Independent Infantry Brigade stationed out at Barrackpore. It is appropriate that his brigade be kept in the picture in case anything develops which could require a British armed response. On my right here is Captain Duncan Reeder, Intelligence Corps and in operational command of this unit. Finally over there," he paused to give the meeting an opportunity to swivel heads, "is Sergeant Harding. He is in the Signals."

A man dressed in khaki-drill trousers and white bush jacket strode into the room and in a soft Highland voice announced his apologies for lateness and said, "Oliver MacNair, representing the Viceroy. Hope I haven't missed anything."

Grindley assured the newcomer that his assumption was correct and for his benefit made a speedy re-run of the introductions. He then asked Captain Reeder to run through the background narrative of the operation and clarify any features of Harding's report as it was progressed.

Reeder waited until the meeting had settled and launched into his presentation.

"Sergeant Harding was sent up to Assam earlier this year to keep in touch with selected Naga village headmen who remained loyal to the British forces during the Burma campaign. The object of this liaison being to locate any packets of the INA who were still at large with a view to having them captured and brought back to India to face trial as deserters. It was thought that if they remained on the loose they could be recruited to support any armed insurrection that could be fired up by nationalists intent on seizing power in the more remote regions of India and Burma. Sergeant Harding was lined up for this job because of his experience in undercover work gained in signals intelligence and counter signals operations in enemy held territory. OK so far?"

After a brief pause for questions he went on…. "As a result of Sergeant Harding picking up some information that some aircraft were using the abandoned airstrip at Tamu on the Assam/Burma border, an RAF photograph reconnaissance mission was tasked to scan the area. You will see the upshot of that flight on your copy of the report sent to GHQ Delhi marked with the codeword KINGSMAN. That codeword, by the way, was assigned by Colonel Grindley and duly registered as the title of the developing operation."

Grindley nodded his head in silent appreciation of the acknowledgment to his creative spirit. Again Reeder waited until he was satisfied there were no questions to be put, then continued with his narrative.

"GHQ Delhi told us to mount a ground recce to fill in the gaps opened by the RAF operation and the situation dictated that the most appropriate means was to task Sergeant Harding for the job. At this point I will ask the sergeant to take over and guide us through his report, but before he does, I will pass round photographs and descriptions of five chummies, so far unidentified, who dropped by at Tamu for a bit of a convention. Sergeant, it's all yours."

Harding was waiting until he had the full attention of the meeting when Colonel Grindley intervened.

"I see, Sergeant, that you have given codenames to these descriptions. Was this inspired by the notion that they could be termed 'big fish'? If that's what you had in mind, I would suggest that one of the species you named is quite small. I refer of course to the piranha."

"You are right, of course, sir. As these people had no known identity I thought it convenient to give them names purely for reference purposes. As they were arriving at a jungle airfield and therefore loosely connected with flying, I was reminded of the opening words of Chesterton's poem: The Donkey … 'When fishes flew and forests walked….' So, as I was under the impression that they were up to no good, I thought the names of some unfriendly fish might be appropriate. You do remember the poem, sir?"

"Er … yes, did it at my school. Let's get on with it then."

Harding poured a glass of iced water from a Thermos jug and after a couple of sips began his account.

"My instructions were to carry out a ground recce at Tamu airfield. I was not aware of the nature of the target: was it friendly or unfriendly? What was the number strength of personnel there? Could I expect to be in any danger if I were discovered? And finally, what exactly was I looking for? The only pre-knowledge I had was what had been reported to me regarding aircraft movement at an old wartime airfield. I therefore decided I would go armed, approach from jungle cover and carry rations for about five days with suitable emergency medical supplies. On day one, I made a halt at a Chinese eating house in Imphal. The proprietor there told me that a trading company had set up house at Tamu and he thought the company was in the business of dope smuggling. This came to light when I asked him about a brand of Singapore beer he was selling. I thought he must have been a pretty resourceful chap to be able to fix up a supply from that distance."

Chief Superintendent Sedley interrupted, "This dope rumour sounds rather interesting. You don't seem to have included any reference to it in your report. Do you have anything to add? Where it might be sold, for instance?"

"I have no idea where it might be sold or anything other than what I have just told you. I didn't include it in my written report because it was hearsay intelligence and rumour-based. I would have been unable to substantiate it if called upon to do so at some future date."

Captain Reeder spoke up. "I suggest we leave this dope business for the time being. I believe the Chief Superintendent has got a few things to say about this stuff later, OK? You can please continue, Sergeant."

"Thank you sir. After my lunch break I drove on towards Tamu and left the road to follow a disused timber track into the jungle arriving at 1730 hours to a position at map reference 013215, two thousand yards approx from my objective. I bivouacked for the night and started out the following morning at 0700 hours. By about 1630 hours and having covered a fairly demanding eight hundred yards, I decided to make camp for the night."

"Tell me, Sergeant, why do you wish to include all this guff about lunch breaks and bivouacs? I thought your job was to produce useful intelligence about Tamu?" Colonel Grindley looked around the table to muster support for his criticism, but he was disappointed. No-one made any comment. They waited for Harding to carry on with his story.

"I thought, sir, that it was prudent to include as much information as I could in case it might be useful for any further recces that might be called for in that area."

Before Harding continued MacNair said, "I think we should let the man get on with his account of the operation as he experienced it. Do you agree, gentlemen?"

Heads nodded in agreement signalling Harding to press on.

"Thank you, sir. I got under way again at 0700 hours on day three and at about 1100 hours I came across a well-used track and feeling a bit yacked by this time I decided to follow it, seeing that it generally followed my planned line of march – 30 degrees magnetic. In mid-afternoon I was having a rest break when I saw the party which you see I describe in my report. I had withdrawn into cover when I heard the party approach. Unfortunately I was spotted by one of the women who had fallen out for a piss. I had seen her at Mr Ong's place in Imphal a couple of days previously and knew her as Jasmine, an employee of Mr Ong."

Harding paused when he heard some clearing of throats and a suppressed giggle or two. He was about to ask what the joke was when Grindley sneered, "I suppose she was a brothel *bibi*, hey what? Does she account for your missing couple of days at the end of your mission?"

"Yes sir, I did spend some time with her when I came out of the jungle and she was very good to me. It seems she found me by the roadside in a pretty sorry state – suffering from some kind of fever, I believe. Don't know what the trouble was, could have been dehydration or a touch of blood poisoning from some leeches I picked up – I haven't a clue what happened, but old Ong gave me a bed and kept my Jeep secure in his compound until I was fit enough to travel. If it hadn't been for Miss Jasmine, I probably wouldn't be here now trying to give you a report on the job I was ordered to do. Does that satisfy you … sir?"

Harding delivered the account in flat tones and ended it with a sarcastic emphasis on 'sir' – setting the seal on his response to a bloody stupid comment. If the colonel thought he could deliver the old talk-down bullshit to him then he was way off target … Harding was confident in his own ability to identify and report accurate intelligence and he wasn't going to cave in to this jumped-up commander of native troops. Grindley averted his gaze and after a throat clearing "harrumph" told Harding to "get on with it."

"It was at this location that I picked up some leeches when I had to take cover from the INA *wallahs*. I managed to get rid of them, then continued on the same track as they were taking. At 1700 hours I arrived at the airfield and after an initial survey set up my observation point from where I could get a fairly good view of the inhabited part of the place. As I have set out in my report, it seemed a well organised set-up with a very obvious military input."

"I suppose we can all float our individual speculations on what could be going on up there based on what Sergeant Harding saw," said MacNair. "However, I would like to hear from the sergeant what interpretation he puts on it all."

"From what I observed, I would think the airfield is going to be occupied for some time. I assess that from the semi-permanent accommodation shelter and the use of a large output generator. Apart from providing mains lighting, this power source would be required to drive the transmitter associated with the long range aerial array. The bulk fuel dump, as well as providing derv for the generator, held 100 octane petrol for aero engines, suggesting that the aircraft using the airfield need to be refuelled to cover flights outside the limits of their normal operating ranges. As there was no sign of road vehicles I can only assume that the MT 74 was for the field cookers. My theory about the distances flown by the two aircraft I saw is backed up by the fact that they keep a couple of draught elephants on site to haul them to and from their take-off and arrival points to conserve fuel normally expended on taxiing. The Junkers 52 has most certainly got a Russian connection because I saw the evidence in the aircraft log book. But I couldn't start to guess what that indicates, and as for the Dakota, that could possibly be linked to the Americans – its tactical star and wing bands were still identifiable in spite of being painted over. Oh, yes, the pilot had a cigar jammed in his mouth – I spotted that as the elephants were towing the Dak along the runway."

MacNair spoke again. "Thanks, that's most helpful. Just one more thing. Do you consider that the transmitter could work Moscow?"

"Fairly certain. The rhombic aerial was pointing in the right direction according to my reading and considering that type of aerial is used on the Army Wireless Chain operating world-wide from the UK, it's a safe bet."

"You'd better stay in the chair whilst we consider the identities of the flying fishes," Grindley said. "We can get on with this job now we appear to have got the airfield set-up out of the way, at least for the time being."

"Certainly, sir. We have the photographs available now to help things along. First there is the character I call SHARK. As you can see from my report he is of European appearance and was obviously running the show. His civilian dress – diamond check pattern pullover, cord trousers and desert boots – gave me the impression that he could be English. Jasmine told me later that he spoke English but he also used Urdu to the INA and sometimes a local language she didn't understand to the chap I code-named PIRANHA. She also said he was referred to as Mr Cambridge."

"Mr Cambridge, hey?" said Captain Reeder. "That's a bogus name if ever I heard one. But that apart, I go along with Sergeant Harding's belief that he could well be an Englishman and by the look of his picture we could be pretty near the mark. So we are looking at a chap, possibly English, who has obviously spent time in India if he is at home with Urdu and possibly a local language. Good stuff, Sergeant. Who's next on the list?"

Harding put up PIRANHA as the next candidate. "From watching him I gained the impression that he was a fellow of some importance. Unlike SHARK, he wasn't in the business of running the show, but he seemed to command respect when he was in conversation with his cronies. His style of dress was certainly Burmese, similar to that of the local hill-men but of a more affluent style – scarf turban-tight to his head and a colourful sarong. His height was average – about five six, I would say, and a bit on the skinny side with a pale brown complexion."

"You are fairly certain he was Burmese? Or as certain as you can be from what you have seen of the locals and their form of dress?" MacNair asked Harding, then turned to Captain Reeder. "I want to signal Delhi. I have an idea who this character could be but I just need a few queries answered first. I'll classify it Top Secret so it'll have to be transmitted in cipher. I don't want it to be revealed to the Indian Government's intelligence people, it's politically very sensitive, so I'll address it for the Viceroy's Eyes Only. Good, we seem to be making progress. Shall we carry on?"

Colonel Grindley said, "Right, two down and three left to go. What are you going to tell us about them, Sergeant?"

"Well sir, with your permission I will deal with the Buddhist monk fellow ... the one I code-named SWORDFISH. I managed a good camera shot of him as he came out of the jungle. He was accompanied by a boy who was carrying a bedding roll head load that indicated that he was a bit of a traveller. I know that many Buddhist monks tend to wander about the place begging a living, like the Hindu holy men, but this chap was no sack cloth and ashes type. In fact when I caught a *dekko* of brown knee boots under his yellow robes, a well-nourished olive tinged face and a definite military bearing, I could have sworn he was a Jap officer. I know that sounds a bit far-fetched but that was the impression I picked up."

Kendall, the BM from 73 Brigade said, "I might be of some help here. When the war ended, dozens of Japanese officers fell on their samurais rather than surrender but quite a number took off and disappeared into the countryside. They were generally senior officers who would have been brought to book and made to answer for serious war crimes, especially for the treatment meted out to POWs and civilian internees. My brigade headquarters carries a roll of Jap officers who haven't yet been accounted for and with whom we would like to have a word. If you'd like to leave it with me I'll have a look at the roll and see who might fit the bill."

MacNair looked at his watch and said, "I move we have a break for some refreshment. It'll give me time to get my signal off to Delhi and shall we reassemble at, say, four-thirty?"

The group agreed and went outside to stretch stiffened limbs or disappear for a comfort stop. A runner from the Sergeant's Mess was waiting outside the security area with a message for Harding. It was from Laura asking him to telephone her after seven-thirty. The thought of perhaps arranging a date cheered him and he made up his mind to press on with the remainder of the debriefing session – only MARLIN and BARRACUDA to be landed.

★★★

"MARLIN and BARRACUDA came in on the Dakota, as I said in my report. They walked up the runway to the admin area and I got a good look at them as they passed my hide. MARLIN had the look of a man who had spent some time on military ops. He had a confident stride and was alert to his surroundings. I would say that he was Chinese and was dressed in British jungle green with a '44 pattern web belt and ammunition pouches. He was armed with a Sten gun. His mate was of less robust appearance. Again, I would say he was Chinese but with finer features, average height and dressed in a black *samfoo*. He didn't seem to be a military type, but he was wearing a US pattern waist belt with a pistol holstered in cowboy fashion on the right hip. That's about all I can tell you about them. They seemed to be the important people up there at Tamu. I hope you can make some sense of it."

After a short silence during which notes were completed, Captain Reeder said, "If we don't need Sergeant Harding and if there are no more questions I would like to suggest that he is given tomorrow off. He has had nothing in the way of a break since he got back from his recce and I think he is due a rest."

MacNair replied, "I'll second Reeder's proposal and I would like to thank Sergeant Harding for the quality of this intelligence and particularly the professional way in which it was presented. He didn't dwell on the enormous difficulties he obviously encountered in the planning and execution of the enterprise. To enter the jungle alone, with no back-up or an evacuation plan with the risk attached to the possibility of facing a bunch of armed traitors, called for courage and a high sense of duty." He faced Harding and said, "On behalf of the Viceroy and for myself I thank you ... well done."

Harding bowed his head slightly to the ripple of "hear hear," stood up, replaced his cap, saluted and left the room.

Chapter 27

"That sounds good to me, I have no idea what's showing but it'll be pleasant to enjoy a bit of cinema air conditioning as a change from this sticky heat."

"If you'd like to come over in the afternoon you could have a dip in the swimming pool. I'm sure my host wouldn't mind." After giving him the address and directions she laughed lightly, "See you tomorrow … g'bye."

★★★

Harding called in to the ops centre and warned out for the remainder of the day. Then, at the Fort Contractor's shop, he invested in a pair of blue Jantzens. His old trunks were hardly fit to be worn in a private swimming pool. He walked out to the *maidan*, hailed a taxi and ordered the driver to take him out to Tollygunge, the high class residential district of Calcutta, which contained the homes of retired Indian Army officers, civil servants and wealthy businessmen. He left the taxi a couple of hundred yards from the villa and walked the rest of the way.

He pulled the bell chain set in a recess on a gate pillar and, whilst waiting to be let in, surveyed his surroundings. The villa stood in a wide leafy avenue and was protected, like the neighbouring homes, with high walls topped with spikes set in concrete. High trees shielded the villas from the eyes of passers-by. He was let in by the *chowkidar*, a tall, turbaned Indian of soldierly bearing who sported a large black moustache. He carried an old, brass-bound rifle that had probably seen service in the hands of rebel tribesmen up on the North West Frontier – perhaps in the hands of the chap who now held it.

Harding followed the *chowkidar* along a wide, sweeping drive laid through well cut lawns and bordered by herbaceous plants of variegated leaves which bore exotic flowers. Laura was stretched out on a steamer chair on the shady veranda with a cotton wrap over her swim-suit. She poured him an iced coffee from a vacuum jug and invited him to sit down. Although the sun was passed its zenith, the air was still hot and heavy and Harding, thirsty from his journey, quickly finished the welcome drink. The monsoon which had been raging in from the Bay of Bengal through the hot summer months had made the afternoons almost unbearable. But many Britishers, denied a summer retreat to the hill stations during the war, now worked through the morning and spent the afternoons playing badminton, tennis or swimming, thus breaking the myth that a 'summer spent on the burning plains of India could send a fellow mad'.

The swimming pool, protected from the direct effect of the sun by high canvas screens, and tiled in pale green, looked cool and inviting. Harding ducked behind a screen to change into his swimming trunks and emerged to see Laura, her figure now almost fully revealed in a white two-piece swim-suit, stride to the edge of the pool, adjust her swimming cap, and with a high curving dive enter the water. After swimming a couple of lengths she called Harding to join her. They swam a dozen lengths together, changing from breast-stroke to crawl to butterfly to side-stroke, then gently floated on their backs until they reached the steps to clamber out. After a sluice under the shower they lay on deck loungers to enjoy a glass of ice-cold *nimbu-pani* which an ever attentive bearer had brought out for them.

"When you 'phoned me last evening you suggested going to the cinema, but if you want to you are welcome to spend the evening here. The D'Silvas are away until the weekend and Jeanne, Mrs D'Silva, has left instructions with the house servants that they are to look after me and my guest."

"That's very kind and they don't even know me."

"I told them who you were and how we met … anyhow they are having a dinner party on Saturday and I have been ordered to invite you. Jeanne must be keen on giving you the once-over … say you'll come."

"I'll have to see what the score is with this duty visit of mine, so leave it with me. I'll let you know when I've checked up."

Harding was tempted to go along with Laura's invitation to spend the evening at the villa but chose instead to stick with the original idea of the cinema visit. "If you prefer to go to the pictures, that's OK with me. But you'll stay here for tea, then we can go on straight from here if you like. Oh yes … I meant to ask what could possibly have caused those rather brutal wheals over your shoulders and across your back, and also those scars across your chest and tummy. They look like leech bites to me. Have you been on a jungle trek or something?"

"I did have a run-in with those little blighters in the woods when I was doing some survey work up near Imphal and those wheals were caused by the straps of the pack I was humping. I had to do a bit of footslogging – couldn't get the Jeep up to the point I was making for. Peacetime soldiering makes a chap a bit soft, I expect, hence the marks."

Laura bent over and kissed him tenderly on the cheek. "Poor you," she teased. "Come on, let's get dressed then see what's for tea – I'm starving."

★★★

The Metro Cinema lacked a rising Wurlitzer, but in most other features it was similar to the thirties neo-classical architecture of the Odeons that had blossomed in the provincial towns and cities of Britain. A chilled blast from the air conditioning was a welcome relief from the warm, sticky atmosphere of the Calcutta streets and Laura, wearing a sleeveless cotton frock, was grateful for the comfort of the cardigan she had brought with her.

The newsreel that opened the show was of American origin and reflected the Hollywood view of world affairs. The Nuremburg trials of Nazi war criminals lined up in the dock and guarded by white-helmeted US military police and shots of death camps was watched in silence by the audience, mostly represented by British servicemen. It was followed by a commentary of the political leaders of India going to or returning from yet more talks aimed at finding an independence settlement. The sight of Mahatma Gandhi surrounded by his followers somewhere in Bihar was greeted with calls from the audience of "Jai Hind, keep your bloody country. Let's go home." The mood changed to sharp disfavour when some shots of American servicemen waving goodbye to the Ocean Terminal at Southampton as the liner Queen Mary carried them away from the quayside brought shouts of "Why have the bloody Yanks pinched our big ships? Half a dozen trips on that and the Queen Elizabeth would clear India in a month." After a short current events documentary everyone settled down to watch the main feature: a Boris Karloff horror film. As one terrifying scene followed the other, Laura snuggled up to Harding, her fingernails digging into his arm. He was more than happy to comfort her.

"It seems as if your comrades don't have a particularly high regard for the Americans," Laura remarked as they left the cinema. "Do they upset you as well?"

"They are OK when you get to know them. Not much different from our blokes really. I think the main gripe is the pay, but after all, both countries fought the same war and if they hadn't come in when they did we would have been hard-pressed to cope with the Germans on our own."

"That's generous of you … no complaints about our American friends?"

He gave a brief chuckle. "Don't really think I have but I must admit I get a bit fed up with only being able to get their toothpaste, shaving cream and rations out here. But that's a minor bellyache.

It's been a long day, time to see you safely home now."

★★★

Harding recalled the high points of his short acquaintance with Laura as he made his way back to Fort William. The sight of her in a swim-suit. Her nearness in the cinema. The taxi ride back to the D'Silva home as she lay back on the seat smiling with happiness. He remembered how petulant she was when they first met: stranded at the roadside with a broken down wagon and her display of temper as he teased her about her possible lack of petrol. Her annoyance over the tea samples with Narayan Rao. He thought that she must have been under some strain not knowing if her husband was alive or even dead and then being landed with the responsibility of helping to run the tea estate. He felt she had started to loosen up a bit during the evening he had spent at Erskine-Jalpai and again on the train journey to Calcutta when he had seen her back to her compartment after an enjoyable interlude with himself, the VCO and a liberal share of Rosa rum and peaches. He was confident that she held him in some regard if not in some affection. If there were to be any sort of affair with her it would be on his terms with no commitment until her status as wife or widow was clear. He was not going to be inhibited by any difference in their social levels – even in class-conscious India with its strict protocol and status values. "Damn them all, she's a female. I'm a bloke. So what? She's had a bloody difficult time and she is entitled to a bit of fun."

Chapter 28

"Good morning, Sergeant. Take a seat, we've got a full day's work to face. Hope you feel up to it after your day off, what?" Colonel Grindley leaned back in his chair and raised his eyebrows to elicit a reply but Harding did not respond. Instead he went to an empty chair, laid his document folder on the table and waited for the session to get under way. He felt better after the time spent with Laura – swimming, afternoon tea and the cinema, and then there was the Saturday night do to look forward to. He had decided to ring her and confirm it would be on after he had cleared it with Captain Reeder.

Grindley opened with, "Let's get on with it. Mr MacNair has offered to be ringmaster today as it now seems there are more political than military implications developing … so instead of trying to round up a few army deserters we are looking at a state of affairs that could gravely affect our colonial possessions in South East Asia, plus the interests of the French in Indo-China and the Dutch in the Netherlands East Indies. Mr MacNair, over to you please."

"Thank you, Colonel. Good morning gentlemen. I trust we are all in possession of Sergeant Harding's report and the photographs of the players he brought in from Tamu. This will serve as the basis on which to build up our intelligence picture. All set? Let's go then … in response to my signal sent to Delhi the other day I have received a pretty complete dossier on the chappie codenamed Piranha. It is a racing certainty that he is Aung San, a known anti-imperialist of Burmese nationality. Long before the war he and a chappie called U Nu fired up a lot of unrest in the student community of Rangoon University and by fomenting strikes, used them as a protest weapon which led to anarchy and violence. It is fairly certain that, but for the start of the Second World War, he would have had a shot at gaining direct rule over Burma. In 1941 Aung San founded a group known as the Burmese Thirty. They approached the Japanese with an offer of support in their plans to rid the Eastern countries of their European masters. The Japanese gave them some military training to form a cadre element for a Burmese Independence Army. When the war came and the British were driven from Burma, Aung San and his cronies turned out to be an unreliable bunch and instead of being given a combat role were employed on harmless admin duties. The Japanese ordered them to be disbanded, reformed under their close supervision and renamed the Burma National Army. Aung San soon discovered the Japs were worse tyrants than the British so, when he saw the British were winning the Burma campaign, he scuttled over to our side, formed a resistance movement which became known as the Anti-Fascist Peoples Freedom League and sucked up to Lord Louis Mountbatten, our Supreme Commander in South East Asia. This crafty move eventually saw him installed, by Lord Louis, and without reference to London I might add, as the leader of Burma. When civil government was restored under Dorman Smith, the previous governor, Aung San set about creating mayhem in the country by reverting to his long practised activity of organised agitation. That is where we now stand, gentlemen, in relation to Mr Piranha. We knew he was running much of the lowland areas of the country. It is now apparent that he has some presence in the northern hills. Does anyone have anything to add or raise any questions?"

Harding spoke up. "Does this mean, sir, that there could be a revolution in the making in Burma if this bod is allowed to roam about the countryside? Can't he be stopped?"

MacNair said, "We don't know the full extent of his power or how difficult it would be to curtail his activities. With the rundown of our forces and lack of reliable intelligence, one could stir up a hornet's nest of political chaos if we went for him without being absolutely certain that he could be … shall we say, taken out of the picture. Before we can come up with a plan we have to make sure who the other laddies are, who is running the aeroplanes and what the hell Tamu is being used for. Any more observations … anyone?"

With interest mounting at this revelation by MacNair, the group remained silent as the possibilities of a developing situation were considered. Eventually MacNair glanced round the table and looking at Major Kendall said, "Did you dig out anything on Swordfish? Is he indeed who you thought he might be?"

Kendall passed around some photographs of a man dressed in the uniform of an officer of the Japanese Imperial Army. He explained that it had been selected from a captured enemy newsreel shot in Singapore when General Percival surrendered his garrison to the Japanese in February 1942. Kendall continued, "Before I go on I would like to ask Sergeant Harding if this picture compares well with the chap he saw dressed up as a Buddhist monk on the airfield at Tamu."

Harding replied, "I'm not absolutely certain, but from memory, and supported by the photo I took, I'd put evens on it."

"Hardly a racing certainty," broke in Grindley. "However, I think we should hear what the major can tell us about his picture. It might give us a lead worth following."

"This Swordfish *wallah* could be one Colonel Masanobu Tsuji. He was listed as a war criminal but was clever enough to avoid capture. A careful examination of Japanese records didn't throw up any evidence of his last unit or whereabouts, he was neither posted as missing nor killed in action. The latter would have been a doubtful possibility. Staff colonels, even those in the Japanese Imperial Army, didn't enjoy front line soldiering."

Harding smothered a chuckle as Grindley glowered at Kendall's last remark.

"Many Japs, especially those in the lower ranks, not having received a direct order to throw in the towel and finding themselves cut off from their parent units, took to the jungle and by following standard survival techniques, managed to exist and, what is more important, avoid the disgrace of voluntary surrender. Intelligence gleaned from remote villages in Malaya and Burma indicate that a number of Japanese officers also fled and took refuge in the jungle where some of them managed to bribe village headmen to give them food and shelter. To get back to Colonel Tsuji, it is thought that he could be a rather formidable character, having studied at the US Military Academy at West Point, so we can take it that his English and knowledge of Western military organisation will be more than useful. It is known that he was the planning brains behind the pre-invasion intelligence operation in Malaya where he set up a network of agents posing as teachers, rubber plantation and tin mine managers, geographers and even tourists to build up a profile of military installations. These agents produced local maps to guide an invasion force through the maze of plantation roads, jungle tracks and swamps. When the Japs launched their military operations in Malaya, our friend Tsuji was appointed Chief of Staff to General Yamashita, the commander of the 25th Army. As we all know, he ran our forces out of Malaya and the island of Singapore in a brilliant ten-week campaign that brought down the curtain on the age of British superiority in the East, and as the Chinese would insist: we 'lost face' over that business."

"I must say," said Colonel Grindley, "so far as one can tell, he was an efficient officer doing his duty by his country. Why should he be listed as a war criminal?"

"There is strong evidence that he led the interrogation of Allied prisoners and was not averse to using physical methods to extract information over and above that which is allowed under the Geneva Convention. Although, as I have already explained, his whereabouts was not confirmed from Japanese army records, it is known from intercepted wireless communications that he was present in Burma right up to the fall of Rangoon."

"How do you know that it wasn't false information that was intercepted? Remember the Japs were up to all kinds of tricks to mislead our intelligence effort?"

"I understand that the intercept was in high-grade Japanese cipher, system 6633 to be precise. It is unlikely that the Japs would go to the trouble of encoding a signal in high grade cipher if they wanted it to be broken by the enemy. If it was the intention to mislead, such a signal would have been sent in clear."

MacNair said, "If this fellow who Sergeant Harding observed at Tamu airfield is indeed one Colonel Tsuji, we have a problem on our hands and I'll tell you why. Many of the people in the countries overrun by the Japanese looked to them as liberators from the 'foreign devil's yoke'. We have only to remember what happened in Indo-China when the French administration welcomed the Japanese with open arms to see how quickly enemies can collaborate with each other. Now the war is over and Japan is a defeated power, I fail to see how the Japanese can have any direct influence on matters outside their own country, whatever they might be. It therefore seems reasonable to assume that this wee laddie dressed up as a Buddhist monk is in league with Mr Aung San, alias Mr Piranha, and with the others who so far remain unidentified. I think we must agree, gentlemen, that something dire is afoot up yonder and I'll lay a bottle of best malt it's got something to do with India."

Grindley glanced at the time. "Talking of malt reminds me we are due for a midday noggin and some *tiffin*. I suggest we break off for the afternoon and parade again at 1800 hours for a quick study session before dinner. Let's see, you are playing hockey this afternoon, I believe, Duncan, so you might as well give the evening parade a miss and that goes for you too, Sergeant. You might as well stand down until tomorrow … that OK everybody? See you later then. Oh yes, before we break off, I've agreed to invite Chief Superintendent Sedley to join us for tomorrow's session. He has a special concern that just might be linked to this business."

★★★

Harding decided to spend the free afternoon catching up on some overdue mail. It had been almost a week since he had received two letters: one from his mother and one from a school friend now serving with the RAF at Gatow in the British Sector of Berlin. It occurred to him that Richard might have an inkling about how a Junkers 52 came to be spotted on an abandoned airfield in North Burma with a suspected Russian crew.

After forcing down a corned beef fritter selected from the restricted menu offered in the Sergeant's Mess, he resolved to give Firpo's cuisine, available at the renowned Calcutta restaurant of that name, the benefit of his custom at the earliest opportunity. He stored the idea that he might like to take Laura there and share a meal together … might even run to a bottle.

Harding retreated to his room, wafted the damp sheets of an airmail letter pad under the ceiling fan to dry them sufficiently to bear the ink from his pen and settled down to write. The first two pages written to his parents were soon filled with comments on aspects of home news and commiserations on the post war shortages and food rationing – "was it true that bread was about to be rationed?" Even during the darkest days of the war the idea that bread could be rationed was an undreamed-of possibility. After telling them of his temporary duty visit to Calcutta and the air-conditioned luxury of his evening at the cinema, he closed the letter with thoughts on a long awaited reunion in the near future.

Before responding to his second letter, he read it through again to get a feeling for life in occupied Germany. Richard had described the service life there: clubs, good food, duty free booze, cigarettes, Leica cameras. He read how the non-fraternisation policy was gradually eroding and about the shortage of adult German males: killed in the war, missing or prisoners in Russian hands. Harding compared his present service life with that of Richard. Always more men than women in India, available ones that is. Some luxuries were on tap in the big cities but forever in sight of the most appalling poverty, hunger and the harsh conditions imposed by the climate … life on the Indian sub-continent, Harding wrote, "was lousy." After he had set down a few comparisons he continued in a general way to invite Richard to comment on the disposal of captured enemy equipment. Were they all up for destruction or did the victors retain some for their own use? "Just wondering, old mate."

Chapter 29

"Right, gentlemen," said Colonel Grindley. "Now we have had a little time to digest the character references of Messrs Piranha and Swordfish I would ask Chief Superintendent Sedley to outline some concern he has which may help to throw some light on our problem. As you are aware, he has been operating with us on the apprehension of INA deserters but now he is in possession of some information that could be of extreme importance. Mr Sedley, it's all yours."

"Thank you, Colonel, and good evening gentlemen. This information is about drugs … opium to be precise." He paused for impact. "Yes, gentlemen – opium. Most likely no-one present has knowingly come into contact with opium but in recent history it was a very live topic in this part of the world. You will have heard of the Opium Wars with China but you will not have heard about how the old East India Company grew it by the ton, mostly in Bihar, slapped excise duty on it, then stepped back leaving it for private traders to traffic the stuff to China where it was used to foment unrest to the commercial advantage of our traders. It was of course widely used in England for medicinal purposes but fell out of favour as recently as the nineteen-twenties with the advent of the drug aspirin. Even the miserable buggers who slaved in the dark satanic mills of Victorian England used opium, but as a narcotic, to give them a temporary escape from the drudgery of their daily lives. A coolie in this part of the world will obtain a direct and precisely induced euphoric haze by taking a small pellet of the stuff, stick it on a needle then burn it through a pipe. Half a dozen breaths and it's gone. Some coolies, when they can afford it, will consume up to thirty pipes a day. The point I want to get over is this. About three weeks ago, a police constable at Kushtia, up in East Bengal, picked up a tea chest he found at the side of the tracks just outside the railway station. The chest was full but the contents were not entirely tea. A consignment of opium about the size of a house brick, weighing two and a half pounds and enough to keep seven hundred addicts happy for a week was hidden inside. It had been consigned from the Erskine-Jalpai estate in the Megalayah district of Assam to an East Howrah *godown* in Calcutta. The particular concern I have is that opium is being given to religious activists, both Hindu and Muslim, in reward for their willingness to indulge in the kind of communal riots we saw here in August. The only evidence I have is that a certain *rickshaw wallah*, unsure as to what it was, handed a pellet of the stuff over to one of my agents after the August killings. I am of the opinion that some people are in the business of creating political instability to make the country impossible to govern and thereby hasten the departure of the Raj."

A long silence followed Sedley's revelations, broken at length by Grindley.

"Perhaps, Maurice, you would like to tell us how this affects us and what help we can give."

"Thanks, Colonel. I have a fairly extensive intelligence network, not all directly employed by the police service, you understand. They have their limitations and in spite of co-operation from the local police in Assam and North Burma I am having some difficulty in making progress. It is clear someone at the Erskine-Jalpai tea estate is involved and as the dope has been confirmed as originating in Siam or Indo-China, it could be the estate is being used as a staging post in the smuggling operation. If Sergeant Harding, with your permission, could be made aware of the problem he might be able to have a look at Erskine-Jalpai and help me with this line of enquiry."

MacNair looked up at the wall clock and checked the time against his slim, gold pocket watch. "Time we called a halt, I believe. I suggest when we reconvene in the morning we put the question of Erskine-Jalpai to Sergeant Harding."

★★★

Harding listened with growing alarm as Chief Superintendent Sedley recounted his disclosure of a dope smuggling route traced back from Calcutta to Erskine-Jalpai. He quickly realised that he was in a position to fill in a few blanks in the unfolding narrative.

There had been the sight of an armed escort guarding the transit of haversacks from the American crewed Dakota at Tamu airfield. Could they have contained dope? There were Mr Ong's suspicions of dope being brought into the country and an implied link with Tamu. And finally the late night visitor to Erskine-Jalpai and the shady behaviour of Narayan Rao when Laura enquired about the late consignment of tea samples.

Normally, Harding wouldn't give a second thought about reporting anything he discovered in the course of duty. But now, with the strong possibility that Laura and Julia were becoming linked with some shady business, he began to have doubts about disclosing all he knew or suspected. He could not betray Laura and Julia, neither could he protect them. "What a bloody mess."

"Are you still with us, Sergeant?" Harding re-focussed his attention and looked across the table to see MacNair gesturing.

"Yes sir, I'm with you...."

"Right then, let's get on with it. The evidence seems to suggest that this dope is being used to reward activists who are intent on creating trouble to make the country ungovernable and lead to a state of revolution."

"If I may have a word." They all turned to Captain Reeder to hear what he had to say.

"Sergeant Harding has told me he picked up some gossip from a certain Mr Ong, the eating house fellow in Imphal. He did not include it in his written report because he had no hard evidence to support it."

166

Harding was not paying much attention to what Reeder had to say; his mind was churning over what the connection was between dope smuggling and Erskine-Jalpai.

"Wake up, Sergeant ... got something on your mind? You don't seem to be with us this morning. Not overdoing the social life are you?" Grindley was not slow to get a little jibe in just to let everyone know that he still had a presence at the meeting.

"No sir, just getting my thoughts together regarding this opium business. Yes, I did let Captain Reeder know about my conversation with Mr Ong. My interest was raised when he offered me a bottle of Tiger beer which is brewed in Singapore. When I expressed some surprise that he had managed to import it over that distance he hinted he had black market contacts that could be linked to dope smuggling and maybe to a trading company which had been set up at Tamu airfield."

MacNair said, "I think this is as far as we can go. If Captain Reeder can put our meeting minutes into a full intelligence summary for the Viceroy, I will put wheels in motion to try and find out more about the identities of the people and aeroplanes seen at Tamu. We may have to refer it to London to see if the Foreign Office laddies can help. I shall be leaving for Delhi tomorrow morning, so I'll take this opportunity to thank you all for your efforts. I'm sure the Viceroy would also like me to extend his thanks. Goodbye."

Before the meeting dispersed Captain Reeder suggested that Harding should stay on for a few days in case he could be of further help in answering any queries that might come down from Delhi. Harding made up his mind to grasp the chance of some extra time in Calcutta to take a look at the Assam Bengal Trading Company set-up, the consignee of suspect tea samples.

★★★

The off-duty civilian dress of a British Other Rank in India was fairly similar to that worn by Europeans employed in civilian jobs in India: khaki shorts, white shirt and knee-length cotton stockings. To bring him a more authentic civilian appearance Harding wore a solar topee, which had the extra advantage of giving him some protection from the mid-afternoon sun.

He walked across the *maidan* to Kiddapore Road, where he waited under the welcome shade of the tattered awning of a soft drinks stall for a bus to Dalhousie Square. He refused repeated offers to buy a tumbler of freshly squeezed cane juice, which seeped like watery milk from the rusted rollers of the vendor's fruit mangle.

When the bus, nearly hidden under a covering to sides and roof with passenger overload, wheezed to a halt, he shouldered his way onto the conductor's platform into a tight pack of sweating bodies. He was fully aware of sensitive fingers testing for the location of a wallet or loose change, but Harding, well experienced in avoiding the covetous attention of pickpockets, carried little of value when outside the security of barracks, other than cash for immediate use and of course his paybook which was stowed in a body-belt underneath his shirt and next to his skin. When he felt an over curious hand slither into the waistband of his shorts he grabbed it by the thumb, levered it back against the wrist joint and pressed very hard. The hiss of breath being sucked in between clenched teeth signalled that he had no more to fear from the owner of a very painful hand. On reaching the old East India Company Writer's offices in Dalhousie Square he thrust a couple of annas, representing uncollected fare, into the bus conductor's hand and without waiting for a ticket to be punched leapt from the bus to join another mass of bodies on the crowded pavement.

From Dalhousie Square he hired a cycle *rickshaw* to convey him to Strand Road South where he picked up a tramcar to take him as far as the eastern end of the Howrah Bridge. Harding could have taken the more convenient and comfortable way of making the journey by taxi from start to finish but he did not want to betray his movements to any interested bodies. One never knew when one was under surveillance in this country, especially as he had the distinct feeling that he was becoming mixed up in something that carried a rather sinister, but so far, unidentified connection.

He decided to walk across Howrah Bridge, jostling with sacred cows, pedestrians and sweat drenched coolies stripped to the waist. The natives were hauling carts with enormous iron-shod wheels piled high with bales of jute, cotton and animal hides over the burning tarmac road to the *godowns* spread alongside the wharves of the muddy Hooghly. A pair of bored looking policemen armed with rifles squatted beneath the overhang on the far side of the bridge. If they were there to keep watch on potential trouble spots following the Calcutta killings of August, it seemed most unlikely to Harding that they could be of much use, penned in as they were by thousands of swarming Indians moving in a seemingly endless stream in pursuit of earning a few annas for a day's work.

As Harding, keeping a sharp lookout for the *godowns* of the Assam Bengal Trading Company, walked on the shaded side of the river, he caught occasional glimpses of freighters moving slowly upstream on the incoming tide. They reminded him that trade continued no matter what politicians and national fanatics said or did. Over to his left and sprawling into the distance behind a miscellany of dockside sheds and high cranes lay the hideous Howrah slums, housing a limitless supply of cheap labour, which being self-generating and not written in to balance sheets as capital assets provided a non-accountable business resource. Much of the dockside plant and infrastructure was in a sorry state having been established during the last century with *godowns* crumbling from the ravages of tropical weather and indifferent maintenance. The Assam Bengal Trading Company *godown* was a new, steel framed structure having been constructed, probably with government funding, to transit military supplies brought across the Pacific from the United States.

He walked on some twenty yards before cutting through an alleyway to double back to the rear of his goal, which he approached with caution, pausing only to listen for sounds of movement inside the warehouse. Loading doors were wide open which allowed him a restricted view of part of the dim interior. He called out to attract attention, having the excuse ready that he was lost and was trying to find his way to Howrah Railway Station. There was no response to his repeated "hullos" as he climbed the few rungs of an access ladder to take a closer look. Some bales of jute and coir were stacked head high next to drums of chemicals, wooden boxes of Sunlight soap and bundles of mattocks, pick axes and shovels. As he moved back to the loading bay his stocking caught on the jagged edge of a piece of metal. It was the corner binding protruding from a pile of empty tea chests. As he stooped to free the stocking threads he saw the binding was nailed to a small sample chest stencilled Erskine-Jalpai and marked with a red spot.

The ringing of a telephone and the sound of an answering voice froze him. The conversation was indistinct and as it was conducted in what he thought was Bengali, made no sense to Harding. When the caller hung up Harding crept on hands and knees in the direction of the sound. An Indian clerk was settling down on a *charpoy* to continue his disturbed afternoon sleep. Except for the lack of small-pox scars on his face, Harding saw the clerk was a near double to Narayan Rao, the Erskine-Jalpai estate manager. He was now sure that there was a connection between the late night visit to Erskine-Jalpai, Narayan Rao, opium trafficking, Tamu airfield and the Assam Bengal Trading Company … but how do Laura and Julia fit in to all this?

Harding couldn't bring himself to believe the two women were playing any part in this game but they were implicated if only by association. He had a clear responsibility to inform his superiors of any relevant information, but he had to find out from Laura if indeed she was knowingly involved. How could he tackle Laura without betraying his cover?

★★★

A message in the mess letter rack told Harding to telephone Calcutta Civil 8379. An orderly said it was a memsahib who had called but did not leave her name.

Laura apologised for any inconvenience. Harding detected a note of anxiety in her voice and she seemed relieved when he suggested taking her for dinner. She agreed to be ready for seven o'clock.

★★★

As Harding and Laura drove through the tree-lined avenues of Tollygunge heading for central Calcutta, she grasped his hand and said in a low voice, "I just had to see you. Something is going on and I had to speak to someone I felt I could trust … I can trust you, can't I?"

"Tell me what's worrying you,' Harding said gently and added with a smile, "I'll let you know then if I can be trusted."

"It may sound trivial to you but yesterday when Mr D'Silva returned home he told me the police had been making enquiries at one of his *godowns*. He said they were particularly interested in Erskine-Jalpai: was all our tea shipped through him? Who was running the estate? How long had it been in the present ownership and for how long had Mr D'Silva been acting as our agent?"

"Did D'Silva have any idea what the police were after? Could it be they were acting for the Customs people, for instance?"

"No, all they would come up with was that they were following a routine enquiry, but they would say that, wouldn't they?"

"There's no point in getting worried about it until you have some clear facts to go on. I'm glad you told me, but if neither you nor Julia have done anything wrong, and I'm sure you haven't, there should be no cause to worry. I don't suppose there is anyone up at the estate who could attract the attention of the law? What about the manager? He seems to have his finger on the button. Do you think he might be up to a bit of skulduggery?"

"You mean Narayan Rao? Wouldn't think so. Uncle Carter took him on and from what I could see, Mark seemed to get on with him OK. I must admit, I'm not all that enthusiastic about him but he has kept his side of the business going pretty well for us."

"Well, you know the estate better than me. Let's leave it there, shall we, and enjoy the evening. How do you fancy Firpo's? Top rate food, small orchestra, give us the opportunity to talk … better than the pictures."

"I'm hardly dressed for a sophisticated rendezvous…."

"You look absolutely smashing, Mrs Erskine. You'll beat anyone else hands down. I'm the one who should be apologising. All I've got is a tie to conform to the dress code of Firpo's."

When the taxi turned onto the busy Chowringhee, Harding ordered the driver to drop them off at Firpo's. He asked, "You go BOR Firpo, Sahib, or Officer Firpo."

"What's the difference?" Laura asked. "Don't they both have food and dancing?"

"I can see this demands an explanation. First, there is a restaurant where the management supplies the steak, egg and chips needs of the common soldier, and then there is the number one Firpo's which carries the implied sign 'Officers Only Please'. It's a civilian establishment outside the protocol published in King's Regulations and that is where we are going. Yes, driver, we are going to Firpo's, not the bloody works canteen."

"Well spoken, Sergeant. I second that proposal. Let's make a night of it. You've got your orders, driver … let's go."

The driver chuckled into his beard, nudged his companion and said, "*Thik hai* Memsahib, I go there quick."

Chapter 30

White table cloths, fantail-folded napkins, crystal glasses and gleaming cutlery, white-robed, red-turbaned and cummerbunded waiters, palms standing in brass planters, sparkling chandeliers, oak panelled walls and the acoustic backdrop of soft orchestral music delivered a style of taste and luxury standing in harsh contrast to the crushing misery of Calcutta's squalid streets and rotting slums.

As Harding and Laura were being conducted by the tail-coated head waiter to their table, Harding fingered the fold of five rupee notes tucked inside his paybook with which to honour the financial outcome of this special occasion. He made an approximation of the menu prices to those of a silver service dinner on the King's Cross – Leeds Pullman and concluded he could meet the bill and even afford to splash out on a bottle of something reasonable to be chosen from the calf-bound wine list flourished by tail-coat.

Throughout their meal, and during the dances that followed, Harding saw the glances of 'lucky sod' envy from some of the unaccompanied men crowded in the bar as they gazed in admiration at Laura. She appeared to be oblivious to the male hunger she was attracting and gave her full attention to Harding as they moved gently to the swaying rhythm of a Glenn Miller number.

They decided to leave when the bar area began to overflow into the restaurant area as late night drinkers came in to ease thirsts brought on by cinema air conditioning or simply plain boredom at hanging about waiting for homeward-bound movement orders.

★★★

"It seems we've got a choice of whisky, gin or you can mix a martini. There's a bottle of vermouth and a supply of ice in the 'fridge."

"Your host certainly looks after you pretty well. The guest bungalow all nicely set up and a night tray to welcome you … very nice too. Thanks for the offer but I don't fancy any more to drink. I reckon it's time I hit the road now I've seen you safely home."

"I'd like you to stay for a little while, please. I told you earlier this evening about the police snooping around the D'Silva *godown* enquiring about tea sample shipments from our estate. Well, something else has cropped up which is giving me a headache. Look, just have a coffee with me and I'll tell you about it … won't take a minute to fix up."

"Go on then, don't want to overstay my welcome."

Laura quickly produced a couple of coffees from the kitchen and led Harding out to the veranda. From a folder she produced a bundle of papers, some of which carried the War Office crest.

"Amongst other things I had to see to in Calcutta were some matters connected with Mark's affairs, his personal bank account, a few outstanding bills and so on. Amongst some papers sent from Pay and Records at Jhansi is this cancelled cheque. It was cashed in Karachi and according to his last statement just about cleared his current account. Here, take a look."

Harding examined the cheque issued by Lloyds Bank (Cox and Kings). It was signed M Erskine, Captain, and made out in favour of the Field Cashier Karachi for the sum of five hundred rupees and dated 19 Sep 1945. He turned it over a couple of times, held it up to the light and returned it to Laura.

"I assume that's his signature? And if the cheque didn't bounce, what's wrong with it?"

"You remember that day at Erskine-Jalpai when you came to dinner, I told you that Mark had been reported missing on Operation Zipper? Well, that operation took place in September at about the time the Japanese gave in and logic tells me that if it was mounted to invade Malaya the troops would have been mustered somewhere on the east coast of India, a port area on the Bay of Bengal or even as far south as Ceylon where much of the Royal Navy was based. Now if Mark was involved in that operation, which, according to official sources he was, and he had gone missing there, what the bloody hell was he doing getting a cheque cashed in Karachi?"

He could see she was angry and upset at this cheque turning up and was frustrated at being unable to understand what it was about. He asked her for the cheque, looked at the date again and drew a deep breath.

"The date on the cheque is the nineteenth of September, the Operation Zipper landings took place on the ninth – ten days before that cheque was cashed and the date when your husband was officially reported missing. Now how do we account for that? Missing officers don't sign cheques and I doubt if the Army Pay Corps accepts post-dated ones."

He could see she was still confused and uncertain of how to respond to Harding's analysis, which was clear in its implication that either someone had got hold of her missing husband's cheque book or that he was alive and had gone absent from his unit before setting out on Zipper. Harding placed his arm across her shoulder to reassure her. He knew that something was seriously adrift and he tried, for Laura's sake, to avoid thinking that Mark was not the man she thought he was.

Laura looked up at him and said, "I know I shouldn't saddle you with my worries, but I have to talk to someone I can trust and who can help me understand what is going on. First there was this police questioning about the estate. That links up in my mind with Narayan Rao's shifty behaviour when I challenged him about delaying our tea samples. Now there is this cheque that was cashed in Karachi at about the time Mark was reported missing. Then … there is something else that I just have to tell someone. It's been worrying me for ages and I'm afraid it's very personal."

Harding could see she was having difficulty in finding the right words to tell him.

"I hope you can trust me and if there is anything, anything at all I can do to help I promise you I will do all I can."

She paused for a moment and said, "When Mark asked me to marry him and go to live on a tea plantation after the war, I was filled with the very romantic idea of leading a life like a character from one of Somerset Maugham's novels. It became obvious that Uncle Carter was looking to Mark to produce a male heir, preserve the family name and ensure the future of Erskine-Jalpai. Although Carter had married Julia, there was no prospect of her giving him an heir, for whatever reason I don't know and I never asked. Our honeymoon was a snatched three days in Nani-Tal, a hill station in the Himalayas. This was the first time I had really slept with a man. Oh, I had been out with a few boys and enjoyed pretending to make love I suppose, like many young people do, but that was all … never the ultimate, too scared I expect. The very worst thing about our honeymoon was that he didn't touch me. Whenever it seemed the time was right it just didn't take off. Mark refused to discuss it even in veiled terms. He just mumbled something about being worried about the war and changed the subject. He left me the same day we returned to Erskine-Jalpai and that was the last time I saw him. I reported back for duty at Comilla and got on with my contribution to the war. Then, after Carter died and Mark was reported missing, the war came to an end and Aunt Julia begged me to take an early discharge and go to help her run the estate. So here I am, failed marriage and now a war widow. A bloody good start to the rest of my life and there doesn't seem a lot I can do about it. If it weren't for leaving Julia in the lurch, I'd be booking a passage home on the first ship I could. Sorry to bother you with my troubles, but I really do feel browned off with the whole bloody issue. One other thing, my wedding ring is now in my purse and I declare to all that I'm a single woman again."

"You seem a hell of a sight better than you did half an hour ago, good show. Hope you feel more at ease now you've got that little lot off your mind. Let's have that quick nightcap, then I'll leave you to it. We'll talk about all this later after I've had the opportunity to do a bit of research on this Zipper operation to see if I can find out more about Captain Mark Erskine's job and where he fitted in to the picture. I think I know a bod who might be able to produce a few answers."

"Thanks, Harding, I'd be very, very grateful, and I think a nightcap's a super idea ... but, you don't have to go ... do you?"

Chapter 31

The next morning, true to his word, Harding broached the Operation Zipper matter to Captain Reeder. "Yes, we've still got monitor intercepts from Zipper," he said. "They are stashed away in our intelligence registry where, in the fullness of time, a Board of Officers will be convened to sift through them. The more routine stuff will be destroyed and anything considered to carry ongoing security implications will be sent off to Troopers in London for them to have a go at before consigning the juiciest bits, liable to cause political embarrassment, to the archives under the thirty-year rule. Even those will be carefully censored to make sure certain institutions can't be called to account for errors of judgement. Anyhow, what's your sudden interest, Sergeant? I thought that now you were off the hook, you were enjoying a bit of free time before heading off up country again."

Harding replied, "I'm not able to give you the full reasons why I would like to have a look through them, even to you, sir. It's partly private, but it could have serious connections with the matter which brought me down to Calcutta and the briefing sessions I have since been involved in."

Captain Reeder knew that if it were revealed that he had allowed anyone other than a properly authorised body to examine the registry records he would be for the chop. He looked directly into Harding's eyes as if trying to harvest his thoughts. He unlocked the key-press held in a combination-locked safe and pointed to a set of three Yale keys.

"They will get you into the registry. If they aren't back within two hours I will raise the alarm and it will be you who'll be for the high jump. Is that understood?"

"Thanks sir, I won't let you down."

Harding let himself into the registry and wondered why the lights had been left switched on, until he realised the dry heat from the 150 watt lamps was to protect the stored documents from the warm humidity which encouraged mould and would severely damage anything left in a damp atmosphere, if only for a few days. He made a mental note to leave the lights on when he had finished his search.

He quickly located a file index. Enemy wireless intercepts entered on red printed forms and clipped into open folders were stacked in date order on slatted shelving. Harding, through sheer curiosity, glanced at a couple of bundles of messages but being in code they meant nothing to him; the only understandable content were date-time groups and the receiving operator's signature entered in clear. Monitor intercepts from own forces wireless traffic were mostly written in log form and stored in a different section. Some entries were annotated to show that minor breaches of procedure had been committed but that no further action was to be taken. Breaches of security when messages sent in clear containing classified information had been endorsed to show that the guilty formation had been informed for appropriate action to be taken against the offending individuals. The amount of own forces intercept material was reduced to a few scattered files from the 12th of September 1945, three days after Operation Zipper.

Harding gathered an armful of files and began to run through the information they contained. They began with a week of wireless silence that usually preceded a planned operation. Except for a few recorded instances of carrier transmissions, when an apprehensive operator would check that his equipment was serviceable and that he was netted to the correct frequency, the logs were blank except for date and NTR (nothing to report) scribbles. When the Command Net opened up at dawn on the day of Zipper there was an immediate increase in the amount of recorded intercept material: signals to and from Land Force HQ down to radio telephone traffic in clear, with increasing irritation being expressed by landing craft commanders reporting that allocated landing points were inaccessible because of sand bars in places where they should not have been, at least according to pre-operation recces. Harding grinned when he read the messages straight from the beaches that confirmed at first hand the rumours that had gone the rounds. On the second day of the operation he found an intercept from the Force HQ to HQ South East Asia Command asking for confirmation that an unnamed officer, responsible for parachuting into the jungle to liaise with local resistance commanders, had indeed been dropped as planned.

So, Harding concluded, at least one bod had gone adrift on an alleged 'no casualty' operation. Hardly sufficient evidence to identify Captain Erskine as the missing officer but enough to provide a suspicion that it was so. Coupled with the cheque cashed in Karachi and the uncertainty of how he came to be missing, circumstances were coming together to suggest that Erskine's disappearance could prove an embarrassment to the army.

After sorting through the remainder of intercept traffic up to the end of September 1945 he found nothing of any relevance to his search. He replaced the files where he had found them and left the registry, remembering to leave the lights switched on. With less than fifteen minutes to go he returned the keys to Captain Reeder's safe.

Chapter 32

Saturday had duly arrived and Harding pondered the invitation to the D'Silvas. 'Carriages at Midnight' was a polite way of saying "the party's over, please arrange to get moving at that hour." In Harding's inventory, the term was well understood but he thought 'Seven-thirty for Eight' was ill-defined almost to the point of indifference. For the five years of his military service he had been trained, by instruction and experience, to treat time as essential to the planning and execution of an event or operational engagement. Being primarily involved in operational communications when the order to open up a wireless link at a precise minute meant just that, with no excuses short of enemy action accepted for failure to comply, Harding had played it safe and stepped down from the *tonga* at seven twenty-five on the dot.

The drive was lit with an avenue of coloured lamps slung from trees and pitch-fuelled torches in iron cages spiked into the lawn. A band could be heard scraping and blowing into tune led by a repeatedly struck piano key giving out middle 'A'. There was no sign of guests and, not wishing to be mistaken for an intruder, he decided to take a stroll along the deserted street until the *ram-sami* came to life.

He returned after some twenty minutes to find a couple of dozen cars parked bumper to bumper outside the gardens with groups of *syces* chattering, smoking their evil-smelling *bidis* and chewing the equally objectionable *betel nut*, which required the user to spit blood-red streams of saliva at frequent intervals, adding to the sun-browned stains left by previous users.

Laura met him at the head of the drive. She looked beautiful in a soft peach evening gown. Her pale blonde hair was swept up in the Edwardian style and held in place with a silver dress comb. She took his hand and offered her cheek for a greeting kiss. As his lips touched her skin he became aware of her perfume – fresh, alluring and in perfect harmony with her unconcealed aura of vibrant sexuality. Before taking him to be introduced to the D'Silvas she took him aside and asked if he would "Please forgive me for the other night in the guest bungalow. I don't think there is anything else to add."

He gave her arm a reassuring squeeze and said, "There's nothing to forgive. It's me who should be apologising for not staying. It wasn't that I didn't want to stay, but I thought that with all this worry about your husband and that cheque it wasn't the right time and we may have been sorry afterwards. Shall we get on parade then? Don't want to keep our host and hostess waiting, do we?"

She looked up at him, face flushed, and with an emphatic voice said, "It was nothing to do with either my missing husband or the cheque business or any of the dozen other things that have been worrying me. Can't you see, you idiot, I want you because I love you and if that isn't a good enough reason, we might as well call it a bloody day and you can forget all about me. In the meantime let's honour our hosts and get on with the evening."

She turned to walk away but Harding grabbed her arm. "If you don't mind hanging on a minute, I think you should hear what I have to say first … let's go over there." Still holding her arm he led her away from the veranda steps and out of earshot of other people. "Maybe I haven't made it clear, but there is a hell of a difference between us. You are soon liable to be the owner of a bloody great tea estate and all the trappings that go with it in India – big house, servants and an exclusive social life. I am a sergeant in the British Army and Raj protocol tells me we are not on the same frequency. But, that apart … you are a damned attractive woman and I wouldn't carry on saying no if I thought that's all there was to it. Until tonight I wasn't entirely certain how you felt about me. I love you, Laura, and I have done since the evening I spent at Erskine-Jalpai

… and before you say anything else let's go and you can get me introduced to the D'Silvas before they start a search and rescue operation."

They moved back into the reception and sought out their hosts.

"So you are the chappie who came to the rescue of this dear young lady in the wilds of Assam," said D'Silva. "I owe you a great debt of gratitude. I have tried to keep an eye on the estate and its business since Mr Carter died and poor Mark was reported missing in action. If anything had happened to Mrs Erskine I would have been unable to forgive myself."

Harding reassured D'Silva that there had been no danger as he retrieved his hand from the dry, bony grip of the Eurasian. He assumed with that name there were a few drops of Portuguese blood running through his veins and was fairly convinced that his concern for Laura was secondary to his trading concerns and the demand for Assam tea on the world markets, which he was in an advantageous position to help satisfy. After exchanging "Pleased to meet yous" with the dumpy Mrs D'Silva whose bleached hair was at some variance from her more than dusky complexion, presumably from her mother's side, Laura led him down the carpeted ramp into a maple-floored marquee to join the flow of couples dancing to the now reasonably well tuned band playing a slow foxtrot number in the strict tempo style of the Victor Sylvester School of Dancing.

The honest exchange between Harding and Laura had added an electricity to the air and as they danced, she pushed in closer to the soldier. He could feel her breasts flattening against him as they pivoted through the forward turns in rhythm to the number 'You are Dancing on my Heart'.

When the music ended they stood for a moment, unwilling to end their closeness: he with his right arm round her slim waist, she with her body arched up to him and her head on his shoulder.

She whispered, "I do love you, Harding."

★★★

Harding surveyed the buffet dinner laid out in the base of the L-shaped configuration of the marquee. His thoughts were on the austere life still being endured by the people back home which they had put up with throughout the war and now in peacetime, still waiting for the plenty they were hoping to be rewarded with, especially as they were under the impression that they were the citizens of a victorious nation. He felt the lavish presentation of fine foods was also verging on the obscene when millions of people were constantly on the edge of starvation throughout the sub-continent.

He viewed with astonishment the serving points supervised by liveried servants offering foods separated in accordance with the tastes of the diners whose choices were dictated by religious dietary edict: Halal meats for Muslims and non-beef dishes for the Hindus. There was a sea-food bar displaying lobsters, king prawns and crayfish, all smothered in chipped ice and garnished with parsley and wafer-thin slices of lemon and cucumbers. The dessert bar had tiers of mangoes, oranges, pineapples and bananas piled high amongst trifles, blanc-mange, and the violently hued *jellabies* greatly favoured by the Indian palate.

A nudge from Laura reminded him to grab a few goodies and follow her to a corner table partly hidden by some tall potted plants. A hovering waiter served glasses of champagne and left them with the bottle in an ice-bucket.

"This is a bit extravagant, isn't it? If you'll excuse the expression, it's what we in the army would call a load of bull."

"Don't be shy … you mean bullshit. I'm not offended. Don't forget, I've also been in the services and can probably match you with word choices. Hold it, I think I have spotted the reason for some of this extravagance, over by the buffet talking to our host – see? I think he has a couple of bodyguards with him."

Harding stood to get a better view. He saw a man of medium height, about five six or seven. He was wearing a white linen suit, which, although he could see the jacket was well cut, hung from him as if it were slung on a coat hanger. Piercing black eyes shone from a bony face structure behind a hooked nose. Thin grey hair was brushed straight back. He held an ebony and gold cigarette holder in his right hand which he moved quickly to flick ash into an ashtray held by a servant between puffs. Two burly men with the pale complexion of Frontier tribesmen flanked their charge ready to discourage anyone who ventured to stray over an invisible boundary. Mr D'Silva was engaged in a whispered conversation with the guest.

"Yes Laura, of course, that's our friend Mr Jinnah, the leader of the Muslim League. He's the fellow who declared that he would have a separate state for the Muslims or he would have India destroyed when the country is given independence. I wonder why D'Silva should invite him here? A very high-powered local *wallah* to be found at this sort of *ram-sami*, I would have thought."

"My guess is that Mr D'Silva, who has wide business interests in Bengal, is making certain of his future should it become part of the state of Pakistan," Laura said, with a hint in her voice which suggested she had no illusions about the business methods of her host.

Harding was silent for a while, then said, "If he is settling his plans for the day of independence I wonder just what is going to happen to all the other Brits and Eurasians who live in the country? Have you thought how it will affect you and Julia?"

"Of course I have. My main concern is what will happen to Erskine-Jalpai. I've become very attached to it and would hate to see the place taken over at the point of a gun or by whatever methods are encouraged by the new rulers. I'm lucky, I have a home in England, but Julia will be stuck out here. She has no-one back home."

Harding shook his head. "Don't know the answer to that one, I'm afraid. My guess is there's going to be a hell of a bust-up when we pull out. There'll be no British Army to try to keep the Hindus and Muslims from each other's throats. I meant to ask you, have you heard anything else about those bods who were making enquiries about the estate and sniffing about at the *godown*?"

"Not a word. I think the police were following a line of enquiry aimed at some employees of Mr D'Silva who had apparently been up to no good. I'm told this information came from a senior officer of the Bengal Police and that D'Silva's set-up has been given a clean bill of health, so it seems there is nothing else to worry about on that score. Happy?"

"Tell me, was the police *wallah* called Sedley by any chance?"

Laura lifted her eyebrows. "Yes, that was the name. Do you know him or something?"

"Well, yes, but don't let on to D'Silva. I'll tell you in due course why I want to keep it quiet for a while. Shall we drop this business now and get on with enjoying the evening? It's going to be our last get-together for some time."

"Let's dance," she whispered.

They fell into the slow rhythm of the music with their bodies touching. He could feel himself responding to the hardness of her breasts as she clung to him with an increasing urgency. He allowed her to guide him to a shaded corner of the floor where a banked chicane of potted plants offered a discreet exit.

"I'm going to the powder room," she said. "I'll join you at the guest bungalow. Best not to be seen leaving together."

★★★

Chapter 33

January 1947 and Britain was held in the vice-like grip of a savage winter. Fierce blizzards transformed snowflakes into ice-hard shot that banked into high drifts blocking country lanes and city streets alike. The nationalised coal industry was in deep crisis. A snowbound transport system was unable to carry fuel to power stations and electricity cuts had reduced manufacturing capacity to almost zero. Acute food shortages extended wartime rationing into a hard-won peace. The raw austerity of the dollar-hungry economy added misery to Britain's distress with the debt burden of Lend-Lease. American supplied war materials expensively bought at the price of a once asset-rich empire, dragging the harsh six years of war over into the days of peace. Hopes invested with the celebration of a Labour election victory with promises of a better life for war heroes and their families were turning into cringing despair.

Rowena Taylor shivered as she stepped out of the War Office building into the biting wind that swept along Whitehall, bringing with it the sour smell of Thames water and the rancid undertone of bomb-damaged homes and office blocks. She buried her face into the high beaver lamb collar of her overcoat and leaned into the wind to adjust her balance. The road and pavement were slippery with rutted ice offering bone-shattering hazards to the unwary. Except for an official car that pulled away from Number Ten, the roads were empty of traffic and people. She had been instructed to report to the Foreign Office at 3.30pm and entered through the Downing Street archway where a uniformed messenger stepped forward to greet her.

"Miss Taylor?"

She nodded.

"Please follow me."

The temperature inside the building was little different from the outside chill as if to demonstrate that even the offices of state enjoyed no privileged dispensation from the prevailing post-war misery. She followed her guide up a wide staircase. The lift gate carried an 'Out of Use' placard. At the first floor her guide knocked on a door bearing an engraved plate: 'His Majesty's Principal Secretary of State for Foreign Affairs'. Rowena Taylor was ushered in and greeted by a middle-aged woman. She wore the tired look typical of the type: greying hair caught up in left and right plaited coils that flanked her temples like a telephone headset, no make-up and plain cream blouse under a mauve cardigan. A wide carriage Imperial typewriter and a dictaphone standing on her desk bore testimony to her secretarial skills: confidentially employed in processing classified material originated by her minister. After stroking the call button on a one-to-one intercom, a voice came back to her. "Ready now, Helen. Ask her to come in … and some tea please." The request was delivered in grating tones with a West Country accent, 's' pronounced 'sh'.

The minister was seated at a large leather topped desk lit by a green-shaded banker's lamp. The grey daylight from the opened curtains was the only other light source throwing dim shadows into the sparsely furnished room. Open dispatch boxes tiered over a corner of the desk spilled documents and telegrams over a large blotter.

He looked up from his task to give a slight nod of welcome and motioned his visitor to a deep armchair near the fireplace. Although the basket had been designed to generous proportions, bricks had been placed to reduce the amount of coal space. The meagre fire made a brave attempt to cast a glow barely reflected from the heavy brass poker stand and black iron fender.

Rowena settled in the chair and examined the room. It was spacious and what little furniture it contained was in the style of eighteenth century country house. Some paintings of classical subjects in frames of rococo gilded design hung against the dark green walls. The blue carpet showed signs of wear and there was no doubt, she thought, it would be a priority item in the post-war refurbishing schedule of the Ministry of Works when funds became available.

After reading through and initialling a final paper with a fat Conway-Stewart held between his middle and index finger, the minister leaned back in his chair, screwed the cap on his pen and clipped it into a waistcoat pocket to join its matching propelling pencil.

"Good afternoon, Miss Taylor. Good of you to come over at such short notice. I'm very grateful to your department for their assistance. Ah yes, here's the tea. Thank you Helen, we'll have it by the fire. It's a bit cold, I'm afraid, but do make yourself comfortable."

Rowena slid out of her coat and pushed it over the back of her chair. She removed her woollen cap and gave her short-cut hair a quick finger comb. After a period of silence, broken only by the chink of cup and saucer, the minister cleared his throat.

"I understand that you spent a couple of war years in the Far East and for much of that time you worked from the British Military Mission in Chungking where Generalissimo Chiang Kai-shek set up his government after the Japanese invaded China in '37. The Director of Army Intelligence tells me that as a result of your experience and the special work on which you were employed, you're in a good position to help throw some light on a sensitive matter that's giving the authorities, in India especially, some concern." He paused to elicit Rowena's response.

"Thank you, Minister," she said. "I will carry out whatever orders you give to the fullest extent of my experience and ability, but I would like to hear more about the job first."

"Of course, young lady. The information so far is a bit scanty. I want you to go away and with the intelligence so far produced, analyse it and try to put a name to some descriptions we have. A number of people were observed at a meeting held at an ex-RAF airfield on the Assam/Burma frontier. A couple of these characters have already been identified by Army Intelligence. One is a well known Burmese political leader by the name of Aung San. His history became suspect when he went in on the side of the Japanese, but when the war ended and he had time to review his future, he returned to the fold. Mountbatten, the then Supreme Commander in South East Asia, thought fit to make him head of the Burma Government. The reason was to reassure the population and attempt to neutralise anti-British feelings. Is he by any chance already known to you?"

Rowena thought for a while. "I can't be certain for the moment. We had our eyes on masses of local leaders and personalities who were thought to be worth watching, but if I can sift through our files, I could no doubt come up with something useful. What about the second fellow you mentioned?"

"I thought you might say that, but this could have some connection with, and I say this in the strictest confidence ... our wartime allies. I'll go no further than that until you have read this report. Then I will tell you why I have ordered Army Intelligence rather than my Secret Intelligence Service to look at it."

He handed Rowena a foolscap-sized envelope marked KINGSMAN and classified TOP SECRET.

"Read this."

He levered himself from his chair and walked across to the window to look out over the stripped trees and frozen lake of St James Park to the Victoria Monument and Buckingham Palace. The flagstaff over the balcony rooms was bare. Instead, the Sovereign's Standard would be flying over Sandringham, the great country house in Norfolk where, according to established custom, the Royal Family would be spending the first few weeks of the New Year. No matter where the King happened to be in residence, he would be kept up to date with affairs of state from documents delivered in the familiar red dispatch boxes. There was much to demand the King's concern: the economy, almost at a standstill, but facing an on-going demand for funds to pay for the country's needs and to prop up Eastern European countries in their attempts to resist the expansionist ambitions of Russia. Even the agreements made at Yalta in the final months of the war – where Churchill, Roosevelt and Stalin agreed to carve up Eastern Europe in the best strategic interests of the victorious allies – were in danger of falling apart.

Britain's Empire in the East was under pressure from the Americans who held the firm belief that for most of the nineteenth and twentieth centuries Britain's overseas presence had successfully underwritten peace and, by exporting capital, had also underwritten economic stability. This was now to change since the war had been conducted largely on American terms that, under the Atlantic Charter of 1941, peace should bring liberty and self-determination to all peoples of the world. This aim was of concern to both Churchill, the imperialist, and Stalin, whose eyes had long been firmly fixed on the Indian Empire. The King, fully aware that the days of the British Empire were numbered, had recognised this outcome when he promised the co-operation of his government to help India achieve independence.

The minister closed the heavy curtains to shut out the darkening London evening and turned to Rowena. She closed the report and looked up to invite further explanation.

"Let me share my understanding of what you have just read and how it came to our notice. A local operation was mounted to apprehend some key figures in the Indian National Army who fought with the Japanese during the Burma campaign. This operation had to be conducted in a covert manner so as not to arouse suspicion amongst nationalist agitators who carefully watch and note any unusual military activity. An army sergeant, well experienced in special operations, was sent up to Assam where he made contact with a number of Naga headmen who could supply him with useful leads regarding the INA. It was one of these leads, describing aircraft movements in and out of Tamu airfield, which demanded some explanation. The RAF had none of their aeroplanes operating in that area and the Americans, the only other people with any air capability, were long gone from that part of South East

Asia. An air recce confirmed that Tamu was indeed being used by somebody or other as you will have seen from the photographs in the report. The sergeant carried out a ground recce and brought back the information that you have just read."

Rowena said, "It is quite an interesting project and if my chief thinks I am the right person to take it on, as I have already said, Minister, then fair enough. Is there anything else I should know at this stage?"

"Yes … two things. First, I have kept nothing back. You have seen all the information so far made available to me. Second, and the reason why I want your people rather than MI6 to deal with it, is that I have certain reservations about some of them. There is a strong chance that Russia has a finger in this pie and I know that some people, whose names I know, are playing a double game. They think that Joe Stalin holds the key to a new world order based on his version of Communism. They were students at Cambridge in the thirties when active recruitment to the Communist cause was the order of the day and a hard core formed a group which called themselves the Apostles – an inner circle of intellectuals dedicated to their Communist beliefs. In addition to their distorted political opinions they were also playing what I would call 'pat-a-cake' … in other words they were practising homosexuals. I'm sorry to have to tell you this, but it's right that you should be fully aware of these facts."

She took this revelation with a wry smile.

"I understand, sir, but it's nothing new to me … I came across some very odd sexual behaviour during my time in China. In fact it was a source of compromise which as intelligence operators we had to be continually alert to."

She glanced at her watch, anxious to get back to her flat in Chelsea before the few available buses became overloaded with the home-going crowds.

"How much time do I have to produce some answers, Minister?"

"I can't afford more than a month, but if you come up with

some important information let me know immediately instead of waiting to submit a formal report. Use the codeword KINGSMAN. That will get me straight away. You will work at a house in Yorkshire which we use for certain purposes. You will find that Army Intelligence will have made available all profiles on VIPs and political figures compiled from your observations submitted through the Military Mission in Chungking. If you need access to any other data, the Director of Military Intelligence will get it to you. Ah yes, the army chap who did the Tamu ground recce will join you up there. He is due to land at RAF Northolt tomorrow night."

Chapter 34

Harding hurried across the tarmac apron from the Transport Command York in which he had flown from Karachi Air Trooping Depot. The aircraft, modified from the Lancaster bomber, had been noisy with an incessant roar from the four aero engines, frustrating serious attempts to read or even doze. On-ground spells to refuel, carry out system checks, change crews and give opportunities for the passengers to feed and stretch legs at Baghdad, Cairo, Rome and Lyons had extended the journey time to almost forty hours. Thin khaki trousers and a jersey pullover were hardly appropriate clothes to wear, but the rush to get him airborne with priority movement orders had permitted no time to get kitted up for the biting cold of a harsh English winter.

A supply NCO at the terminal building issued him with a second-hand RAF greatcoat from an emergency stock held to bring a little weather protection to personnel arriving from tropical stations. After signing for a two weeks advance of pay, ration allowance and food coupons, he was given instructions to report to HQ War Office Signals, Eton Square for onward transmission to an unknown destination. He was given a late supper of sausage and chips prepared by a disgruntled cook in the Sergeant's Mess and by midnight was in bed and shivering under four blankets and a RAF greatcoat in an unheated room.

His presence at breakfast the following morning raised no question from any of his fellow diners. They were accustomed to Senior NCOs passing through London on routine transit. Before reporting to the Orderly Room to collect movement orders and travel warrant for onward transmission to somewhere in Yorkshire, he was issued with a new battledress uniform complete with sergeant's stripes, War Office troops Crown and Lion formation signs and a greatcoat to replace the RAF garment which he had been very happy to wear and supplement his blanket allocation during his first winter night in London. When he enquired of the quartermaster how they could possibly know his size and rank in advance of arrival, he was told not to ask silly questions and get on his way.

The train left King's Cross on time. After stops at Peterborough, Grantham and Doncaster he reached Leeds in mid-afternoon where, according to his movement order, he was required to report to the Railway Transport Officer who gave him a telephone number to call when a car would be sent to pick him up.

★★★

The car turned out to be an Austin Utility, a modified vehicle that was half saloon and half cargo space. The driver was a civilian who assured him they would "Get there in about an hour if we don't have to shovel our way up the hill."

In reply to Harding's "And where is 'there', may I ask?" the driver said, "Just up the dale. Moorside Hall it's called. Used to belong to the Rushworth family but when the war broke out it was taken over by the army as some sort of training centre."

Harding thanked him for his enlightening information and concentrated on the passing countryside. They had left the slush-blackened city streets and were now driving over hard packed snow which, in some exposed places had drifted high against dry-stone walls to leave clear stretches of road surface. With the engine pulling in third gear the driver maintained a steady pace on the traffic-free lanes. When the driver turned the car into a narrow lane he halted and requested Harding to assist in securing skid-chains to the rear wheels. He explained that without them he would be "Hard put to it to reach the top of the hill."

Harding, whose legs were stiff with cold, was swift to oblige, glad to seize the opportunity to dance around to ease his muscles and get the blood circulating again. With the chains fastened in place they resumed their journey, now climbing up slopes which took them higher and higher from the valley floor in a series of zig-zag bends bounded on the drop sides with collapsed walling where centuries of Pennine winds and ground movement had left huge gaps now fenced with barbed wire to keep sheep from straying.

The car rattled over a cattle grid then turned off into a long dip, shielded to the west with a huge outcrop of millstone grit that gave some shelter to a large house built in the Scottish style and set in an enclave of gale-ravaged blackthorn, alder and gaunt elm.

Harding eased his half-frozen body out of the car and followed the driver up some well-worn stone steps, through the great doorway, along the stone-flagged hall and into a small room where a corporal, hugging a pint pot of steaming tea, stood up from behind a trestle table to greet him.

"Sergeant Harding? If you would please complete this pro-forma and let me have your food coupons. We need all we can get these days. I'll show you to your billet." Harding quickly filled in the details required: name, rank, number, medical category, next of kin, religion – what if a chap didn't have a religion? Would that excuse him anything apart from church parade....

"Last unit, Sarge? We need to know this because you are still officially on their posted strength and they will have to publish any Part Two Orders regarding your rate of pay and ration allowance."

Harding thought for a moment. He did not know how much this chap knew about what went on at this place and he could hardly identify the intelligence set-up he had been working in ... "Right, just put me down as Headquarters India Command. That should fit the bill, OK?"

"Cor, you've come far enough. I'll bet yer feeling brass monkeys."

"Just a bit. Now, where's my billet and what time is supper?"

"Served at 1900 hours, Sarge. Everyone usually gathers in the ante-room before going in ... there isn't a bar waiter but there is a night tray and a book if you fancy a drink. Just help yourself and sign for it."

The corporal took Harding's bag and led him up a wide staircase, along a gallery and into a room where a blazing log fire welcomed him. He quickly unpacked and divided his kit between a chest of drawers and a mirror-fronted wardrobe, both of Victorian origin. A bottle of Black Label, bought in the transit mess at Karachi, was stowed in the back of the wardrobe.

After a long soak in a hot bath to warm his half-frozen limbs, he wrapped himself in a blanket, pulled a large armchair up to the fire, poured a large tot from his bottle to further relax him and contemplated this new situation.

A light knock dragged him back from the edge of sleep. The door opened slightly and a girl's voice said, "Can I come in?"

Harding gathered his blanket which had slipped from his shoulders and shuffled towards the open door where the owner of the voice smiled and enquired, "Kingsman?"

He was not feeling too happy at having his doze period interrupted and not being completely alert was already forming his reply to say, "You're in the wrong room," when he remembered the codename. His 'need to know' briefing, sketchy as ever in the specific operational culture of intelligence procedure, had disclosed the name Taylor, detailed to be his mission contact in the UK.

"Would your name be Taylor by any chance?" he countered.

"Yes, it certainly would. I am Rowena Taylor of Army Intelligence based at the War Office."

"Right, well, my name is Harding, Sergeant Harding, at present based wherever I find myself these days. India last week, somewhere in Yorkshire this week and who the hell knows where I will be next week … perhaps back in India with a bout of pneumonia, thanks to this weather." He paused and smiled. "You are a female. Are you in the army or a civilian attached or something?"

"Of course I'm a female. Don't I look like one? And yes, I am in the army, or at least the women's part of it. My official title is Junior

Commander Taylor of the ATS. I think Junior Commander is about the same as Captain, three pips you know."

"Beg your pardon, I didn't know … Ma'am … er Miss …."

"The correct form is Ma'am, but let's not get caught up in the rank business. Miss Taylor will do, but I would prefer you just call me Rowena. After all, we aren't on the parade ground and as I won't be appearing in uniform there's no need to salute either. Come on, then, what's your first name?"

"Harding will do or even Sergeant if it's a formal meeting. I never use my first name since I lost it when I joined the army."

"OK, have it your way. I'm sorry I spoiled your nap but I was told you'd arrived so I thought I'd jolly along and introduce myself. It'll be nice to have some company in this place. I've been here since yesterday and they all look upon me as if I'm a spy." She laughed and went on, "Well, I suppose I am in a way, just like you. No, they seem to be a bunch of cloak and dagger merchants, from all three services plus a couple of our friends from the US of A. God knows what they are up to but they seem OK, loaded with chocolate, fags and scotch and, although they haven't mentioned it yet, I'll bet they have a few dozen pairs of nylons to charm the knickers off the ladies. I see you've brought your own liquid reserves. Good show, don't keep it all to yourself … it's depressing to drink alone, you know."

Harding was taken aback at the frankness and casual approach of this woman. He thought she seemed, at least on the outside, to be a good player, but having had no experience of female commissioned officers he made up his mind to step with caution. He had, of course, come across female operators of the Special Operations Executive, Churchill's underground agents in Occupied France and Belgium, but trusting no-one for fear of being given away to the Gestapo they made no social contact with other operators, working either alone or in tightly organised cells. He would see how Miss Taylor tackled the work they had been tasked to jointly undertake on Operation KINGSMAN, to assess her worth as an intelligence officer and the level of experience she could call upon.

Rowena eyed his blanket garb and chuckled, "If you can find

something couth to wear in public, dinner will be dished up in half-an-hour. I'll save you a seat. See you there."

Harding dressed in the trousers, shirt and pullover he had worn during the flight. The new battledress issued in London was in a bit of a mess after helping to fit skid-chains to the Austin Utility, could do with a press if he could root out an iron. He thought the corporal would be able to fix him up.

She seemed attractive enough, tall, almost as tall as he was, soft brown hair, good teeth and a wide generous mouth. Her age, perhaps about twenty-six. Bit young to carry three pips but promotion had been a bit rapid during the war years. He wondered how many men had been on her list....

★★★

After the meal, which owed more to the cook's resourcefulness than the quality of the ingredients, he joined his fellow diners in the ante-room for coffee. He looked around trying to remember names and identities. The Commandant of the Technical Study Centre as it was called had introduced himself as Lt Col Harry Parker, Royal Tank Regiment. His job was admin and security – beds, rations and sentries as he put it. Harding was to learn later that he spent most of his day out on the moors, taking off after breakfast with a half loaf, a can of bully or Spam and a bottle of scotch to return at dusk with perhaps a hare or rabbit caught in one of the traps he had illegally set. The two Americans, who wore lieutenant's bars, introduced themselves as US Army Air Force personnel but declined to say what work they were engaged in. The remainder included a language specialist from the Education Corps, a Royal Navy marine engineer and three civilians of no known connection.

A pretty mixed bunch, he suggested to Rowena, who explained that the centre was a sort of retreat where people engaged on sensitive research could work in complete seclusion away from the daily routine of operational units or establishment.

"Another coffee?" Harding looked up from the *Yorkshire Post* and the pictures of snow-covered countryside and sheep cowering in makeshift shelters he had been studying to see Rowena waving a pot at him.

"No thanks, but I'd like a quick word with you when you have finished yours." He glanced round the room but no-one was taking any notice of him or Rowena. "Not here though."

She nodded in the direction of the door and Harding followed her through the hall and into a small room, spartanly furnished with a couple of chairs and two six-foot trestle tables covered with the ubiquitous army blankets.

Rowena pointed to a small safe cemented into the wall. "If you have any classified material with you, it is obligatory that it is kept in there when not being worked on. Everyone else here is working on classified tasks of some sort or another so I think we can be reasonably confident about them. I don't know about the admin staff, but I'm sure they will have been vetted. Anyhow, here is a spare key if you have got any stuff to stick in it."

"Yes, I have a few notes which would be better under lock and key. I'll shove 'em in then I'm going to hit the sack. See you here after breakfast. That OK with you?"

Chapter 35

"Look, Harding, we can be absolutely open with each other. We both know why we have been sent here and what we have to produce. The reason you are here is because you first made contact with the subject, you saw certain individuals and events at first hand and have been involved in high level de-briefings in India. I have been informed about your background in general terms, where you have operated and the value of the work you have produced. Bearing all that in mind I think it is right that you should know what I bring to the job in hand, OK?"

"Yes, that's fair enough. Fire away."

"As I told you last night, I am a Junior Commander in the ATS. I spent two years during the war with the British Military Mission in China. My job was to collect and analyse political and military intelligence from all sources. That of course included keeping an eye on our Allies as well as the Chinese and especially on the Vichy government who were collaborating with the Japs in French Indo-China. I operated through a number of agents. Some were even citizens of the relevant countries. So, you can see I managed to collect a lot of information, especially by watching the degree of infiltration of the Chinese Nationalist forces by Chinese Communists who were almost openly supported by the Russians. Much of what I picked up has been of some value already in settling post-war agreements and who can be trusted as leaders sympathetic to our policies in that part of the world."

"How did you come to find yourself posted out there? Did you have any local languages, for instance, or experience of the countries?"

"Until the age of eleven I lived in China, mostly in Shanghai where my father worked in the Diplomatic Service. My mother ran a medical practice. As I had a Chinese *amah* you could say I spoke Cantonese from the cradle. I began my education at the local English school where I learned Mandarin and a great deal about Chinese history and customs. I was then packed off to boarding school in England followed by three years at university. I was virtually picked up from my degree ceremony and strongly invited to join the ATS. After a minimum of formal training I was sent off to the Army Intelligence Training Centre, given a quick course on relevant subjects and sent out to Chungking. That do for you?"

"I'm impressed, good for you. Now shall we get on with it?"

"Good, I'll lead in from my initial briefing. I was sent for by the Foreign Secretary no less, and given the Kingsman report to read. Apart from that, he made it very clear that it had to remain with the Army Intelligence people. He didn't want MI6, the Foreign Office Intelligence Service, to become involved. He had some misgivings about some of the MI6 people, especially a little coterie that had been at Cambridge and were … what shall we say, unreliable because of a degree of sexual ambiguity and some uncertainty as to where their patriotic duties lay?"

"Well, I don't know any secret service chaps, so I think they can be ruled out so far as I am concerned."

"Glad to hear it. Now then, two of the people you spotted at Tamu airfield appear to have been positively identified as a certain Japanese colonel and a war criminal to boot, and Aung San, the Burmese leader put in by Lord Louis himself. I see they were codenamed Swordfish and Piranha respectively. I won't ask who gave them these names or why, but they sound better than Mr A or Mr B etcetera. I managed to dig out some field intelligence files which include profiles on many people who came to our notice during my time in China on the off chance that they might reveal a clue or two. I'll sift through these and see if there is a pattern that fits the remainder of the Tamu people. Then, if I can turn up a few possibilities, we can perhaps go through them together. That OK?"

"Good plan. In the meantime I'll give some thought to the aeroplanes and the wireless station – see if I can make some sense out of them."

A knock on the door and a couple of mugs of tea appeared. With the door re-locked they kicked off with clean sheets of foolscap, each with a copy of the full Kingsman report. The sheets of paper were quickly covered with notes, spider diagrams and references. They worked in silence except for an occasional muttered query and time off for a walk round the room to stretch stiff muscles. It was after midday when they decided to break for lunch. They numbered and signed their work sheets then placed them in the safe in separate files.

"Come on Rowena, time for a swift half before lunch. I'm ready, I don't know about you."

★★★

The smell of burning wood from log fires hung on the still air. The wind had dropped and it had stopped snowing. From a viewpoint a hundred yards from the house Harding looked out over the wild moors covered in grey-white snow to the black crags shouldering out of hillsides. There had been no further snowfall overnight but the air was at reading zero. He contrasted this cold northern country with the heat of India and the steaming Burma jungle. He had been unable to contact Laura to let her know he was being sent back to the UK. He was under strict orders to maintain absolute secrecy about his movements and not even to communicate with his family.

He turned at the sound of snow-crunching footsteps. It was Rowena. She had taken the lunch break opportunity to maintain her appearance. She stood close to shield herself from the icy wind, close enough to give Harding a smell of what he judged to be an exclusive toilet soap. She looked up at him. "Come on soldier, let's get on with it. We have a long way to go. I don't know how you are doing but I'm still casting around for clues."

"I've got a bit of groundwork done, I reckon. I want to approach it from the geographical angle, build up a framework using the wireless aerial as a guide, which might link up with identifying those aircraft that I saw and which the RAF photographed. It's going to mean more guesses than probabilities but I can only try. I want to see if I can drum up a map of the region. See you inside."

★★★

The corporal did well. He produced a political map of South East Asia and a sheet of clear talc overlay on which to mark up significant locations. They worked steadily until tea time when they went off to enjoy tea and toast with Gentlemen's Relish. Harding had never before come across this standard spread widely used in officer's messes world-wide. It was a bit sharp and according to the jar label was rather reliant on anchovies to produce its special flavour. After that refresher they returned to work and by six o'clock Harding was satisfied he had produced a reasonable battle plan and was ready to run with it.

"Come on missee. Time go home, likee flied lice for supper?"

Rowena looked up from the mass of paper spread over the blanket and pressed her fingers against her forehead.

"I like your accent. I hunnerstan. Chop-chop, let's bugger off then. See you at dinner."

★★★

"Can I get you a drink, brandy or something. It's been a long day and I think a noggin or two is indicated."

The after-dinner atmosphere of restrained consideration in the ante-room did not appeal to Harding. He was more comfortable with the open behaviour of the Sergeant's Mess when a chap could settle down for the evening with a few mates and get gently pissed if one felt like it. He recognised that he was in rather odd company here with service and civilian personnel from varying branches all trying to be at one, but were held in check by the unusual business they were engaged in.

Rowena's voice broke into his thoughts. "Good idea, a G and T for me please. We ain't got no lemons, I expect, but I do insist on fresh ice."

Harding poured a measure of gin, fizzed in some tonic water and a lump of ice. He fixed himself a whisky, again with ice, and joined her near the fire.

By nine o'clock Harding and Rowena were the only two left. Everyone else had either gone to bed or back to work. He was happy to listen as she filled in more of her background. As well as Chungking she had served in Moscow during her three and a half year tour abroad. She had opted for an extended service commission to give her the opportunity to study on an outside bursary for a PhD, with her army pay helping to finance her plan. She was single and her parents were now living in Norfolk with her younger sister who helped them run an expanding market garden enterprise. After a pretty awful war, when her father had been interned in a Jap prison camp, he had retired from the Diplomatic Service. Her mother had been home looking after her sick mother when the Far East war began and had avoided becoming a guest of the Japanese Imperial Army.

Chapter 36

Harding started off before breakfast to get his map set up and marked with an overlay to show a range plot of the two aircraft seen dropping in at Tamu. He first re-arranged the two six-foot tables to form a single six-foot square work surface on which he laid the map. After covering it with the transparent talc sheet he described four concentric circles measured from Tamu in Chinagraph pencil to indicate the ranges and maximum point-to-point flights of both a Junkers 52 and a Dakota.

The inner circle, drawn to a scale radius of six hundred miles showed the inward and outward flight journey the Junkers 52 could make carrying a full load of fuel. The second circle at a scale distance of twelve hundred miles showed its maximum flight. He marked both circles in red then calculated the distances for the Dakota at sixteen hundred miles and three thousand, two hundred miles respectively and marked them in blue. These figures had been extracted from the specifications of World War Two aircraft he had picked up in Calcutta, but he was prepared to mark down the distances he had calculated in the knowledge that ranges could vary considerably in the extreme flying conditions experienced over tropical and mountainous regions.

When Rowena joined him they set to work on first analysing the presence of the Junkers 52. Bearing in mind that it was fairly certain to have been crewed by Russians and that the log had been made out in Russian, they agreed that the aircraft could almost certainly have set course from a base in the Soviet Union. The orientation of the wireless aerial, aimed in the direction of Moscow, gave further support to that theory. With all these factors demanding attention they set about plotting a theoretical flight plan into Soviet territory.

Given the theoretical maximum flight distance of twelve hundred miles requiring a full load of fuel at take-off, it would have to cruise at or near its ceiling of nineteen thousand feet to overfly even the lower regions of the Himalayas that lay beyond Indian air space. With accurate navigation and careful fuel usage, Harding estimated it would have to put down in Tibet, either at Gartok or at Rutog one hundred miles further and at the absolute limit of its range. He was ignorant of what, if any, flight support there may be at either location, but given that they obviously started out for Tamu from somewhere in Russia, it was a fair bet the flight plan would have been carefully surveyed. It was now clear that the pair of draught elephants at Tamu were employed to conserve fuel by hauling the aircraft about when on the ground.

He discussed his analysis with Rowena who agreed that, lacking any evidence to the contrary they must draw the conclusion that there was a Russian connection with the goings-on at Tamu. But the questions remaining to be answered were with what aim and how that aim was being underpinned.

"Let's add the tall European fellow to our clue list. You remember, the one I codenamed Shark. I reckon we have to identify him before we can chase up the Russian connection."

Rowena dug Harding in the ribs. "So, it was you who allocated the codenames. Aren't you a clever sergeant? It must have an obvious link to fish life but I'm terribly puzzled as to what it could be. Perhaps you'll tell me when you divulge your Christian name?"

"In the fullness of time all will be revealed, but for now let's put this lot in the pending tray and fall out for lunch. Then, suitably re-fuelled, we'll have a look at the Dakota connection."

★★★

Rowena returned from lunch to find Harding completing some

notes he had made from his survey of the operating ranges of the Dakota.

"You are going to tell me you've got the Dakota connection solved," she said.

"Afraid not. In good running order and given fair weather, this aeroplane has an operating range of three thousand, two hundred miles, sixteen hundred out and sixteen hundred back. The blue circle on my map takes in the whole of Burma, Siam, Malaya and Singapore. Add to that the French Indo-China territories of Laos, Cambodia and Vietnam, plus a slice of the Dutch interest of Sumatra, and we have a pretty big area to play in."

"What about India and, of course, China? Don't these deserve a look at?"

"Well, those possibilities can't be ruled out, but the RAF has got India well covered, so I don't think any stray aeroplanes could operate over there without being quickly picked up. So far as China is concerned perhaps you could raise an idea or two."

She tapped her teeth with a pencil, giving the proposition some thought then said, "I think things will be in a bit of a froth in that country just now and liable to get worse if my information is correct. Although Chiang Kai-shek is still running the place with his Nationalist government, a certain chappie called Mao Tse-tung is busy trying to gain support for his Communist movement. It's fairly strong in the north and liable to spread a bit rapid if he is getting help from Moscow, which is not beyond the bounds of possibility."

"OK then, we'll strike those two from our list. That still leaves us with a lot of ground to cover. Let's run over what we've got so far. One, a Dakota widely used by both the Americans and the Brits during the war, the Allied markings of a star and white bands painted out and new lettering – CAT – stuck on. Two, I'm certain American crew; you know, the cigars and baseball cap bit, so there is a fairly strong chance that some organisation connected with the 'land of the free' should be considered."

"So much for the management. Now, what about the two

characters who emerged from it when it landed. Let's concentrate on seeing who they could be or where they sprang from. I'm not too sure about the one dressed in jungle green with four red stars in his cap and sporting a Sten gun. I'll leave you to dig around about him … I've got access to files of many personalities who played a part in the war in South East Asia so he might be on record there. About the other one, the one you labelled Barracuda and wearing a black pyjama suit or *samfoo* as you described it, I think I can put a name to him. Just one point you can help me with. Are you certain he was kitted up with a US army issue web belt?"

"A month's pay on it, and he was carrying a pistol, but I couldn't see what it was from my hide. Is that important?"

"Yes, very. I'll leave you to get on with your detective work. I'm off to pull out one of my profile folders. See you later?"

Chapter 37

"Never mind the post prandial, I'll join you in your room and we can have a go at your Black Label while I fill you in on our friend Mr Barracuda. I've got a super match for him. I am pretty sure we are looking at a Vietnamese called Ho Chi Min and he is a confirmed friend of our Russian maties. Here goes: he was born in 1890, that puts him at about fifty-six now. Does that age seem to fit?"

"These Orientals are a bit difficult to pin down as regards age but I'm certain he's past the first flush of youth … yes, I suppose middle age is a fair bet … bash on then."

"Right, it seems he was involved in forming the Indo-China Communist Party in 1930 and later initiated a guerrilla campaign against his French colonial masters until it was put on ice with the arrival of the Japanese in his homeland. Don't forget, the Japs invaded that region after the French surrendered and formed the Vichy administration, friendly to the Axis powers, so they entered French Indo-China on friendly terms. This made no difference to Ho Chi Min who was intent on getting all foreigners out of his country, so he went off to China to whip up some support from his underground Communist friends for his resistance movement. This was not a good idea because when Chiang Kai-shek's intelligence people heard about him they picked him up and slung him in jail."

"Funny lot, bit difficult to work out who was on whose side and when during the war. Here we have a chap who is an enemy of the Japanese trying to drum up help to continue his resistance campaign and he gets himself locked up. Anyhow, carry on, you've got my full attention."

"Some time in '42 the Americans overcame Chiang Kai-shek's prejudice and gained Ho's release. In spite of his Communist reputation they trained him in wireless operating and intelligence-seeking techniques and let him loose in his own backyard to work for the good old US of A. Smart thinking eh?"

"As I've already said, war's a bloody complicated business when it comes to sorting out which side one is batting for. Anything else on this chap?"

"Oh yes, there's lots yet. It's a pity you didn't know the codename the Americans gave him, might have saved your creative thinking … it was Lucius. How about that? Sounds a lot nicer than Barracuda."

"I still prefer Barracuda, but continue please."

"What really put me on track was the US army issue web belt and the pistol which I'll bet was a Colt automatic. Given that my line of logic is accurate it could give us a lead in to the identity of the Dakota aircraft on which Ho Chi Min and his pal flew into Tamu."

"Good, press on then."

"Back in '37 Chiang Kai-shek's wife, no shrinking violet in Chinese politics, was instrumental in hiring an American to set up an effective Chinese air force. His name was Lee Chenault, later to be promoted to the rank of brigadier and Commanding General of the 14th US Air Force operating from bases in China during the war. Anyhow, to return to the Mrs Chiang Kai-shek initiative, Chenault recruited aviators from various sources and formed what came to be known as the Flying Tigers."

"Yes I've heard of that lot, a sort of private army. Think I saw film of them shooting down Jap aeroplanes over Manchuria or somewhere like that. Very intrepid … blazing guns and burning aeroplanes. Thought it was just another Hollywood blood and guts job."

"Well, before Pearl Harbour, at the beginning of '41 when the Japs were giving the Chinese a good going over, formal authority was given by Washington for Lee Chenault to form the American

Volunteer Group using American aeroplanes and American pilots backed, I suppose, by American funds into the bargain."

"Makes one wonder just how much warning the Americans had about Pearl Harbour if they already had a military, and no doubt an intelligence, presence, so close to the Imperial Japanese war machine for up to four years before that fiasco."

"Yes, doesn't it? You are going to enjoy the next bit. When the Americans eventually set up shop in China in support of Chiang Kai-shek and as a base to pursue the war closer to the Japanese homeland, the Flying Tigers became an official element of the US Army Air Force. That was in the middle of '42, at the same time as the Americans obtained Ho Chi Min's release from chokey and recruited him into their intelligence network. Ho Chi Min had long been an admirer of Lee Chenault who it is thought was the prime mover in getting him to co-operate with the Americans. Before taking up his duties with the Americans, Ho Chi Min went to see Lee Chenault and asked him to give him some Colt automatic pistols which he could dish out to some of his chums who were to form part of his spying operation. He was issued with six and to further authenticate his role as an American agent, Chenault also gave him a signed photograph of himself. Thus equipped, Ho Chi Min, alias Lucius, alias Barracuda, set about his pro-American duties in Vietnam."

"If all this wasn't so outlandish, I'd swear it was fiction."

"There, I promised you'd enjoy it. Another tot of your Black Label and I'm off to bed. I reckon we've done a good day's work and put some overtime in as well."

"Good. Now how about this for intelligence work? The corporal tells me he has received special word the village pub has got a supply of York ham and that ham, egg and chips is on the menu tomorrow night, but only for special customers and to be served in the back room. I reckon a plateful of that and a couple of pints of Tetley's Bitter would go down extremely well. Like to join me? The Utility is leaving at seven."

"It's a date. Goodnight Harding."

Chapter 38

"Good morning, Junior Commander, Ma'am," said Harding. "No hangover from your ham and eggs? Did me the world of good – almost forgotten what decent fare tasted like. The beer was not bad either. Anything else on friend Lucius? I'm beginning to feel he's a lifelong acquaintance with all the griff you've given me."

"Yes, there's more to come yet. I am sure that he's still taking a very active role in the politics of South East Asia with or without the connivance of the United States. Once we've found out who that Dakota belongs to we will be striking out into some murky waters."

"Well, from carrying out a simple surveillance job in Assam in connection with a few layabout deserters, this has certainly developed, in theory at least, if not in practice. Do I see some letters in your hand?"

"Yes, one each. Glad someone remembers us."

Harding noticed re-addressing endorsements on the envelope from India and London before it reached his hands. It had been posted at a British Air Forces of Occupation Post Office in Germany some eight days earlier. He read it through then said, "How about this, that sighting of a Junkers 52 at Tamu was almost certainly Russian and officially Russian at that. I made an off-the-record enquiry with a mate of mine serving at RAF Gatow in Berlin. He hears on the grapevine that the Russians made off with hundreds of aeroplanes when the Germans packed in. Fighters and bombers were sent for scrap but they hung on to transport and light communication aircraft like the Storsch for instance. They even asked the Americans to let them loose on the BMW factory in

Bavaria so they could stock up on power units and spares. Now if we add that little snippet of information to what we have already got on the Tamu log book, the type of helmets the crew had and that they kept apart from the Dakota crew, we have just about established a firm Russian link. This leads us on to the tall chap, who I'd like to bet is a Russian agent but what's his nationality? Could he be Russian, American or even British?"

"I have an idea how we can maybe find out, but more about that later. I think I would like to chase up this Dakota business, so I'm going to have a word with one of the Yanks who are working here. I might just be able to get a lead in to a bit of inside info if I mention Chennault ... just in passing, you understand."

Harding walked over to the window and looked out, mentally comparing the frozen landscape with its bare trees and grey sky with the humidity and heat of teeming, noisy Calcutta or the steaming, jungle-clad hills of the Assam/Burma region. And Laura, back at Erskine-Jalpai, trying with Julia to hold the estate business together. Wonder if she often thought of him or that night in the garden bungalow. He hadn't seen her since....

He turned to Rowena. "We've still got a lot of work to do to get this stuff done with. Any idea how long it's going to take?"

"You're not in a hurry to get back to India, are you? What's the present tour there for a regular soldier? Seven years or something a bit primitive? The army hasn't moved on much since the days of Wellington, has it? Don't tell me you've got a thing going with ... now, what's her name, Mrs Erskine."

"No I haven't. As I have already said, I met her by accident, then a couple of times in Calcutta when I had to go there to deliver my recce report which involved me in this caper. I expect I'll have to return to that jewel of the Empire, but I can't see anyone staying out there long with all that civil unrest boiling up. We'll soon be handing over to Ghandi and his mates."

"Bugger India and the Empire. It's you I'm asking about. Look, we've been working together for over a week, we've had a few drinks together, oh, and don't forget the ham and eggs social evening so … I thought … oh, forget it. Look, I'll have a friendly word in my Yank's ear and see if I can get him to spill a few beans."

"Yes, I think you should. Let me know how he reacts. Don't want you to endanger the special relationship with our transatlantic cousins."

★★★

"I have now established that there is a definite link with our American allies regarding this mystery Dakota and I reckon that except for Shark we have just about finished our analysis. I've made some notes so I'll read from those."

"So your Yank contact came up with the goods, did he?"

"Not exactly, but he did put me on track to chase some info from our military attaché's Washington station. You see, I just couldn't raise such a sensitive matter with them unless I had a bit of evidence to validate my enquiry. The Yank provided this snippet of evidence when I mentioned Lee Chennault to him. He was more than happy to go on about the exploits of a fellow countryman going to the aid of a beleaguered country with or without official authority."

"How did you get in touch with your Washington friends without breaching security? Telephone lines are a bit open, you know."

"I got permission from my chief in the War Office to use the secure line which is available from the Commandant's office … anyhow, listen to this, it's absolutely exquisite."

"Test me … I'll make some notes as you go along that might help glue the whole business together."

"Good thinking. Well, the story goes like this. We have already established the special connection between Chennault and the Chinese Nationalist Government which extended right up to the end of the war, but it starts all over again, when he becomes involved in ferrying relief supplies to the areas of China which had been affected by the Communist revolution led by Mao Tse-tung.

These supplies were provided by the United Nations to help relieve civilian hardship. It seems they were piling up in dockside warehouses and, without any sort of efficient transport system to move them to where they were urgently needed, just lay there festering. Well, along came our intrepid aviator and founded an airline which was quickly licensed by the Nationalist Government and named CNRRA, Chinese Nationalist Relief and Rehabilitation Administration, a company name to give it a level of esteem linked with UNRRA, the United Nations relief organisation. CNRRA was later shortened to CAT, China Air Transport."

"Small old world, isn't it? So that's who our Tamu Dakota was operated by. So there is a link with America after all and I'd lay money on it that Washington was well in the picture regarding the doings of one of its late generals."

"Indeed. The aircraft you saw at Tamu must have barely got its paint dry because the name CAT appears on the founding document registered in Shanghai only last October and bears the signatures of Lee Chennault and a certain Mr Whitling Willaur, whoever he may be. According to my information they now have a fleet of almost twenty cargo aircraft, Dakotas and Curtiss Commandos supposedly bought in from war surplus. I'm told the airline will take on anyone with a pilot's licence who can put up with servicing their own 'planes and working under impossible conditions in and out of primitive airstrips with no search and rescue back-up. Now it's a racing certainty that Chennault and his partner didn't have the cash to buy these 'planes, fund spares and fuel and pay the pilots into the bargain. I know the Chinese Nationalists are just about broke so where do you think the money is coming from?"

"Could be Moscow, but if that was the case the Reds would be running the firm themselves and not relying on ex-US Army Air Force generals. That only leaves the Americans. Their people, according to the founding document, will be running the show and bearing in mind that I identified the crew at Tamu as almost certainly Americans, what is there left to say?"

"It was hinted that the Office of Strategic Services has a connection with the enterprise."

"Is that so? Well, I've heard about this lot, a bit like our Special Operations Executive, an undercover sabotage and resistance set-up. Probably the same people who recruited Ho Chi Min to their flock during the Japanese occupation of Vietnam."

"No doubt in my mind. I happen to know that the OSS was formed in 1942 and trained by the British Intelligence Service at a school set up in Canada. Prior to that, the only sort of external affairs intelligence system the American Government operated was set up to provide commercial information dealing with finance houses, law firms and international companies. So, if a secret intelligence organisation is connected with this CAT Airline, then the means are available to transfer government funds to any sort of clandestine operation without being subject to the normal regulations of detailed audit and accountability, as well as existing outside the normal forms of democratic control and direction. A wide open job, eh? I have been promised even more revelations from my Washington source because my enquiry has set something of a ball rolling there."

"We are making progress, aren't we? There is only Shark and Marlin to track down. Then we can call it a day, I hope. Got any plans to ferret these two out?"

"Yes, as a matter of fact I have. How do you fancy a couple of days in Cambridge?"

"Cambridge? Who would want to go there at this time of the year? Hardly punting weather and just think of that bloody icy wind blowing across the fens straight from Siberia via Germany and Holland."

"You might be surprised at what I have in mind. When I was briefed by the Foreign Secretary about Kingsman, I naturally asked why he wanted Army Intelligence to do it rather than his own intelligence people – MI6."

"Funny you mention that. The same thought occurred to me when I delivered my report to my bosses in Calcutta."

"It seems the Foreign Sec doesn't entirely trust them in certain areas of intelligence. He is in possession of information that some people employed in the FO have Communist affinities, even to the extent of passing on intelligence summaries to Moscow during the war. Some MI6 agents stationed in the Middle East had unofficial contacts with the Russian Secret Service, the NKVD, probably in Turkey, a hot bed of international intrigue where, I understand, both friends and enemies dined in the same restaurants. The Foreign Sec even went so far as to tell me that the common denominator in this double game was Cambridge University, where a few practising homosexuals formed the 'Apostles', a group of intellectuals dedicated to the theories of Russian Communism."

"I thought that sort of thing was a criminal offence. How, I wonder, did they manage to get away with it … both activities I mean, spying and the other."

"No idea, but they did, it seems. I, perhaps like you, am more at home with army intelligence, fairly uncomplicated principles where one is directly responsible for harvesting information about the military potential of both friendly and not so friendly nations and with battlefield intelligence critical to the forming of operational plans. On the other hand, our secret intelligence services work directly for their political masters and play the political game of finesse, bluff and double bluff to confuse another country's secret intelligence service according to what appears to be a set of rules observed by both sides. It would be reasonable to assume that sex, both normal and different, are devices frequently used to encourage loyalty, if you see what I am getting at. We were, of course, warned of these devices when posted to Military Attaché sections in overseas capitals where one came into social contact with any number of spies often posing as trade delegations or technical advisors."

"Very interesting, but what about this Cambridge jolly then? How about giving me time to rustle up some civvy clothing, overcoat at least and a couple of shirts. I have been promised some clothing coupons from the special supply held by the Commandant for people who are required to work out of uniform, so I thought I'd take myself over to Halifax and get fixed up."

Chapter 39

Harding slung his holdall and Rowena's weekend case up onto the luggage rack and settled down in a corner of the compartment with his feet on the heating pipes. The non-corridor carriage of pre-First World War manufacture was divided into separate compartments, with each compartment seating about five or six passengers each side. The floor was wet with melting snow brought in from the platforms and the smell of stale tobacco smoke, soot and damp clung to the threadbare plum coloured moquette upholstery. Faded sepia prints of northern holiday resorts, framed and screwed to the compartment walls, served to attract the gaze of passengers who had not equipped themselves with newspapers or other reading matter before boarding. The train had probably been running since early morning as a workmen's special with the heating system operating at its optimum temperature of just better than lukewarm. Engine drivers were well briefed to conserve fuel and provide motive power rather than consider passengers' comfort.

Harding looked out on a cold grey landscape as it rattled past the carriage window to the rhythm of wheels, the sound rising and falling as the train steamed under farm-track bridges and across towering viaducts, a feature of high Pennine railways. The rattle of porters' carts, the banging of carriage doors and the shriek of whistles from engines and guards signalled arrival at and departure from branch-line stations.

As the train made a stop-start approach to Leeds City station, Harding watched lines of coal trains with empty trucks waiting the signal to move out to pit heads and load up. The station was very busy with passenger movement but it was tired and drab looking after serving the nation's needs during a very demanding war.

"Over the footbridge, change at Peterborough. Train due out in ten minutes." The porter looked as tired and drab as his railway.

Harding escorted his companion to a First Class saloon carriage furnished with back-to-back seating, tables and starched headrest covers. White jacketed stewards were taking orders for late breakfast or morning refreshment.

"Sorry about this, I'm afraid it's where we split up, because there is First Class on this part of the journey and being an officer I have been issued with a First Class travel warrant so I'm stuck with it. If you feel bad about it I'll gladly join you in your grade with the poor and struggling masses."

He responded to her laughing sarcasm with a wry smile and shrugged his shoulders. "Don't worry about me, Ma'am. Enjoy it whilst you can. See you at Peterborough." A half salute, a mock bow and he withdrew.

The final part of the journey into Cambridge found them sharing a compartment in a single class train again. It carried the same dismal smell as its Yorkshire counterpart, the same plum coloured upholstery but the framed prints were different – Yarmouth and Lowestoft instead of Scarborough and Bridlington. The countryside looked even bleaker as they trundled out from Peterborough with mile upon mile of flatlands, frozen dykes and isolated farm buildings. Work gangs were trying to prise frozen vegetables from the ice-bound soil to help the nation's food supply. It was late afternoon with fading light as the train pulled into Cambridge.

Harding had booked the hotel from the telephone number he found in an old AA motorist's handbook he discovered at Moorside Hall. He was relieved to see it looked tidy enough from the outside and was not disappointed with the enthusiastic welcome they received inside. After signing the register their bags were taken up to their respective rooms, whilst they were given tea with toast and jam served in front of a blazing fire in the resident's lounge.

"Shame we couldn't be incarcerated in this place instead of that gloomy mansion in Yorkshire."

Rowena gave him a soft smile. "Yes, nice and private too … no odds and sods wandering about. Hope the rooms are as welcoming."

"Twos up on that and let's hope the food is on the ball. Could manage a steak if there's half a chance of it appearing on the menu. I've just about had enough of Spam, corned beef and powdered potato. We can hardly go tramping around the university areas tonight, so I vote we wait until the morning to see what we can dig up about the educated classes of the nineteen-thirties. Hope you are more familiar with the local geography than I am. Although I spent a bit of time out in the countryside in '43 when we were in the business of setting up phantom divisions into fooling the Germans that East Anglia was designated as the jumping off point for the invasion of Europe, I haven't a clue about Cambridge itself."

"Don't worry about finding our way around. One university is much like any other with porter's lodges, halls of residence and libraries. If you are familiar with the culture we shouldn't have much trouble. Although it's officially vacation time I think some colleges will have students in residence who are stuck here because of travel difficulties. I'm informed there is plenty of hot water so I'm off for a soak. See you at dinner."

★★★

Of the dozen or so tables in the dining room, only four were laid for dinner. Their hostess showed them to a table near the fire. Even if she thought they were out to enjoy some snatched moments, she did not betray her thoughts. The war had changed many things and she knew well enough that many Smith or Brown couples did not share the same names on their identity cards. But these two were different – they had booked separate rooms.

They dined well enough on sweet white fish landed probably at Lowestoft, followed by lamb chops and rounded off with home-made treacle sponge pudding and custard, all accompanied by a bottle of French white. Coffee and brandy nicely lubricated the remainder of the evening as they relaxed to enjoy each other's company.

Rowena, still curious about Harding's private life, ventured, "We don't know a lot about each other's previous history except for what I told you about my early days in China and what you disclosed about your service activities," she said. "Do you have any skeletons in your cupboard? I mean anything a friend should be aware of?"

"Nothing sinister or very personal as far as I can remember," Harding responded. "In fact, I think I've led a very sheltered existence. I suppose my army service has taken up most of my later teenage years, leaving me with little opportunity to explore many possibilities. But for the war I might have been well on my way to gaining an architectural qualification and even contemplating marriage. As it turned out, the army broadened my outlook, offered a lot of excitement and not wishing to put it all at risk, I decided to take on a regular engagement. So, there it is, an abbreviated history. How about you?"

"University and a decent all-round degree which doesn't pin me down to any specific discipline, and a future that doesn't yet include marriage."

Harding felt that events were moving gently along without any effort on his part. They were sitting close together on a sofa near the now dying fire. He invited her to have another brandy but she declined. "No thanks, I already feel dangerously sloshed. Another of those will put me out, then some kind soul will have to put me to bed ... and that would never do."

She cupped his chin to turn his face towards her and kissed him. "Come on, Sergeant ... don't want to spoil your evening ... or mine for that matter."

He walked her to the stairs and up to the bedrooms. She took his hand and steered him to her room.

He ran the zip down from neck to waist and slid her dress down over her shoulders and onto the carpet. She was wearing a white silk slip. She gave a little twirl, lifting her slip to reveal a bare bottom and closed up to embrace him, forming her body against him as he eased her backwards to the bed. She sat up to remove her slip and brassière as he tore off his shirt, trousers and underpants. She moaned with desire as he leaned over to kiss her breast and abdomen and lifted her body to his touch as she pulled his head back to kiss her hardened nipples.

"Your turn now," she whispered as she rolled him onto his back to caress him with her tongue.

"Are you sure you want to?" he asked.

"Stop now and I'll report you for leading a girl on then falling at the last fence," she said.

★★★

Rowena was happy and relaxed as she walked with him through the fresh overnight snowfall. She glanced up at Harding, gave him a mischievous wink and closed up to him. They stopped to admire the soaring majesty of King's College Chapel.

"Where light and shade repose, where music dwells."

"What's that all about?" Harding asked.

"Only recalling a bit of a sonnet Wordsworth wrote in praise of the chapel. He did write about things other than daffodils, you know."

"Alright, Miss Smarty Pants, 'Upon Westminster Bridge' didn't refer to daffodils either. Don't go on any further about the fellow – that's about as far as my poetic memories go."

"Before we end this literary discussion, I'd like you to know that I think I have worked out the source and reasoning behind the codenames you gave our Tamu air landing chums. If I said you were inspired by Chesterton's 'When fishes flew ...' etcetera, would I be on target?"

"If I said you were nearer the mark than a certain Indian Army officer I know, would that satisfy you?"

"OK, let's get cracking on this Apostles lark. Trinity was it? I'll ask at this newsagent's shop. They are usually well clued up about the locality with their delivery rounds."

The newsagent was muffled up in an overcoat, woolly cap and scarf and was crouched behind the counter close to a smelly paraffin stove.

"Do you mean College or Hall? Two different places you know. A lot of folks get the two mixed up."

Harding and Rowena looked at each other trying to work out which would be the best bet. Rowena said, "If you can direct us to both of them we'll know which will be the right one when we get there."

After an assortment of "straight ons," "but don't take that roads" and "just ask theres," they decided to take their chances and proceed with their quest.

Harding said, "When we find the right place we can't just barge in and ask if the Apostles are at home, can we? If they are what we are so far led to believe they are, we might be treated as spies and either reported to Special Branch or simply invited to get lost. I propose you do the asking, just get your charm working and I'll keep my fingers crossed."

"I was told by my brother to look up his old college if ever I found myself in Cambridge. Now here I am and I thought I'd like to see where he wasted his years."

They arrived at the porter's lodge. After a tap at the half-open window, the porter appeared. Rowena explained that she and Harding were taking up her brother's invitation to look up the college and wondered whether they might be able to take a look around.

"Well, miss. It's fairly quiet just now, so I'd be glad to show you how to get to the most interesting places, libraries, common rooms and the like. You might even find a picture of your brother somewhere. There are any number of group photographs hung up, rowing eights, rugby and cricket teams and the like. Famous place for private clubs, it was. When I first got a job here, before I was promoted to porter, that is, I was employed as a servant, making beds and cleaning up, that sort of thing, and bunches of young gentlemen formed all sorts of societies, some academic and some political. You'll find 'em all here. I'll show you to the big library first then you can go on from there. Now I know you are here you'll be alright. If anybody asks any questions just say Mr Kemp sent you, that's me."

They walked through the Great Court pausing at Mr Kemp's behest to admire a fountain of flaking stone, now in frozen lifelessness. Used to supply drinking water when it was first set up back in 1602, Kemp explained. As they entered the library Kemp, warming to his guide mode, told them the building had been designed by Wren and the ornate carvings were the work of Grinling Gibbons. Pointing to a statue of Byron he said in a lowered voice, "Refused by Westminster Abbey, you know … must have been on account of his wild goings-on. Could have been taught a thing or two by some of the young gentlemen I've known. Some right old capers they used to get up to, I can tell you."

Remembering that he had left some tea stewing in a can on the lodge stove, Mr Kemp asked to be excused and left.

The walls were almost covered by the mass of prints, photographs and paintings. They concentrated their search on the photographs, most of them dated in recent years but many going back to Victorian times. An early photograph portraying a group of bewhiskered individuals sporting top hats was in faded sepia and labelled The Society of Apostles. Later photographs bearing the same identity showed young men wearing blazers or full evening dress.

Rowena said, "I think these groups of the nineteen-thirties might yield some information. The Foreign Sec wasn't very specific about the vintage of his Stalinist suspects but if they are now holding down jobs in the Foreign Office or the Security Service they would probably have come down about the mid to late thirties. That's about the time the Russians were gaining a lot of admiration in some quarters for the effectiveness of their five year plan periods."

Harding nodded in agreement and continued to scan photographs with two identity clues in mind: a tall man codenamed Shark and the name Erskine. The possibility of a link between the two had grown in his mind since Laura had told him of her concern at the cheque apparently cashed by her missing husband at the Field Cashier's office in Karachi after Operation Zipper had gone in.

Rowena drew Harding's attention to a glass topped display case that contained a writing by one Henry Sidgwick, a professor of philosophy: 'Absolute candour was the only duty that the tradition of the Society enforced. The greatest subjects were continually debated, but gravity of treatment … was not imposed, though sincerity was'.

She said, "This seems worthy of analysis if we are to get an insight into the way of thinking of these people and the possibility that they could embrace the ideology of a totalitarian regime even to the detriment of our own national security."

"Funny bunch and no mistake. I'm what's often called a simple soldier. Follow orders and get on with it, no time to become mixed up in political debate even though our masters are politicians, but that's just the way things are. If soldiers betrayed their country they would be lined up against a wall and shot. Damned if I know why the same shouldn't apply to government officials even if they do sprout from the intellectual classes."

Rowena shrugged her shoulders and edged further along the rows of photographs, eyeing each carefully, taking note of names. "Come and have a look at this one, Mr Harding. Does this picture answer any questions?"

The photograph was dated 1935 and depicted individuals in formal pose – ten seated and ten standing. Harding scanned their features. One man, noticeably taller than the remainder and standing on the right attracted his gaze. His suspicions were confirmed when he read one of the names in the caption … M Erskine.

She stood back whilst Harding digested this revelation. "You had a good idea all the time that it was something like this, didn't you? You realise of course that now we have made a positive identification on Shark, the information will have to be disclosed in our analysis report. Are you going to tell his wife or are you going to leave it to come through official channels? That is, unless they want to keep it under wraps for security purposes."

Harding said, "I have no difficulty with that. Apart from confirming his identity it also supplies the answer to what happened on Operation Zipper. Army records and next of kin like to know for certain where assumed casualties end up."

Rowena said, "I don't think there is anything more to be learned here. If you are agreed, I suggest we go and find some food, then see about the train services for tomorrow. I want to spend another night with you."

Chapter 40

Two messages were awaiting their return from Cambridge. One, a signal to be decoded, carried the sender's call sign JAJA. It was from Troopers, War Office. The second was a letter contained within a sealed inner envelope and franked with a Top Secret stamp. When the signal had been decoded using One Time Pad, a system which, being non-repetitive, was virtually unbreakable, it advised Taylor to look up the profile on a certain Chin Peng, a Chinese Malayan who had led a Chinese Communist guerrilla force in the Malay jungle from 1942 through to the end of the war.

They retreated to their task room after dinner and set to work on the Chin Peng file which they eventually rooted out from a file marked Force 136. Rowena had no idea what Force 136 represented until Harding told her it was Special Operations, which as part of its role worked undercover in the Malay jungle after the fall of Singapore. Some elements of Force 136 had maintained communications links with HQ South East Asia Command in Ceylon to call in air drops and keep sabotage groups supplied.

Harding was pleased that all the main players he had spotted at Tamu had been identified when it seemed fairly certain that Marlin had now emerged as Chin Peng. The profile on Chin Peng was rather thin. He had been highly regarded by Spencer Chapman, the British officer who had founded Force 136 as a fine guerrilla leader. He had joined the Communist Party at the age of eighteen and although starting out from poor beginnings was said to be fluent in six languages. That he was a member of the Communist Party was of little importance during the war when the common enemy was Japan. But it was also well understood that his primary aim was, like other Communist Party activists in the region, to drive out their colonial masters secure in the belief that the once powerful British, French and Dutch, who had been humiliated by the Japanese Imperial Forces, were not quite so invincible as had been thought. It was known that the bulk of arms and ammunition supplied during hostilities had simply gone underground to be brought out once a credible revolutionary force could be brought together to free Malaya.

They turned to the Top Secret letter after they had drafted the identity report on Marlin to find it was from the British Military Attaché's Office in Washington. It expanded on previous information unearthed on the CAT airline and described its unconfirmed sphere of activities. After they each read it through, they added the new information to their draft report.

"This is absolutely priceless," burst out Rowena. "This Chennault character puts together a bush operation to support the Chinese Nationalist Government against Mao Tse-tung's Communists and turns it into a revenue earning business, flying arms, ammunition, food, livestock and passengers all over South East Asia. It received a multi-million dollar loan from UNRRA for its humanitarian work. But hark to this. It is suspected to be also running as a cover for the CIA and in support of para-military operations in that theatre. Shouldn't be surprised if they are also in the opium running game."

"That just about wraps up this job," said Harding. Here we have a bunch of anti-colonial nationalist leaders sharing Communist tendencies apparently directed by the Russians with, most likely, deniable support provided by the Americans. Nice picture. Wonder if we'll ever find out what our politicians will make of it."

★★★

Rowena showed him the message: KINGSMAN RETURN AND
REPORT

★★★

The following day Harding departed RAF Northolt.

Chapter 41

Rowena watched the Foreign Secretary as he read the report put together by her and Harding. He spoke sporadically to query a point or to emphasise previous suspicions. As she watched him she tried to imagine the life he had led and the events that had taken him to this high office of state. After early days as a farm boy in his native West Country he had spent time as a carter before branching out as a trade union organiser, then as a Labour Member of Parliament in Churchill's War Cabinet where he played a vital role in charge of the nation's manpower. After the Labour election victory of 1945, Attlee, the new Prime Minister, appointed him to his present job right at the very centre of world politics with many urgent problems to settle. Jews were demanding a homeland in Palestine in the face of Arab opposition, their demands reinforced by the Hitler regime of the 'Final Solution'. Greece and Turkey were in danger of falling under the Russian sphere of influence because Britain was finding it increasingly difficult to fund their defence. With Germany broken and most of Europe in ruins, millions of displaced people were crying out for help. But shattered economies, unable to respond to the need for industrial production and the means to purchase even subsistence levels of food, meant eyes were being turned towards America, the only country to come out of the war richer than it was before.

When the minister finished reading he said, "I want to tell you that I think you have done a good job in the time available to you. It is an excellent report, well written and clear, and although I didn't expect you to present a conclusion, I'm glad you did with all the supporting evidence."

"Thank you sir. However, with your permission I would like to add some comments which have no real place in the report but which I think are worth mentioning."

"Go on, please."

"The work which Sergeant Harding produced from his ground recce was invaluable in identifying the personalities and institutions involved. It is almost entirely due to him that we can now put together an appreciation of what is liable to happen in India and South East Asia in the not too distant future. On top of all that he also brought to light the tea estate link with the opium smuggling trail. I understand that the links we uncovered with Russia and America could be a source of diplomatic embarrassment, but it could not be avoided."

"Yes, that's true, but it is well known on both sides that Russia has had its eyes focussed on India ever since the mutiny. Most of the tribal unrest which kept our troops active on the North West Frontier was down to them. The information about the Americans and that private airline came as no surprise either. Roosevelt made it absolutely clear during the war that the Americans were not in the business of restoring colonial rule in that part of the world. They made things deliberately difficult for the French when their forces tried to re-enter French Indo-China after the Japs surrendered."

The minister stopped for a few seconds, then said with a wry chuckle, "That's got our Allies accounted for so you have no need to exercise caution when you refer to them … now would you like to sum up what you make of it all?"

"I appreciate that sir, thank you. I think the conference that Sergeant Harding dropped in on at Tamu was to finalise the arrangements for carrying out a destabilising operation in India with the leading nationalist activists in the region brought together to agree a plot, backed by Russia, to rid India of the British in the hope that if that part of our Eastern Empire goes down, the remainder of our colonial territories plus those of France and Holland, for instance, would also achieve self-government."

"Are you suggesting that there will be an armed revolution or even a series of coups to watch out for?"

"No, I don't believe anything as confrontational as that would take place, not without direct support from Russia and I don't believe Stalin dares risk a confrontation just yet. I do however think there will be Russian Communist elements working to create civil unrest, perhaps based on the Indian Congress passive resistance scheme, plus engineering an attack on local economies through selective opium distribution to further undermine the social structure."

"Correct me if you think I misunderstand, but I thought opium was a soporific or happy mood drug. I don't see how that can excite disorder."

"That's absolutely true. It is a happy mood drug and it's my belief that the opium coming into India is being given as a reward to encourage the hotheads who hit the streets to kill and maim. We have already seen how religious differences can be stimulated to generate civil unrest as experienced in Calcutta last August. And there are large areas of India, the Punjab for instance, where significant minorities of one religion could be in great danger from the majority population of a different religion. Also there are states like Kashmir where the majority, which happens to be Muslim, is ruled by a Hindu Maharajah, a ready-made cause for concern...."

A buzz from the intercom and a voice announced, "There is a very urgent communication from the War Office. Shall I bring it in, Minister?"

The minister slipped Rowena's report under his blotting pad and told Helen to enter.

He opened the double envelope, looked at the signal and passed it over to Rowena who quickly read: CONFIRMED MARLIN IS CHIN PENG.

The minister said, "It seems this signal from SIC Calcutta just about wraps it all up, at least so far as the people seen by Harding at Tamu are concerned. D'you know anything about this Chin Peng fellow?"

Rowena thought her way through this information and glanced at a notepad she took from her briefcase.

"I think this might help, sir. Sergeant Harding reported that he saw two passengers land from the Dakota, the aircraft that was eventually identified as being American, or at least sponsored by the Americans. One of the passengers was Barracuda, the one I identified as being Ho Chi Min, a Vietnamese."

"Yes, making that connection was a smart piece of intelligence work … but go on, you were saying?"

"Prior to this Dakota landing at Tamu, SIC Calcutta received a signal from one of their operatives in Malaya. A local contact had reported seeing a Dakota land at Batu Pahat, an airstrip on the South West coast of Malaya, embark a passenger, and take off immediately heading in a northerly direction. That would put them on course for Burma. These facts hang together well."

"Have you got anything on Chin Peng? Ever hear of him during your time in China?"

"Afraid not, sir. He could be Chinese-Malay though. I understand that the Malayan Communists who were agitating to get the British out of Malaya and the Straits Settlements became an active guerrilla group harassing the Japs during the occupation. They received a huge amount of arms and ammunition from the British and it's a fair bet they would hang on to them and stockpile them in jungle hides ready to carry on with their original mission."

The intercom buzzed again and without waiting for her boss to speak, Helen said in an urgent tone, "Sorry to trouble you, Minister, you are down for a cabinet in ten minutes."

He looked at his pocket watch. "Give the Cabinet Secretary's office a ring and pass on my apologies. I'll be there as soon as I can." Turning to Rowena he said, "Before we close this chat, have you any theories to offer on Colonel Tsuji's input to this business? It seems a bit odd because, apart from Aung San and the INA element, none of the others were ever kindly disposed to the Japanese."

"Well, according to the brief put together by SIC Calcutta, Tsuji was the staff brain behind the invasion of Malaya. It seems he planted Jap agents in the country posing as teachers, geographers, rubber planters and tourists. They provided the Imperial Army with maps of jungle tracks and bridges not recorded on Ordnance Survey maps that enabled them to advance down the peninsula at such an alarming rate."

"Mm, so it seems as if our friends in South East Asia are going to use this fellow's know-how and what remains of his intelligence network to carry out a repeat performance. You've done a remarkable job, thank you, and if you ever see Sergeant Harding again you can tell him from me that he has earned any promotion that is his proper due."

Rowena inclined her head as she felt a blush rising on her cheeks. "Don't think there's any chance of seeing him again, so far as I can see."

Chapter 42

Harding dumped his kit on the mess veranda and wafted away the cloud of red dust kicked up from the wheels of the departing duty truck which had picked him up from the river ferry at Pandu. He called for a drink. "A large one and make sure it's cold. Oh yes, and make it two, one for Sergeant Davies."

He shook hands with Davies, a mess friend and sergeant in the Royal Engineers Movement Control Unit who was already relaxing in the shade provided by the mess building.

Davies said, "Hullo stranger, didn't expect to see you back here. Disappeared a bit sharp, didn't you? Going to tell me where you've been? No, I don't suppose you will, always a bit secretive, your lot … should be called the Royal Corps of Secrets. Cheers."

They both took a deep swig of the ice-cold beer and stretched out on some rattan chairs.

"Well, Harding, me old mucker, it's a good thing you came back today. Another day and you'd have missed me. We've got all the vehicles, tanks, guns and general gear out of Assam and backloaded to the Ordnance Depots ready to be handed over to the Indian Army, or a new Pakistan Army if Jinnah gets his way. Personally I don't give a shit who gets it. Our part of the job's done and I'm off back home. Got to be at the homeward bound transit camp in Deolali by the fifteenth. Red Road in Cal has closed down, so there'll be no hanging about there, spending my hard earned. Cheers … get you another?"

Harding nodded, stretched out further on the long chair and said, "So, what's the score then? I've been travelling non-stop for almost three weeks, buggered around from transit camp to transit camp so I haven't kept up with the local news."

"It's not what's been going on out here, it's what's been going on back home ... Attlee has told 'em straight. These *wallahs* have got to get themselves sorted out and start running their own country ... been dithering about far too long. He's sending Mountbatten to take over from Wavell. He's the boyo to get Nehru and Jinnah moving. Old Ali the canteen *wallah* reckons that if Jinnah don't get his own independent Muslim state, last year's Calcutta riots will seem like a tea party. Pity the poor sods who will be left here to sort that lot out."

Harding slid his empty glass across. "Your turn mate, time for another then it's a shower, dinner and an early night."

"Yes, and if you're still mixed up with that Posts and Telegraph job you'll have to find yourself some civvy digs, if there is such a thing out here. All British troops are out of this part of India during the next couple of weeks. You'll find that the wireless kit you left here has been sent back to Ordnance and there is a packing case for you that came up from Cal last week. I suppose you'll be reporting to the Camp Commandant in the morning, just to let him know you're back on the ration strength. He'll probably brief you about accommodation; suppose he'll recommend a Government Rest House, they're pretty well fixed up. Got pissed in one once and had to stay the night ... not too bad. Ah yes, nearly forgot to tell you. A female with a very cuddly voice telephoned asking for you one evening last week. Said just mention station wagon ... you'd know who it was."

"I hear you. See you at dinner. I'll get myself sorted out then I might put off my early night and take a farewell noggin or two with you. Hope Prem Lal is still around. My kit's in a hell of a state; needs a good seeing to."

The instructions enclosed with the replacement wireless transceiver he found in the packing case were brief: 'One. Portable set issued in event of quick move. Two. No change frequencies and schedules. Three. Continue as before.'

Harding examined the wireless set. He recalled having had an introduction to it during his training. It was a smaller version of the B2 suitcase set much used by the Special Operations Executive for its European operations. With a frequency range of 3.2 to 9 megs it did not have coverage of the higher frequencies he had operated on the 53 set and sticking with the 'edge of atmospherics' strategy to foil eavesdroppers could prove to be a little difficult. It had a mains supply power pack and alternatively could be driven by a 6 volt battery thus fulfilling its portability role.

He planned to give it a go at 1900 hours, the original opening up time and hoped that by loading it into the highest frequency he might be fortunate and raise Calcutta. The note about sticking to the original frequencies was balls, he thought. Whoever originated that instruction was certainly not communications wise. He decided to give Laura a call.

★★★

Three duty operators at the Signal Intelligence Centre were manning shifts on listening watch, tuning over a planned scanning procedure on or about the 9 megs frequency as they had done on a daily basis since they were told that Harding would soon be resuming his up-country mission. At 1905 hours, when Harding was about to stop his unknown call sign transmissions, he received an authenticated reply from Calcutta. He confirmed with them that until further orders he would be working his 1900 hours schedule to commence after two days.

★★★

Laura was pleased to hear from Harding. "Did the trip go well? Pleased to be back?" She stumbled over her questions in her obvious joy at hearing the sound of his voice again.

"My answers are yes and yes. How about coming out to see you tomorrow, that is if it's OK with Julia?"

"Of course it will be OK with Julia." She added with a giggle, "I think she has a soft spot for you. When she learned I'd seen you a couple of times in Cal she was more than interested in discovering how we got on. Hope she doesn't make a pass at you so be on your guard."

"Don't worry about that, there is no chance. See you tomorrow, for *tiffin*, if that's OK with you."

Harding replaced the telephone handset and marshalled his thoughts. There was little doubt in his mind that Mark Erskine and Shark were one and the same but without establishing a direct link he was on shaky ground. The facts were that a Mark Erskine had been a member of the Cambridge Apostles; that during Operation Zipper he had disappeared to apparently cash a cheque with the Field Cashier at Karachi on the other side of the sub-continent; that he had spotted a tall chap at Tamu and from the photograph he had seen at Cambridge, Mark Erskine was tall. But it was still left to prove a positive identification. He remembered that he had seen no photographs of Erskine at Laura's place. That set him wondering. Did Laura wish not to be reminded of him and destroyed any pictures she had of him? He had to get to the bottom of it and fast. Erskine was an important piece in the Kingsman intelligence puzzle and if he was found to be responsible for withholding vital information he would be for the high jump. He knew he had to get the most from this visit to Erskine-Jalpai, even if it meant firing direct questions at both Laura and Julia.

★★★

Harding had been unable to lay his hands on any 6 volt batteries so he improvised a power take-off from his Jeep engine battery. A useful alternative if it became necessary to open up communications where he had no access to a handy mains supply. He cut a quarter-wave open aerial from a length of twisted copper wire which he could sling over a tree branch or, in some circumstances even lay on the ground and aim in the direction of the distant station, both options well tried and proved in close jungle locations. With the new wireless set and its ability to operate under variable field conditions, he felt less isolated than before when he was equipped with his static transmitter and a fixed aerial.

With his new set neatly stowed and well concealed in the back of the Jeep, he felt happy about using the vehicle as 'recreational transport' to visit Laura. After all, he was on duty; trying to discover the final link in the chain to prove that Shark and Mark Erskine were one and the same.

Marcus leapt out from under the veranda steps to greet Harding with an excited bark that alerted Julia to his arrival. She offered her cheek to Harding for a kiss.

"Hope Laura doesn't get jealous … anyhow, she will be glad to see you. She's down at the generator shed trying to get Narayan Rao to come to grips with the generator. It seems he can't quite grasp what the three phase business is all about and he keeps cutting off our domestic supply."

From the sound of raised voices coming from the generator shed, Harding suspected that Laura might be giving the estate manager a rough time.

She turned as Harding announced his arrival. "Hullo again, I'm glad to see you. Can you please explain in simple terms just what this three phase supply system delivers and how it differs from the old Parsons machine?"

Harding was not exactly displeased to see Narayan Rao's puzzled expression and, but for the possibility that any malfunction of the estate's electricity supply would have a detrimental effect on the tea business, he would have left him to stew.

"I'm sorry if I didn't make it too clear when I set it up. However, now I'm here I'll run through it again. Got some paper handy to jot down a few notes? With the old generator you had only sufficient power to either run the processing plant, and even that not at full capacity, or supply the bungalow. Now you have what we might call the equivalent output of three generators. One to feed the plant, one to supply the bungalow and one spare. We can't unhitch the spare, so until such times as it's required, I constructed a resistance field to take care of the unwanted output."

Laura said, "Does that mean that if we need more power at the plant to run extra machinery we have a ready-made supply on tap?"

"Right first time. Now, about this resistance field. I set it up outside because it would have generated a high level of heat, rather like the elements of an electric fire, and pose a danger if left in the shed. I surrounded the network with a protective barbed wire fence. Could be nasty to the touch, in fact it could be lethal to most people."

Narayan Rao said, "At night-time, this field thing glow very red, sometimes it look purple but plantation workers not see burning by day and not know to keep away."

Harding gave him a brief smile. "Yes, I know all that, but the barbed wire should be sufficient warning. If you have a chap handy with a paint-brush have him produce a few signs to hang on the wire. A ziz-zag lightning symbol should do the trick. And remember it is dangerous, so make sure everybody around here knows about it. *Malum*?"

"Yes, Sergeant Sahib, I understand. I go for *khanna* now Memsahib, if that is all."

As Laura and Harding walked along the track to the bungalow he clasped her slim waist. She stopped and pressed her body close to him in a tight embrace and taking his head between her hands she reached up to receive his kiss. She whispered, "I'm so glad you're here … I wasn't sure if I'd ever see you again … and I so much want you."

Before this meeting Harding had been uncertain how she would react. He had not seen her for some time and the affair with Rowena was still vivid in his mind. He tried to dismiss that brief episode as an inevitable outcome, given that they had been thrown together by unusual circumstance and neither had been unfaithful to anyone else.

Before he found the words to respond she said, "Please don't leave me alone and go back to camp tonight. I want you to stay and make love to me. I've missed you terribly. The time we had together in Cal made me certain I'm in love with you. I'm sure Julia won't mind if you stay over … I'm a big girl now," she added in a teasing child voice and held out her left hand. "And see, no wedding ring, I'm really free now."

Once more he could not find the right words. A lost marriage was not, in his sight, an event to be welcomed but in this situation he was pleased for Laura by reason of her crushed expectations of Mark, her well-founded suspicions of the circumstances associated with his disappearance and the now overwhelming evidence to show that he was, most probably, a traitor.

★★★

"I know that Laura is in love with you and I'm sure you are aware of that."

Taken off guard by such a direct statement from Julia, Harding carefully lowered his glass of iced coffee and was about to waffle into a sort of reply when she raised her arm to stay his voice.

"Before you say anything, let me finish what I have to say. She has not had a particularly happy time coming to terms with Mark's disappearance and although she had no obligation … none whatsoever, to remain here, she did, and has been absolutely amazing in the way she has helped me run this place. Without her I would have been looking to sell up, once the tangle of legal ownership had been resolved. I don't know if Mark, having become the main beneficiary after Carter's death, made a new will following his marriage to Laura, but it's going to take a bit of sorting out. I believe before going into active service military personnel are expected to make some form of will but I don't know if he did. Without extensive legal advice, it would need to cover a fairly complicated collection of assets."

"Well, we all had to sign a will before going on active service. For Other Ranks there is a section in the Service and Paybook that has to be filled in, then detached and sent off to the Records Office. I expect that something the same applies to officers but I don't know the details."

"Yes, but enough of that. Let's talk about Laura. As I said, she spent a difficult time after Mark went missing, but she is young and has a very full life in front of her. I don't know if she wants children but I do know, without her saying, that she needs a man just like any healthy young woman would. It's a lonely life here, although we do occasionally go to social events at the Planter's Club where there are lots of men. But they are either already married, some maybe have hot-blooded young Khasi women living in or they are too set in their ways and too gin-sodden to care about anything."

Harding quickly grasped the idea that Julia was of the opinion that he and Laura would make a go of it and was enthusiastic about her perceived reading of the situation. He chose his words carefully.

"Yes, I think I understand what you mean. We did see each other in Cal after a chance meeting in the railway station. We went to the cinema and had a meal at Firpo's then she arranged with the D'Silvas for me to accompany her to a reception and dance at their place, and I'm glad to say I do enjoy her company very much."

Julia gave a knowing smile and said, "I'm sure the Calcutta trip did her the world of good. She came back here in a better frame of mind than when she left. A bit less skittish if I could put it that way."

"I have no idea what's going to happen out here with all this excitement about independence. My future is also a bit uncertain – never know from one day to the next where I might be sent, so you must see that I'm in no position to make any sort of commitment. I get the impression that Laura's marriage is over, though I don't know if she has yet had official notice that she can consider herself a widow."

"Look, I don't want you to run away with the idea that you and her should marry. That's not on my mind, but I do hope that you can enjoy each other's company and … I don't want to cause you any embarrassment, but if you want to stay over for the night I would not be disagreeable to the idea."

Harding replied briefly. "Thanks for the offer but I rather think that depends on Laura, don't you?"

Laura joined them on the veranda which put paid to the

exchange. She apologised for her absence since *tiffin* and explained that she had remembered some correspondence that had to be attended to and reply letters written and posted by Monday morning if they were to be delivered in Calcutta before the end of the week. She asked Harding if he would join her in the study for she had something on which she would appreciate his advice.

The Shark business was still occupying a corner of his mind and as Laura closed the door to the study he asked her if she had heard anything more about the police enquiry at the D'Silva *godown*.

"Not a thing. Seems to have been a false alarm."

"Did anyone follow it up by making enquiries at the estate by any chance?"

"No ... why should they? Tell me, is there anything I should need to know. You seemed a bit cagey about certain events in Cal and now you are going on about the police and this place."

"Sorry, shouldn't go on about things like this. Put it down to my concern for your peace of mind. Now what do you want to talk about?"

"I have some letters here. These and some personal effects were waiting for me when I returned from Cal. They had been sent from Mark's regiment now it appears the authorities are satisfied that, subject to further enquiries, Mark is to be presumed dead. That's why I removed my wedding ring ... get used to the eventual idea of becoming a widow. A few weeks after hearing that Mark had disappeared I removed all his photographs from around the house. Julia wasn't too pleased but she respected my mood, a sorrowing wife and all that. In fact I wasn't a bloody sorrowing wife at all, though I was too scared to admit to myself that I was glad. The marriage was a sham and I had no wish to be reminded of him. If it hadn't been for Julia I would have been away from here like a shot. Anyhow, amongst his personal effects was a photograph that was new to me. This one."

She held up a copy of the photograph that Harding had seen at Cambridge. The Apostles. She pointed out the tall one on the right. "That's Mark."

"Is that what you wanted to show me?"

"Not only that but if you glance at one or two of the letters you'll get a better idea of the sort of man I was married to."

Harding took the bundle of letters. All bearing a London postmark; any private letters from Laura had been removed and destroyed by her, she said. He glanced at a few then handed them back to her. They contained words of affection not usually used between males and veiled references to past activities which seemed to Harding to be less than savoury. They served to confirm the fears that had been previously expressed by Laura. He handed them back without speaking. He could see she was upset at the disclosures in the letters and took her in his arms until the sobs she had been unable to hold back subsided.

"Please do me a big favour," she said. "There is an old oil drum behind the garage we burn rubbish in. Get rid of these for me .... Everything."

There was no doubt in Harding's mind that Army Intelligence had seen the letters and gone through Mark's personal effects. They were not going to give up easily on an officer who had gone missing on an assault operation that had sustained no reported casualties. Added to which, the cheque cashed at Karachi would have been recorded in the painstaking accounting system the army maintained. And now there was the photograph. It was only a matter of time before Shark would be positively identified and then there would be questions asked of him, his role in the affair and his connection with Laura and Erskine-Jalpai. He had to get himself off to Calcutta soonest and complete his Kingsman report as much for Laura's sake as for his own.

Harding saw to it that the letters were reduced to ashes but not the photograph. He needed this to back his story about the very likely identity of Shark and the danger he posed to British national security by his link with Moscow. He slid the photograph inside his shirt and went back to confirm that he had carried out Laura's wishes. She was obviously relieved that she had rid herself of the evidence that Mark was homosexual and she had nothing apart from her private experience to remind her.

When Harding told Julia that he was unable to stay for dinner and by implication, overnight, she expressed her disappointment but told him that he would be welcome to visit at any time without making any prior arrangement. He took Laura aside and, assured of privacy from any of the servants, he told her as much as he could about that part of his job that had brought him up to Assam.

She displayed little interest in the INA part of his story but showed great concern and some fear when he explained about the opium smugglers who had used Erskine-Jalpai and its links with the Assam Bengal Trading Company to transport the stuff to Calcutta and out to a wider network of political activists.

"You really are telling me that these horrible people actually dared trespass on our property to hide this filth in our tea? They must have had some inside help to get it into our samples and … wait, I remember how Narayan Rao clammed up when I got on to him about a delayed consignment. You were there at the time – your first visit, wasn't it?"

"That's right. I didn't say anything to you about the lorry creeping in later that night for the simple reason that lorries entering or leaving your place had nothing to do with me, but later when I picked up the first inkling that opium was on the move, I recalled listening to Narayan Rao being given a rocket by someone with an English accent and one of the sample chests that night being marked with a red spot. Then, when I was in Cal, I went out to the Assam Bengal *godown* just to have a look after listening to Sedley going on about a sample chest that had been found on the railway line at Kushtia Junction. I spotted a little Indian clerk there. He was the spitting image of your estate manager. I'd have bet a week's pay that the pair of 'em are brothers."

"I've no idea about that but I don't suppose it much matters now that all this business is out in the open. At least it will be when you get your latest information back to Cal. Does that mean another trip for you?"

"Yes, it means just that. That's why I couldn't stay for dinner.

Got to get some travel arrangements organised. Sorry."

"Let me know as soon as you return … I want to spend some time with you."

Chapter 43

"Can't keep away from this place, Sergeant? Thought you'd deserted us when you went off to the UK," said Captain Reeder. "Got the impression you might have not been coming back to us but the job in Assam is still going on, according to Sedley. He's the chap who's had someone keeping an eye on things up there. We had to backload your wireless station when we not too sure about you returning. Sorry about the cock-up over the frequency range of the B2 set but I hear you got it sorted out. Good chap."

Captain Reeder, balanced on two legs of his chair with his knees locked up against the desk, gestured with an open palm in the Indian fashion to indicate an open mind or even uncertainty in some interpretations and continued, "Now what brings you back here at such short notice? Must be something pretty important to bring you all the way from Assam."

"Yes, it is, I want to get this business about Shark cleared up. I'm very sure I now know his identity. You remember, the chap I described as tall and possibly English. Well, it's all here in writing. Perhaps I should leave you to read it whilst I have a word with the wireless people about future schedules and frequencies."

★★★

"Well, Harding, I've read through this report and you've done a good job both here and during your time in the UK. However, I say to myself, when did the suspicion of a connection between Shark and the tea estate first dawn on you? Would you care to fully explain, and remember I haven't forgotten about you having a look at some wireless intercepts related to Operation Zipper to which I turned a blind eye. You didn't care to confide in me at that time so, old chap, you're now in the confessional … and make it bloody good for all our sakes."

"Yes, Duncan … I can still call you that, I presume? I have been bothered about this connection but someone else is involved, someone who I'm sure is totally innocent and until a few days ago, completely unaware about any sinister link this person may have with Shark or his activities. When I asked permission to scan the Zipper intercepts it was at that time entirely unconnected with Kingsman. I was trying to help a friend."

"Don't try to bullshit me, old chap. This friend was a female, wasn't it? A female whose husband I now guess went AWOL on Zipper. Am I correct? Before you answer I should remind you that if you have kept anything back that could embarrass the Government or even lead to loss of life, you wouldn't even have the privilege of a court martial. You would be dealt with in a way that would be beyond any legal help."

"Please listen first, then make up your own mind. But I'm not prepared to go quietly. I have made arrangements for my case to be put if I am dropped in the shit. All this started with a fairly routine army intelligence task, a task with which the powers that be thought I was adequately capable of delivering. It was pure chance that I stumbled on a connection that blossomed into a tricky political situation with international implications. Although the Shark identity was central to what turned into Kingsman, the side issue was that this character turned out to be the husband of a woman I met by pure chance. That issue, so far as I'm concerned was, until very recently entirely separate and I stand by that conclusion."

Reeder scanned a few notes he had made and said, "So that's how you saw it. I honestly thought you were in the muddy waters of trying to protect a third party. Sorry about that. But tell me, is anything going on between you and … er, Mrs Erskine?"

"Absolutely nothing which could compromise security. Perhaps I didn't fully explain. We first met when I was returning to Shillong from a meeting with our Naga friends. She was stranded, miles from anywhere with a broken down station wagon. I went to her aid as a good soldier would and saw her back to her place; the Erskine-Jalpai tea estate. It emerged that she had been in the services, HQ 14th Army to be precise, where she met her husband Mark. Since that fellow's disappearance during Zipper, as you are already aware, Laura, I mean Mrs Erskine, was given a premature discharge at the end of hostilities to enable her to help Mark's aunt by marriage, herself a widow, to stay out here and help run the show."

"Yes, fair enough, I think I understand all that. But what about your trip to Cambridge when you ferreted out the Shark connection with the Apostles? Didn't that give you a connection to Erskine-Jalpai? I say, what with Mrs Erskine and then this intelligence female from the War Office – these women keep cropping up, don't they? You seem to have enjoyed more time with, I expect beddable females, in the last few months than I have during the last four years."

"Genuine coincidence and I have nothing further to discuss about the ladies. I think I've told you enough to get me off the hook. I will add that I had no confirmed evidence that Shark and Erskine were one and the same until I saw his photograph at Erskine-Jalpai the other day and that's why I came racing down to Cal."

Harding could not leave without making sure. "If I really am off the hook now I think it's time I got back to normal duties, whatever they may be in these troubled times."

Reeder reached for a manila folder nestling in his pending tray. "Just a couple of admin matters you are to be told about. You will have heard that the Viceroy is being replaced by none other than Lord Louis Mountbatten and I have it on excellent authority that he is going for independence by the summer. If they can't agree on a one nation state then he's going to let them have a two nation model: Pakistan for the Muslims and India for the Hindus. In the interim, that is until the two separate armies get themselves sorted out, Delhi has asked that certain specialist officers and NCOs be asked to volunteer for service with one or the other. As a bonus there is to be a special allowance paid and an entitlement for the award of a commemorative independence medal … shall I put your name down?"

"No, thank you. If they think they can run their own show then good luck to them. But if there is going to be an armed showdown with any stray British caught up on opposite sides then neither I nor any chaps I know would wish to be involved. Is that the lot then?"

"Not quite. It is likely that you will still be required to carry out special missions but just where I am unable to say because I don't know. All this has come down from Delhi and you will be under their orders from the end of the month – twelve days' time. This place is now no longer required. Its job is done and I'm looking forward to going home some day soon."

"That's a shame, just as I was getting used to the set-up. OK, what do I do now? Go back to Shillong and pack my kit and retreat to Delhi or what?"

"Go back to Shillong, yes, but you have then a little job to complete at Tamu … destroy it."

"What?"

"I say again, destroy it … with the special demolition training you received before your pre-invasion job in France, you are just the chap. Orders are that if the fuel dump at Tamu is destroyed that will put the place out of commission and deliver a fair warning to the users of the place that the game is up. We can't go and bomb it, neither can we send in a major force of ground troops to do the job. It has to be a deniable operation and as you know the place better than anyone else you are the chosen one."

"You mean I have to go flogging through that bloody jungle again? I was laid up for a few days after the last job up there and I don't fancy a repeat dose of whatever it was I picked up."

"I thought you might see it that way. You will be assisted this time. A rifle section of Ghurkas – about half a dozen blokes I think, but under the command of a Captain for added weight – will go with you. The Ghurkas have been selected because we can't use Indian troops in a situation where they could be ordered to cross swords with their fellow countrymen in the form of INA. We don't have any British troops available either. They will already be stretched to cover a tactical withdrawal from the country if that course becomes necessary."

"We certainly are a bit thin on the ground, aren't we? OK, press on then. I would like to see this Tamu business put down, seeing I was in at the beginning. Is there going to be an operation order issued?"

"No. It is an entirely covert operation completely deniable as I have already pointed out. The Ghurkas' task is to get you within shouting distance of the airfield and at a time to be agreed between you and their commander they will let loose with thunderflashes and blank ammo at the same time as you blow the fuel dump and anything else that might prove interesting. Having created a state of panic, it's anticipated the airfield occupants will be pretty well disorientated and start running around like headless chickens. At this point the Ghurkas are to arrest anyone who seems to be in charge and deliver them to Sedley's men who will be waiting off site."

"Got all that, Duncan. Now, tell me, what do I blow the fuel dump with?"

Reeder passed him a satchel.

"This bag contains three No. 28 commercial detonators. As you know, they are electrically ignited so you don't have to worry about lighting fuses and that sort of thing. There's also three gun-cotton primers and half a dozen pieces of amanol. That should give you sufficient kit to blow the fuel dump. I suppose you can organise some voltage and wire. The stuff is safely packed but don't drop it. Never know what might happen in this heat."

"I suppose the Ghurka rifle section knows all about this job?"

"They will be properly briefed about the main task. It's up to you to tie up the final details with their commander. His name, let me see … is Emmerson. He will meet you at Mr Ong's place in Imphal at midday on the seventeenth. That will give you a week to get yourself up there. If there is any delay on your part, signal us one word: "WAIT." That will give you a day's grace. Repeat if you have to, but any more than three and the job will be aborted. And, I might add, your excuse will have to be bloody good."

Chapter 44

"My standard omelette please, Mr Ong, and a bottle of Tiger. I expect you're still managing to get some supplies in?"

"You right, I fix omelette and beer."

Further exchanges were curbed by the sound of a vehicle approaching. Harding met Captain Emmerson as he dismounted from his Jeep. He was alone and wearing the Ghurka pattern bush hat. That and a kukri, sheathed and clipped to his web belt, asserted his affinity with that indomitable fighting force.

Harding greeted him. "The plan seems to be working so far. You are Captain Emmerson, I suppose?"

"Bang on. I take it you are Sergeant Harding. Let's have some refreshment first then we'll have an 'O' Group if that's OK with you."

After settling the bill and disengaging themselves from Mr Ong's entreaties to stay for an afternoon of pleasure, they walked across the street to an open area where they felt safe from anyone overhearing.

Harding said, "I'll go through my task first. As you are probably aware, I have done a close recce of the target and word from on high has ordered it to be shut down. Method; blow the fuel dump, it's mostly high-octane aviation spirit and should go up nicely. I am also going to destroy the admin installation, wireless transmitter, stores etcetera. Casualties are to be avoided and that's where your chaps come in. OK so far?"

"Just about. I've got a rifle section plus a couple of drivers. They can fight as well as drive. My job is to accompany you to the airfield driving up a track that will get us close enough to the target without giving the game away. At a predetermined time we open fire with blanks and drop in a few thunderflashes for good measure. This should cause panic and scatter the INA *wallahs*, getting them away from the danger areas before you blow your charges. I'm told to take in any identifiable leaders or other interesting characters; the odds and sods are to be allowed to bugger off into the jungle."

"Roger, that sounds fine. I suggest we tie up the final timing when we hit the start point. Are your chaps OK, I don't see any sign of 'em?"

"Absolutely. I've got them laagered up in an old logging camp about ten miles away. They've got plenty of rations and know how to look after themselves. There's also a dozen civilian police chaps mucking in with 'em. They are under the command of a Chief Superintendent Sedley. I asked him if he wanted to come with me to meet up with you but he declined. Said it wasn't necessary.

★★★

The next morning and with about three hours' sleep under his belt Harding awoke to be greeted by a smiling Ghurka soldier who gave him a tin mug filled with scalding hot tea – strong and sweet.

"Gunfire sir, all new made." Harding swallowed a few mouthfuls and put his boots on. He declined a mess tin of what was on offer for breakfast. He did not feel prepared to risk the effect on his stomach. As the troops and civilian police were having breakfast he took the opportunity to assemble his demolition charges. He put three sets together, each made up with two sticks of amanol bound with insulating tape to a cork shaped gun-cotton primer to receive the detonator and provide the primary explosion. For safety reasons he left the detonators clear until the charges were placed in their final position. Not willing to risk the unpredictability of dry batteries in the heat and humidity of the jungle, he had stripped the ringing generator from an unserviceable field telephone to produce sufficient voltage to fire the detonators. After testing the generator output on fine gauge copper wire to make it glow enough to fire the detonators, he was satisfied it was going to work.

After a final briefing from Captain Emmerson his men mounted their transport and with Harding's Jeep leading, they started out on their thirty mile journey. Harding relaxed in the passenger seat, happy to have Emmerson driving and allowing him to concentrate on the task that lay ahead. As they forced their way along the deteriorating track Harding was picturing Tamu airfield as he had last seen it. He was trying to work out what to do about the elephants and their handler. He didn't want to cause harm to them when the charges were blown as they would certainly take off in a panic. He felt sympathy too for the handler. He was most likely an innocent party and simply in the business of earning a living by hauling aeroplanes up and down the runway. If security at the airfield was as lax as it was last time, he didn't think he'd have much to worry about.

The party arrived at the start point with ninety minutes to go before the planned H-hour of 0530 hours. Ninety minutes in which to march to the airfield, about four hundred yards of fairly reasonable going, place his charges, insert detonators and run cables back to his selected firing position.

Emmerson said he would give Harding one hour to reach the airfield and place his charges. He would then lead his Ghurkas up to their agreed position and at 0530 hours on the dot give the order to open fire.

Harding shouldered his satchel of high explosive and a reel of D3 field telephone cable and began his walk. Alone again in the alien jungle he began to get the jitters. In addition to the risk of attracting the unwelcome attention of the INA and perhaps Shark or any of his more dangerous playmates, there was the constant threat from his hazardous load. He tried to shrug off any worries about the latter on the grounds that he would have no warning and should the worst happen, hard luck – not a lot to be done about it. He directed his thoughts towards achieving a successful outcome to the job in hand.

The track took him to the eastern corner of the airfield close to the admin area. The layout of tents, marquees and bashas were much as he remembered it. The fuel dump had been enlarged but of aircraft there was no sign. He saw the elephants were in their resting place to the rear of the perimeter track. With the need to get the huge animals out of the way, he crawled up to the mahout, pulled his machete from its scabbard and holding the edge up to the fellow's unshaven chin, gently prodded him in his belly. Harding held a finger up to his lips to indicate silence then gestured in the direction of the jungle. "*Joa … bahut jaldi*," he whispered. The startled mahout cringed in fear and when Harding indicated he had to take his elephants with him he quickly unshackled them, urged them into an upright position and hurried them away.

Time was running out and he would have to get a move on if he was to be ready for Emmerson and his men. He set the fuel dump charges first, using two sets twenty feet apart and swamped them with the contents of a drum of aviation spirit to accelerate the destruction. As he completed the connection to the second charge he heard the sound of coughing and spitting coming from the kitchen area. An Indian muffled up in a blanket had emerged from his tent and was heading straight towards him. Harding withdrew into the shadows cast by a stack of jerricans and waited. The Indian approached the stack and reached up to take one. As he turned to take the full weight of the can on his shoulder, he spotted Harding crouched within an arm's length of him. Before he could shout for help Harding hit him across the head with the flat of his machete. He fell to the ground with blood trickling from his ear. Harding bound the wound with a field dressing and cursing the delay, dragged him clear of the fuel dump to a place of safety some two hundred yards away.

A glance at his watch told Harding he had just under fifteen minutes to lay the third charge, wire it up to the first two and be ready for H-hour. He had planned to place this third charge between the stores marquee and the basha which housed the wireless transmitter, but that would have to wait until the camp had cleared.

With one minute to go Harding connected the cable to his generator and waited for the fun to begin.

He watched as a thunderflash with its burning fuse slicing through the air exploded to signal the start of the action. There followed the sharp crackle of rifle fire and the intermittent rattle of bulleted blank from a Bren gun together with more thunderflashes.

Dozens of men, shaken by the battle sounds, swept out of their sleeping quarters and made off into the cover of the jungle. After waiting a few seconds for the panic-stricken crew to clear the area, Harding fired the charges and watched with satisfaction as jerricans and drums, ripped apart by the blasts, spilled their contents to fuel the raging fire-storm. Clouds of oily black smoke spilled into the air, choking the animal tree-dwellers and sending them screaming with fear into the shelter of the deep forest.

The Ghurkas entered the camp area at a trot, grinning at the chaos they had created. Some of their number had grabbed a few prisoners but they were not recognisable to Harding. He still had to destroy the remainder of the camp as ordered by Reeder, but before placing his remaining demolition charge he decided to have a look round to see if there was anything of interest. He noted the wireless kit was of Japanese design and probably salvaged from the retreating Jap army during the British advance in the later stages of the war. Judging by the size of the transmitter he estimated its output to be in the region of about 1,000 watts and easily able to communicate with Moscow using Morse, assuming that was the station it was intended to work. The valves were cold, revealing that it had been closed down overnight. Except for a signal pad and some sheets of scrap paper, there were no logs, code books, call sign or frequency lists to be seen. Even the frequency dials on the transmitter and the receiver were tuned off the calibrated arc, indicating that the operator was very security conscious and in a 'ready to evacuate' state at instant notice. After ordering a Ghurka to smash the equipment and drop the aerial masts he went over to the stores tent where he met Sedley poking about in the sacks of rice and other dry rations. He had uncovered several packages which Harding took to be opium and the look of triumph he cast at him suggested he was pleased with the outcome of the raid.

Captain Emmerson also seemed satisfied with the part his men had played in the operation and congratulated Harding on the skill of his demolition work.

"It's a good thing you didn't get the opportunity to get your third charge placed, otherwise our policeman friend wouldn't have found the goodies he so evidently prizes."

Harding said, "Yes, a couple of things happened to reduce the amount of time I had allowed myself, and I'd almost forgotten, can your chaps take care of a casualty? I left him propped up against a tree a couple of hundred yards from the fuel dump."

"It's OK, he's being looked after. My section commander went for a pee and found a fellow staggering about with a bandaged head. We'll take him back with us as a prisoner. By the way, we don't seem to have picked up any VIPs. Must have caught the place at a quiet time. If you're going to give the remainder of the camp the treatment I'll get my men out of the way. See you out on the track when you're ready to hop it."

After making sure everyone was clear of the site Harding quickly set up the remaining charge, blew it and left the place brewing up nicely.

★★★

Back at the Jeep, Emmerson checked the time. "Excellent op, five-thirty in – seven-thirty out, own casualties nil, enemy casualties one, prisoners four, loot unspecified. Bloody good effort all round, valour to go unrewarded." Emmerson laughed at his post-op summary and said, "Well, old lad, I don't know about you but I reckon this will be the last piece of soldiering I'll be called upon to do in this part of the world. I'm due to go to GHQ Delhi on some sort of liaison posting. I'll miss serving with these chaps. Hope the British Government doesn't abandon them – they deserve treating well. And by the way, well done. Look me up if you happen to find yourself in Delhi one day and we'll take a celebration noggin or two."

Sedley, who had returned to the start point, offered his congratulations on a job well done and added, "I don't know how much importance to attach to it, but one of my constables challenged an English chap riding a motor-cycle. It seems he was on his way home after a party. He could barely stand and he said he stunk of whisky."

Harding said, "Did your constable give you any sort of description and say where he was going?"

"You'd better have a word with him yourself. I'll call him over."

"Please, Sergeant Sahib, the sahib was very drunk after party. He own tea plantation, taller than me and on Matchless motor-cycle. Very much wobbling."

Chapter 45

Mark Erskine was restless. He had lain awake most of the night worrying about a CAT flight due in the previous afternoon. It had been due to deliver a load of dope and weapons from Chin Peng's hoard in Malaya.

He slipped out of his bed roll, dressed and decided to take a stroll across the airfield. In the early breaking light he was amazed to see the draught elephants disappearing into the jungle at a lumbering trot with heads forward and trunks swaying. The handler was driving them on and beating their legs with a stick. He was about to give chase when he saw a figure dressed in jungle green carrying a haversack and a reel of cable running into the fuel compound.

Next he was alerted to the sound of someone coughing and hawking phlegm wandering in the direction of the fuel compound. Erskine saw it was a cook on his way to get some petrol for the field cookers. He watched bewildered when, after a short interval, the jungle green clad figure emerged from the shadows and dragged the cook away.

He ran back towards the track to see a body of armed Ghurka troops led by a British officer take up positions to the rear of the admin area.

Erskine swiftly determined that the airfield was about to be raided and the figure he had seen at the fuel compound was about to blow the thing sky high. With panic-speeded purpose he returned to his tent, poured most of the contents of a bottle of whisky over his head and body and ran for the shelter of some undergrowth at the edge of the runway. As he crouched in the cover he heard a shouted order as a blast bomb exploded followed by the noise of rifle shots and the rattle of a Bren gun.

Under cover of the din he made for a camouflaged hide where a motorcycle with spare cans of petrol secured to the panniers was concealed. When the fuel dump exploded and the roaring sound of flames engulfed the airfield he ran his machine along some jungle paths, out onto the vehicle track where he started the engine and rode away from the scene of havoc.

★★★

It was some three hours after sundown, about nine o'clock, when Erskine wheeled his motor-cycle into some bushes at the side of the track leading to the manager's dwelling. Narayan Rao was sleeping on a rope-strung charpoy on the small veranda. He awoke, startled to see Mark Erskine bending over him. "Oh Sahib, what is the matter? I am not expecting you. Please no noise. My family are sleeping inside."

"Come on, jaldi. You know why I'm here. Where is it?"

Cringing with fear, the little manager scrambled into a pair of shorts and pulled a sleeveless pullover over his head. "I show you, Sahib, but I must get a spade first."

Erskine grabbed his arm and half lifted, half dragged him off the veranda. "No time for spades, use your hands." They hurried to a small clearing behind the generator shed where the frightened manager dragged a sheet of rusted corrugated iron away from near the base of a tree. He scrabbled in the soft earth to reveal a black japanned deed box which Erskine snatched from him. The manager tried to sneak away but Erskine grabbed him by the arm.

"You open it … it's all there, isn't it, you bloody weasel? Go on, open up … now."

Narayan Rao slowly hinged the box open. Underneath a few sealed documents were bundles of banknotes: sterling, US dollars and Indian rupees. Erskine quickly counted the bundles.

"There seems to be a bundle of rupees missing … one thousand rupees to be exact. You thieving little pig."

The estate manager dropped the box and turned to run but Erskine managed to catch hold of his pullover with one hand as he tried to lug out a pistol from his trouser waistband with the other. The sight of the weapon spurred the now terrified Indian to break free. He twisted away from his captor, lost his balance and stumbled backwards over the knee-high barbed wire fence. His cry of alarm scaled up to a scream of pain, and fell to a dribbling whimper then ceased as he sprawled across the purple glowing

263

elements of the generator resistance field. The generator slowed as it reacted to the sudden load imposed when Narayan Rao's body short-circuited the lethal current to earth. It picked up again to resume its normal rhythm as the body slumped to the ground clear of the open-wire network.

Erskine recoiled in surprise and horror as the acrid smell of burned cloth, hair and flesh hit his nostrils. There was nothing he could do to help – Narayan Rao was dead – electrocuted. He retrieved the money dropped during the struggle and stuffed it inside his shirt. In a panic to get away from the awful scene he kicked the documents and the box under the sheet of corrugated iron and ran to his motor-cycle. With the gears in neutral, he ran with it up the track until he was out of earshot of the labourer's living quarters. As he kicked the engine into life he thought he heard a dog barking but he had no time to worry about that.

★★★

Harding was certain the drunken motor-cyclist was Mark Erskine. Without waiting for the result of the police interrogation of the few INA people who had been arrested, he asked Captain Emmerson to drive him back to his own Jeep and started out on the journey back to Shillong.

He had a strong suspicion that Erskine, unnerved by the dawn raid and the demolition of his Tamu base, would make tracks for a retreat where he could avoid capture and gain time to assess his position. Two courses lay open to him. He could make a miraculous return from being 'missing in action' and seek help and sympathy from Laura and Julia at Erskine-Jalpai. Alternatively, there was Tommy Young. He could prevail upon the 'old pal's act' to plead sanctuary for a fellow Brit in these uncertain times. Harding could but guess at Erskine's reasoning in arriving at a plan for his next move. Knowing that his role as Moscow's agent in helping to unite the major South East Asia Independence Movement leaders, and hatching a regional revolutionary strategy with them to overthrow the European Colonial Powers had been concluded, and that his key position in the opium smuggling operation via the tea route was terminated by the loss of Tamu, it needed little logic to work out that the only thing left for him was to flee the country.

Harding had little trouble finding Tommy Young's place. It was by far the seediest abode he could imagine a British colonial officer living in. As soon as he halted the Jeep by the prickly pear hedge, Jock the bearer rushed out to greet him.

"Oh Sahib, please to see Young Sahib. He gravely ill. I no leave him three days."

Harding followed the bearer through a gap in the hedge and into the bungalow. He pulled the chenille curtain back to see Tommy Young stretched out on the *charpoy*. He was half covered with a sweat-soaked sheet and by the light of the yellow flame cast by an oil lamp, Harding could see that he was in a bad way. The symptoms of a malaria attack were obvious, but Harding knew it would be dangerous to try to move him without first obtaining medical aid and advice. He forced a couple of Mepacrine tablets into his throat and sluiced them into his stomach with water from his own water bottle. He was not prepared to risk giving him water from the open-topped earthenware *chatti* that stood in the corner. He instructed Jock to try to give him some more Mepacrine after another two hours and told him to make some soup from the compo ration pack he produced from the Jeep and get the sahib to take some when he awoke. Harding assured the old bearer he would send some help for his sahib.

Jock said there had been no sign of anyone at the bungalow, but that he had heard a motor-cycle stop back along the track then start up again after about five minutes.

Long enough for Erskine to recce the place without disturbing anyone.

So much for the 'old pal's act'.

★★★

Laura was running with Marcus at her heels from the generator shed when Harding saw her. She stopped and shielded her eyes from the glare of the Jeep's headlamps with her raised forearm. Harding stopped and leapt from the Jeep and took her in his arms. She was sobbing with shock and unable to speak. She just kept on pointing to the generator shed, shaking her head and opening and closing her mouth. Marcus repeatedly ran a few yards back down the track then returned barking urgently.

Harding gently lifted her into the Jeep and with Marcus still barking as he ran alongside, drove her to the bungalow.

Julia, wrapped in a dressing gown, came out to the veranda, alerted by the dog barking and the sound of the Jeep engine.

"What on earth's going on?" she cried. Seeing that Laura was in a distressed state she placed an arm round her waist and with Harding's help supported her into the living room and laid her on the sofa. "I'll see if she'll take some brandy, there's some on the sideboard. There my love, just take a sip and tell us what it's all about."

Laura choked a little as the brandy hit her throat and mumbled, "Naray ... Nar ...." Her eyes closed and her head fell back onto the arm of the sofa.

"You take care of her. Something's happened down at the sheds. Marcus was trying to tell us to go back with him. I'll go and see what's wrong. Sounds as if someone's in trouble. Look after her. I'll be back as soon as I can."

★★★

"It's Narayan Rao, there's been some sort of accident. Looks as if he's been electrocuted. Better ring the police. Oh yes, and can you get hold of a doctor to go out and see Tommy Young. He's in a pretty poor way. Could be malaria, I think."

Laura, although still very shaken, had recovered from her collapse and was able to explain that she had gone to cut the generator for the night when she found Narayan Rao. And that it was the smell of his burned flesh and charred clothing that had overcome her.

Harding said, "Have you any idea why Rao should have been at the generator shed? I was under the impression that he retires early and that you or Julia arrange to switch off when you have finished with the house circuit."

"Yes, the time at which we go to bed varies and it seemed right that we shouldn't rely on Narayan Rao to see to it."

"Did you see or hear anything unusual during the evening?"

"No, not really ... Marcus made a bit of a noise about a couple of hours ago but he soon settled down again. Could have been that he caught the scent of a mongoose or something."

Julia returned to say that the police would see to it in daylight. They didn't seem to think there was much urgency. "Just make sure no animals get to his body before they have had the chance to have a look."

She continued, "I rather got the impression that we should be able to deal with a simple accident and it wasn't until I threatened the duty constable with the State Governor he agreed to report the case. I also managed to get hold of the local doctor. He promised to go out and see Tommy straightaway. I asked him to pick me up on his way so that I could perhaps help out. Can't see old Jock being much use trying to nurse his master."

★★★

Harding returned to the generator shed at first light and tried to work out how Narayan Rao had met his death.

It seemed a fair bet that Mark Erskine had made for the estate after failing to get any help from Tommy Young. Remembering that it was certainly Mark Erskine who had been in the packing shed that night with Narayan Rao when he had spotted them meddling with sample tea chests, Harding was convinced that Erskine had a hand in the Indian's death. He made a quick examination of his twisted body but there were only some cuts on his bare legs where he had torn the skin on the barbed wire. He noted some gouges in the soft red earth that appeared to have been made by the sole of a boot. Narayan Rao was bare-footed. He followed the marks, irregular and overlaid with deep gouges and bare footprints, back to a sheet of corrugated iron. He lifted the sheet to reveal a black metal box, open, angled into a scooped hole from which spilled some documents.

Chapter 46

Laura sat alone on the veranda. She cupped a mug of Bovril in her hands and although the sun's heat was rising she was smothered in a tartan rug.

"Do you want breakfast? I'll have Ramesh fix bacon and eggs if you like."

Harding said, "Hope you're feeling better. Been a rough old night, hasn't it?"

"Much better thanks. It was the sight of Narayan Rao and the awful smell that hung over him that really upset me. What on earth is going on, Harding? Come on, I've got to know. Mark's involved in it somewhere, isn't he?"

"No breakfast thanks, though a cuppa wouldn't come amiss. Julia's gone off to see Tommy, I expect. This isn't going to be easy but you'll have to know some time."

"Hurry up then before Julia returns. She is closer to the Erskine family and the estate than I am so anything bad directly relating to Mark will be difficult for her to accept."

Taking care to avoid saying anything that could compromise the special work he had been undertaking with the SIC, he told her that his suspicions about Mark's disappearance, confirmed by the date of the cheque cashed at Karachi and the delay by the army in making a clear statement about him going missing on Operation Zipper, was a clear indication that he had been playing a double game. He told her the whole story of Mark's connection to the Apostles Society, established by the photograph that she had seen and asked him to destroy, and his part in using the estate and Narayan Rao to help distribute smuggled dope to anti-British political activists in Calcutta and the surrounding districts. He stopped talking as she fought back the tears that filled her eyes.

"Go on, tell me everything."

"I can only guess at much of what follows, but I tracked him from an airfield up on the Assam border. I'm afraid I can't say what I was doing there. However, this airfield was being used to land opium which Mark then moved on via the estate as I have already explained. He was riding a motor-cycle and I think he called in at Tommy Young's place. That's how I knew that he was ill, by the way."

"Yes, that did occur to me, but I wasn't thinking too clearly at the time when you told Julia. I hope he's going to be OK. He's a decent enough chap and doesn't deserve to live in a hole like that."

"The next bit is going to be hard to swallow. It seems that Mark arrived here about an hour or so before I turned up, met Narayan Rao and got mixed up in a struggle, with your estate manager falling into the resistance field. That's why your lights dimmed earlier when he ran the circuit to earth. Now, I came across a tin box that had been hidden near the generator shed containing some documents. A quick read showed that Mark sold a half interest in the capital value of the estate to our Mr D'Silva and subsequently made over to you the remaining half interest. Here, these are the relevant papers: bill of sale and title deed. I'm no expert in the niceties of such transactions, but it seems the business and all the assets are yours, but half is on a mortgage arrangement with D'Silva. I reckon he needed a supply of cash to fund his permanent disappearance and having let you down in marriage wanted to make amends by making over the residue of the estate to you."

She sat shaking her head in disbelief then said, "The pig. How could he do this to Julia? This is her home and livelihood. I can't take this ... it's hers. Promise me you won't tell her the full story about his treachery? Wonder where he is now? Probably on his way to his little friends in Russia. The authorities will have to be informed of his reappearance so they can complete their records and I can start divorce proceedings. Bit of a bugger isn't it, divorcing a husband I wasn't really married to?"

"I don't think you need bother about telling the authorities. All will be taken care of when the official report goes through the admin machinery. By the way, have you given any thought to having a real marriage?"

★★★

"I've brought Tommy back here. The doctor says he's got over the worst but he needs some careful nursing."

Harding and Laura smiled at each other. Then, together, they smiled at Julia.

★★★

Duncan Reeder and Harding walked along the *maidan* and stood to listen to the faint sounds from central Calcutta drifting over from Chowringhee. Harding looked up into the night sky to confirm that his favourite constellation was where it should be and said, "Well, that's the end of that business, the firm closed down and everyone posted out. Some for home and demob, lucky sods. I'm off to join British Forces Rear until the powers that be tell us to depart … and where did you say you were going?"

"GHQ Delhi, for a start. All British troops are being withdrawn to the west and now that partition is as near a done thing as it can be, we'll all be homeward bound within the next few months, I expect."

Chapter 47

Bombay, March 1948.

… and dearest, if we are to be married when you return home I must know your first name. After all, the vicar will have to know to publish the banns and what not and the wedding invites should have our first names on. When I asked your parents they simply laughed and said "It's up to our son to tell you…."

Harding looked up from her letter and let his mind drift to picture some of the places and incidents of the last two years … Erskine-Jalpai … Tamu and that horrible jungle bash … Calcutta … Moorside Hall … Rowena … Mark Erskine … and six months ago, back to regimental duties and operating emergency communications in support of escort detachments trying to protect Muslims fleeing to Pakistan and Hindus making for the safety of India.

Assassins mingling with passengers on overloaded refugee trains and pulling the communication cords at pre-arranged points, when the stationery carriages would be attacked by henchmen waiting on the track-side…. Sikh women hurling themselves into wells to escape being raped.

At the height of the communal riots during the previous September, it had been calculated that one and a quarter million non-Muslims were trying to get to East Punjab at the same time as almost a million Muslims were heading for West Punjab….

Harding shelved his thoughts and concentrated on writing his reply:

Darling Laura
I expect to arrive at Tilbury about the 10th of April on the last troopship to leave this place … I hope Adam will do….

GLOSSARY

bahut acha	very good
baksheesh	gift or gratuity. Pronounced as buckshee by British troops
bolo	say
charpoy	bed
chatti	water container of brass, canvas or earthenware
chowkidar	watchman
dekko	look
dhal	porridge made from lentils
dhobi	washerman
dom	low caste Hindu, remover of the dead or carrion
dhoti	Hindu loin cloth
durree	rug
ekh dum	at once
ekh, doh	numbers: one, two
ghat	landing place or path to river
ghee	clarified butter
godown	warehouse
havildar	sergeant in Indian Army
khud	steep mountainside
loos wallah	thief
malum	understood
nimbu-pani	lime drink
padi	rice field
pagal-pani	alcoholic drink
pani	water
raja	person of some rank
ram-ram	an invocation of the divinity

rickshaw	man-drawn passenger conveyance, sometimes pedal powered
sari	cloth for female dress
thora	a little
tiffin	midday meal
tum	you
tunda	cold
wallah	man
zindabad	victory for/long live

Eric Firth

Eric served in the Royal Corps of Signals from 1944 to 1969, retiring in the rank of Captain. He was posted to Berlin during the blockade and completed two tours of duty in the British Zone of Germany during the Cold War. His army career pattern largely echoed the 'Retreat from Empire', beginning in India, followed by Pakistan, then through to the Sudan, Egypt, Libya, Malaya and Singapore.

After the army, he established a second career in communications electronics and graduated from the Open University with a BA (Hons) majoring in Modern History.

He served in the rank of sergeant at many of the locations and in some of the situations narrated in KINGSMAN.